eye of the god

eye of the god

ISBN-13: 978-1-4267-0068-2 .

Published by Abingdon Press, P.O. Box 801, Nashville, TN 37202
www.abingdonpress.com

Ariel Allison Lawhon is represented by The Nashville Agency,
P.O. Box 110909, Nashville, TN 37222.
www.nashvilleagency.com

Cover design by Anderson Design Group, Nashville, TN

Library of Congress Cataloging-in-Publication Data

Allison, Ariel.
Eye of the god / Ariel Allison.
    p. cm.
  ISBN 978-1-4267-0068-2 (binding: pbk./trade pbk., adhesive perfect
: alk. paper)
  1. Brothers--Fiction. 2. Hope diamond--Fiction. 3. Jewel thieves--
Fiction. I. Title.

PS3601.L447E94 2009
813'.6--dc22

                                              2009014619

Printed in the United States of America

2 3 4 5 6 7 8 9 10 / 14 13 12 11 10 09

eye of the god

by
Ariel Allison

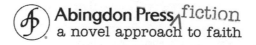
Abingdon Press fiction
a novel approach to faith

For my little sister, Abby.
You make a great namesake.

I began writing my first book at the age of five. And while it is true that I got distracted drawing the cover and never finished, the inclination to put words on paper has stayed with me ever since. Yet this is not a journey I have traveled alone. Many people have come alongside to make this dream a reality. Thanking everyone who had a part in bringing this book to life is an undertaking as big as writing it. I will try to do them justice.

To my editors Barbara Scott and Jenny Youngman at Abingdon Press, your enthusiasm for eye of the god has put more wind in my sails than you will ever know. You made a journey typically filled with nail-biting and self-doubt feel like a long conversation between old friends. I am grateful for every suggestion, every challenge, and every moment spent poring over this manuscript.

It is rare to have a true friend in this business, much less a champion. Yet my agent, Jonathan Clements, is such a person. I thought he would laugh at me when I first approached him about representation. Seven years later, he still takes my calls. A gal couldn't ask for a better agent.

To my husband, Ashley. My love, every bit of it, is yours. You are still the best thing that has ever happened to me. Thank you for dreaming with me. Thank you for believing in me. And thank you for changing diapers, cooking noodles, and doing laundry while I wrote. You put many men to shame.

To London, Parker, Marshall, and Colby . . . Mommy loves you the most (no matter what Daddy says). Thank you for succumbing to bribery so I could finish this manuscript. I knew those chocolate-covered raisins would come in handy.

Melanie Randolph and Leah Walker were kind enough to read the manuscript and point out its many errors. After such an undertaking I am amazed that they still want to be my friends.

I am greatly indebted to John Farkas and his brilliant, quirky mind. Without his suggestions, this book wouldn't be half as interesting.

I send a million thanks to Richard Kurin, author of *Hope Diamond: The Legendary History of a Cursed Gem*. His research gave life to people I first met in eighth-grade history texts. His book was a great source of historical information and fact. I could have never compiled that amount of research on my own. I would be remiss for not tipping my hat and applauding him for such an extraordinary work.

I have, whenever possible, done my best to quote actual conversations and do justice to historic events. Nonetheless, I am bound to have gotten them wrong somewhere, and I expect a flurry of angry letters from studious historians telling me where I have gone astray. I will apologize in advance and humbly acknowledge I am not an expert on anything. I simply enjoy stringing words together and telling the kind of story that I would like to read. I hope it is as fun for you to read as it was for me to write.

Dear Reader,

It has been said that all of history is, in fact, God's story, and that we are just supporting actors. When viewed through that lens, the tale of the Hope Diamond takes on new meaning. But what if the story is much deeper, more intriguing and significant than simply a diamond owned by some of the world's most notorious figures? What if the mystery of the Hope Diamond is relevant to us, our culture, and our faith? *That* would make a story indeed.

In the spring of 1995 I stumbled across an article in *Life Magazine* about the curse of the Hope Diamond. Like fire on gasoline, an idea for a novel exploded in my mind. During the fourteen years that I spent researching and writing, I realized that one of my greatest dilemmas would be taming some of history's most unruly characters. You will recognize many of those who came into contact with the Hope Diamond: Louis XVI, Marie Antoinette, Caroline of Brunswick, May Yohe, Pierre Cartier, Charles Lindbergh, Harry Winston, and Jackie Kennedy, just to name a few. But try as I might, I could not make room for all of them in this novel. Yet their stories deserve to be told. So beginning October, 2009, I will make them available in short story form on Amazon.com.

At the back of this book I have included a series of discussion questions for small groups and book clubs. I would be honored to talk with your group about this novel via speaker phone. You can set up a time to chat by visiting my website, www.arielallison.com, and sending me an email. I look forward to meeting you.

I would like to say that I wrote the majority of this novel while sitting in an Irish pub, or on the beach in Normandy, or while hiking the Alaskan wilderness. I'm afraid not. I have four boys, ages five and under; and although I have traveled much of the world, my days of adventure and unhindered travel are on hiatus. Since having children I have learned that spare moments are the gold dust of time. An hour here and an hour there don't seem like much, but added up over weeks and months and years they accumulate into a precious commodity. So I wrote this novel during my spare moments: early mornings, late nights, and long weekends. I did my best, often after drinking ungodly amounts of coffee, to tell a tale of suspense with a historical twist.

I am delighted that you hold this book in your hands and that it is no longer just a figment of my imagination but a living, breathing story of its own. When all is said and done, and the dust has finally settled over the last great adventure of the Hope Diamond, you will see that no god chiseled from stone can direct the fates of men, nor can it change the course of history and God's story.

It is an honor to share this story with you,

Ariel Allison

Prologue

GOLCONDA, INDIA, 1653

JEAN-BAPTISTE TAVERNIER WINCED AS THE SOLDIER CHOPPED OFF THE man's hand. The thief shrieked and dropped to the ground, clutching the bloodied stump to his chest.

Tavernier turned aside with a grimace and ordered the litter bearers beneath him to move faster. Four slaves, dark from the sun, jostled between the crowded stalls of Golconda's hectic bazaar and away from the public spectacle. The agonized screams faded as they pressed farther into the crowd.

Dense heat settled over the marketplace, and Tavernier wiped sweat off his forehead with the back of his hand. Pungent smells assaulted his senses: sweat and urine, spiced curry and sweet chutney, burning incense and rotting vegetables. His litter bumped and rocked through the hustle and bustle of shoppers and merchants haggling over prices. Red and gold bridal wear and precious gold glittered in the stalls. Elephants carried the elite through the narrow streets while dirty children chased each other with sticks.

Tavernier looked across the sea of dark-skinned faces toward an embroidered tent in the midst of the bazaar guarded by two soldiers wearing the white turban and golden sash of the sultan's army. At his approach the guards stepped aside and pulled back the elaborate flaps.

Tavernier glanced at the heavy wooden chest near his feet and stepped from the litter. "Guard that with your life," he ordered the soldiers as he entered the tent.

Large, colorful cushions and intricately woven Oriental rugs covered the dirt floor. Mir Jumla, Golconda's prime minister, lounged on an orange and peacock-blue silk pillow. The heavy brow, black eyes, and prominent nose of the Persian-born general contradicted his Oriental adornment.

Mir stood and greeted Tavernier in the traditional Indian way, with palms together, hands raised in front of his face, and head bowed. "*Vanakkam*," he said.

Tavernier lowered his head and returned the greeting.

Mir motioned for him to sit, and they settled onto the cushions.

"Good to see you, Prime Minister," Tavernier said.

Mir grinned, "Jean-Baptiste Tavernier. Punctual as always."

"You said it was important?"

Around Mir's neck hung a buckskin pouch, which he untied and placed in Tavernier's hand, "I could lose my head for this."

"Come, come Mir, we both know the sultan would much prefer to chop off your hands and leave you to beg for food like a common slave."

"My hands it will be then if the sultan ever learns *that* escaped his grasp."

Tavernier opened the pouch and emptied the contents into his hand. His eyes widened and the corners of his mouth twitched as he suppressed a grin. In his palm rested the largest blue diamond he had ever seen. He turned it over, running his fingers along the irregular surface.

"This is a great deal more than ten carats. It was my understanding that any diamond over ten carats found in the Kollur mines went directly to the sultan."

Mir Jumla nodded and pushed back into the cushions. In one hand he fingered a gold coin with his long fingers. "That is the edict. But I never said this stone came from the mines."

"Since when did you start dealing in stolen gems?"

Mir Jumla thrust out his lower jaw. "You don't want it then?"

"Of course I do. I am just curious why a man so loyal to the sultan is selling diamonds right out from under his nose."

"Loyalty, like most things, has a price." Mir grinned.

Tavernier smiled. "Indeed." He held up the diamond, letting the light filter through. *"Net et d'un beau violet,"* he whispered in his native French.

Mir tilted his head to one side.

Tavernier repeated in Indian, "A clear and beautiful violet."

"Yes. It is flawless."

Tavernier balanced the stone in his hand for a moment. "One hundred carats, or close to it, I would wager."

"One hundred twelve."

"Excellent. And the price?"

"Two-hundred twenty-thousand livres."

"A little steep."

"We both know you will not find another such diamond for sale in Golconda. They all sit in the sultan's treasury."

"Fair enough." Tavernier shrugged. "But you still have not told me how you came by this stone."

Mir hesitated a moment as he studied the coin in his hand. "I would not give that much concern. The last person to own this was made of stone and sat in a Hindu temple on the banks of the Godavari River. A slave named Raj, starving and half-mad, brought it to me three weeks ago, claiming he had chiseled it from the forehead of an idol named Rama Sita." Mir cast a sideways glance at Tavernier. "*Cursed*, Raj said. The idol cursed the diamond and all who would come to own it."

"And where is this Raj now?"

"In the bazaar. I believe my soldiers just relieved him of a hand."

"That was your doing?"

"I paid him a fair price for the stone three weeks ago, but he came back this morning for more. When I refused, he tried to steal this." Mir held up the coin.

Tavernier laughed. "A convenient story, my friend."

"You don't believe me?"

"Weaving a tale of theft and vengeance is an old jeweler's trick to induce interest in the buyer. One I have used myself, as a matter of fact."

Mir gave a curt nod. "May it be on your head. I am glad to sell it and be done."

"At such a price, I am sure you are. But as far as my head goes, I intend for it to stay in place."

"The curse does not bother you?"

"I don't believe in curses, Mir. Besides, we both know they increase the value of trinkets such as this."

"Then we have only the matter of payment to attend."

Tavernier rose and fetched his treasure chest from the litter. Returning, he set it on the rug before Mir and opened the lock with a small golden key. When he pulled back the lid, hundreds of gold coins spilled onto the carpet before them. Tavernier counted the purchase price before the prime minister, who eyed the gold with hunger. Only a few dozen coins remained in the chest when he was done.

Tavernier slid the great blue diamond back inside the buckskin pouch and tied it around his neck. "Should you stumble across the other eye you will, of course, let me know?"

"Of course," said Mir with great satisfaction. "And thank you once again for your business."

The men gave each other a polite nod, and Tavernier stepped from the tent. Within seconds his litter disappeared amidst the writhing mass of vendors, peasants, and hanging goods.

1

CARNIVAL, RIO DE JANEIRO, BRAZIL—PRESENT DAY

ABBY MITCHELL STARED THROUGH THE WINDOW AT THE FEVERISH DISPLAY of dancing outside. She placed her palm on the warm plaster wall of the Chacara do Ceu Museum and felt the pounding Samba music pulse against her fingers. She observed the frenzied celebration from within the safety of the museum's main gallery. An old mansion, turned resting place for some of the world's most renowned art, the museum was a pleasant combination of low ceilings, cream-colored walls, and quiet elegance.

Her cell phone buzzed, and she took a deep breath before answering. "Good morning , Director Heaton."

"It's not all that good, Dr. Mitchell. We have a bit of an issue." His voice was raspy, the ravages of age and cigarettes.

She cast a nervous glance over her shoulder. "What's going on?"

"The Collectors. They've taken two Van Goghs."

Abby closed her eyes and pressed her forehead against the window. "Where?"

"Amsterdam."

"How?"

"We're not exactly sure. Investigators are baffled. The paintings just disappeared in the middle of the night."

"Prints?"

"None."

"Of course not. In ten years they've never left a print. Or a clue for that matter."

"Abby," his voice prodded on the other line. "You know what this means."

She nodded, staring at her reflection in the window. "They can't get their hands on the Dali. And we know they want it."

"You know what you have to do."

A weak smile spread across her face. "Let's just hope I can."

"Call me when you're done," he said, and then hung up the phone.

A handful of tourists wandered the gallery, trying to study the timeless wonders on its plaster walls, but distracted by Carnival just a few feet away.

Lost in her thoughts, Abby paid no attention to the approaching footsteps until she felt a polite tap on her shoulder. She turned to find a woman, in her late fifties, wearing a white linen suit and a gracious smile.

"Dr. Mitchell, I presume?" she said with a distinct Brazilian accent.

Abby held out her hand. "Indeed. And you must be Director Santos?"

"Please, call me Ana." Though aging quite gracefully, it was obvious Ana Santos had been a sight to behold in her prime.

"Sorry to keep you," she smiled. "With all the tourists in town, I have been running behind all week. But things should calm down now that Carnival is almost underway."

"No trouble at all. I've been enjoying your remarkable collection."

Ana stretched out an arm and motioned Abby to follow. They turned their backs to the window and made their way through the gallery toward a series of priceless surrealist paintings. One in particular caught Abby's attention, and she leaned forward, appreciation evident on her face.

"Now, Dr. Mitchell, you said there was an urgent matter we needed to discuss. I assume more than Carnival brings you to Brazil?"

"I'm afraid so." She ran a finger over the nameplate which read *Two Balconies, Salvador Dali.*

Ana beamed. "Fantastic, isn't it?"

Abby nodded.

"*Two Balconies* is the only Salvador Dali painting on display in Latin America. It is one of the Chacara do Ceu's most prized exhibits."

Abby tapped her lips in contemplation. "I don't doubt that."

"Beautiful ring," Ana said, glancing at Abby's finger.

"Thank you. It was a gift."

She grinned mischievously. "He must love you very much."

"You would think so."

Ana smiled sadly and changed the subject. "So what is your concern?"

"I'm worried about this painting."

"*Two Balconies*? What do you mean? I thought you felt it would be a spectacular addition to your exhibit next year."

"I do," Abby assured her. "My concern is not with the painting itself, but with its safety. I have reason to believe it may be in danger of theft."

Ana relaxed a little and laughed. "I can assure you, *meu caro*, we have strict security measures in place. All of our paintings are bolted to the wall and connected to hair-trigger alarms. If a painting is moved even a fraction of an inch, the alarm sets off our security system. In addition we have state-of-the-art video surveillance and round-the-clock armed guards."

"I wasn't suggesting your security system is sub par, merely that we have gotten word there may be parties interested in this particular Salvador Dali painting."

Ana flashed a charming smile. "Do you mind me asking your source?"

"I've received notice from the art theft division at Interpol. There are rumblings of an illicit interest in Dali and this painting in particular. I thought it prudent to warn you, considering your partnership with the Smithsonian."

"Why is the International Criminal Police Organization interested in *Two Balconies*?"

"There has been a rash of thefts recently, and Interpol contacted me with a warning."

"I appreciate your concern, Dr. Mitchell, but I feel confident we have taken the appropriate measures to protect our facility."

Abby sighed. "All right. But know you have our full resources at your disposal should you need them."

"Thank you, Dr. Mitchell. I will certainly take that into consideration." Ana glanced back at the painting and asked, "I assume the Smithsonian is still planning to include *Two Balconies* in next year's exhibit?"

"Absolutely. Preliminary preparations are underway for its transport and security."

Ana beamed. "We would be delighted to accommodate you in any way. I will, of course, have to accompany the painting to Washington."

"Of course."

Both women turned back to the window as a loud burst of cheering and music erupted from the throng outside. Viktor Leite, the mayor, was barely audible over the din. Flanked on both sides by voluptuous women dressed in revealing Carnival garb, he screamed into the microphone so he could be heard over the pounding drums.

"Let the festivities begin!"

At his command the massive parade, seventy-thousand people strong, erupted in applause and began to snake through the streets.

"You will be staying for Carnival?" Ana asked.

"I'm afraid not. Duty calls me back to Washington."

"I thought this was a working vacation?"

"More work than vacation, I'm afraid."

"Surely the Smithsonian wouldn't object to you staying an extra day or two?"

Abby sighed. "My flight leaves at noon tomorrow."

Ana opened her mouth to argue her case but was jolted into stunned silence by the thunderous sound of a gunshot. Abby and Ana spun around to find two armed men standing at the museum entrance.

2

ALEX WELD STARED DOWN THE BARREL OF HIS NINE-MILLIMETER GLOCK. The small crowd of tourists and museum staff gaped at him with open mouths. Dressed as an average tourist in khaki pants, white linen shirt, and Carnival mask, he looked as though he belonged outside with the multitude of partygoers.

An armed security guard ran into the main gallery. "Now!" Alex shouted to his brother.

"*Coloque suas armas ou eu porei uma bala em sua cabeça!*" Isaac Weld ordered in Portuguese.

The guard slid his handgun across the floor and backed away.

Isaac retrieved the discarded weapon from the marble floor and then pistol-whipped the unarmed guard in his temple. The unconscious man collapsed to the floor.

"*Quem está na carga?*" Isaac's voice rang dead and hollow behind the frozen lips of the resin mask. Almond-shaped openings revealed his cold, blue eyes, the only proof of life in the painted face.

No one answered.

Isaac raised his Glock and fired a single round into the ceiling. Screams echoed thoughout the room, and a shower of dust and small plaster chunks fell to the floor. "I said who is in charge?" he repeated in English, stressing each syllable.

"I am." The well-dressed woman in her early fifties took a hesitant step forward, her gaze locked on the gun in his hand.

"And you are?"

"Ana Santos, the museum director."

Isaac grabbed the back of her suit and forced her toward the security desk at the front of the lobby. "Disconnect the alarm and the security system or everyone here dies."

Ana pulled a thin silver chain from inside her blouse. On it was a single key, that she slid into the console, and then punched a code into the keypad.

Isaac pressed the gun into the small of her back. "How long until the alarm is disabled?"

"Thirty seconds," she said through clenched teeth.

Alex motioned his gun at the captives. "Everyone in the middle of the room, on your knees, hands behind your heads!"

Terrified, the small crowd obeyed the order without complaint. A young boy whimpered and buried his face into his father's chest.

Isaac moved toward the display wall, "If anyone moves, shoot them."

"Picasso, Matisse, Monet, and Dali," Alex said, nodding at the four paintings.

"No," Ana moaned. She shook her head, lips parted and eyes large.

While Isaac cut the canvases from their frames with a scalpel, Alex circled the small crowd, holding them at gunpoint. A woman knelt before him, hands laced on top of her head. Her brown hair was pulled back at the nape of her neck, exposing her face. He had never seen her before, but the ring on her left hand was unmistakable; intertwined gold vines and a single diamond glinted beneath the lights. Alex ripped it from her finger.

"Aahhh!" She screamed, turning to face him.

Their eyes locked for a brief moment, as they studied one another.

Alex stared at her with guarded suspicion and then stuffed the ring in his pocket and moved on.

"Done here!" Isaac shouted as he rolled the last canvas and slid it into a cardboard tube, placing it in a black duffel bag with the other three. Without a word the brothers ran for the door, flung it open, and disappeared into the Carnival procession without a backward glance.

Ana stumbled to her feet, tears streaming down her cheeks, and stared at the empty spots on the wall. "All of them. They have all of them!" The look she gave Abby was one of shock and accusation. "How did you know?"

"We didn't. I mean . . . not yet," Abby said, trying to gain her composure. "I thought we had more time." She rose slowly, rubbing her bruised ring finger, eyes locked on the door the thieves had just exited. She pulled the cell phone from her pocket and turned to Ana. "I have to make a call. May I use your office?"

It took Ana a moment to register what Abby had asked. "Yes . . . of course . . . down the hall, fourth door on the right. Now if you will excuse me, I need to phone the police."

Once amid the stifling crowds of Carnival, the thieves pulled off their masks, slipped their weapons into the duffel bag, and snaked their way through the *Rua São Clemente*, the old city's main thoroughfare. The five-minute walk to their hotel took half an hour as they pressed into the flow of traffic and were jostled by the crowd.

The Hotel Gloria was located just minutes from the *Palacio de Cidade*, on the *Praia do Flamengo*, one of the most exclusive beaches in Rio de Janeiro. They had chosen the white, twelve-story hotel not because it often played home to foreign dignitaries or for the tropical gardens and panoramic verandas, but because it was the only hotel in Rio that offered helicopter transfers. In just over an hour they would board an Augusta A109 Power helicopter and fly 285 kilometers an hour toward their next destination.

Isaac shut the door to their suite and hissed, "What did you think you were doing back there?" He scowled at Alex, blue eyes smoldering. It was the only physical characteristic they shared. His hair was cropped short to the skull in military fashion, and his thin, wiry frame contained a constant nervous energy. Although older by three years, Isaac was shorter, thinner, and generally less handsome.

"You mean this?" Alex pulled the ring from his pocket.

"Yes, that. Since when are we into petty theft?"

He tossed the ring to Isaac. "I would hardly call that *petty*. We made fifty grand lifting it three years ago."

Isaac examined the ring closely and nodded. "Dublin. That batty old lady who sang Irish drinking songs in her sleep."

"Yup." Alex pulled the cardboard tubes from the duffel bag and leaned them against the wall. "That woman either knows the man we stole it for, or she knows one of the Collectors."

Isaac was suddenly interested in the ring. His eyes narrowed. "Or she is one of the Collectors."

"Precisely."

"How do we find out for sure?"

Alex leveled his gaze at the ring in Isaac's palm. "Leave it to me."

———

Abby sat behind Ana's desk, looking out on the parade below. She heard the pounding of drums and roar of the crowd, but it seemed to meld into the migraine that pressed at her temples. She shook her head and stared at the phone. Five minutes had passed since her first attempt to reach Director Heaton, lead investigator at Interpol's Art Theft Division.

Abby took a deep breath and lifted her cell phone again. She pressed the code for Lyon, France, and then the number she knew by heart. It rang six times while Abby tried to formulate what she could possibly say in a voice mail. Then he picked up.

"Director Heaton. And this better be good. I'm in the middle of a filet mignon and my wife is getting tired of me answering the phone during our anniversary dinner."

"It's Abby." Her voice sounded small and weak, defeated.

"Abby, I'm sorry. I thought it was that pest from accounting. He's been after me for my expense reports."

"I'm sorry to interrupt your dinner."

"No problem. Did you get everything taken care of?"

"Not exactly. The painting was stolen. Along with three others: Picasso, Matisse, and Monet."

There was a prolonged silence on the other end and then, "You mean to tell me they got there before you did?"

"No, sir," she said, her voice trembling. "You could say we arrived at the same time. They stole the paintings this afternoon, right in front of my face, not five minutes after I'd warned Director Santos."

"How," he stammered. "How could that have possibly happened?"

Abby gnawed at her bottom lip. It was so obvious now. "Carnival, sir."

"Of course. A ready-made diversion . . . brilliant actually."

"Terrifying is more like it."

"You saw the entire thing?"

"Live and in person."

"You okay?"

"A little shaken up, but I'm fine."

"Abby," he said, with that same prodding tone in his voice. "You realize this ups the ante and pushes us toward a more difficult solution?"

"I know."

"We'll need to debrief when you get back."

"I understand."

"Go back to your hotel and get some sleep."

Abby smiled sadly. "Not likely."

"Call me when you get back."

"Yes, sir."

Heaton hung up, and she put the phone back in her pocket.

A sharp knock on the door startled her. Ana stuck her head in the room, looking frazzled and none too happy. "The police have arrived. They wish to take statements."

Abby followed the director into the main gallery of the museum where they stood as the police questioned all the witnesses.

The detective in charge of the investigation was flanked on either side by officers in sterile gray uniforms who held semiautomatic machine guns. Detective Rodriguez was a burly man with a pencil-thin mustache, thick waistline, and perpetual smirk. His guards did not speak and did not seem interested in the proceedings. For that matter, Detective Rodriguez gave the distinct impression that he would much rather be celebrating Carnival than investigating a theft.

One by one the staff and tourists were allowed to go after giving names, statements, and addresses where they could be reached for further investigation. Abby and Ana waited to speak with the detective privately.

"Director Santos, I need a list of everything that was stolen today," Rodriguez said, handing her a notepad and pencil.

"Of course," said Ana, gracious as always. She rattled the names off while scribbling them on the paper. "Pablo Picasso's *The Dance*. Claude Monet's *Marine*. Henri Matisse's *Garden of Luxembourg*. And Salvador Dali's *Two Balconies*."

Rodriguez took the notepad and stuck it in his pocket without even a glance at what she had written.

"Detective, these men were professionals. They knew what they were doing," Abby interrupted.

Rodriguez glared at her sideways. "And you are?"

"This is Dr. Abigail Mitchell, Director of the Smithsonian Institution's Natural Programs. She is my guest," Ana said, an edge of irritation in her voice. "She has some information you will be most interested in. Just moments before the robbery she warned me of the possibility that thieves might be interested in the Salvador Dali painting."

Rodriquez narrowed his eyes at Abby. "I see. And how did you come by this information?"

"A routine alert from Interpol. The art world is small, and we try to keep one another abreast of illicit activity."

"Detective, they stole something from Dr. Mitchell as well. A ring. Very valuable," Ana said.

"And what does this ring look like, Ms. Mitchell?

"It has a thick gold band, intricately carved with vines, and inlaid with a single diamond."

"Are there any other distinguishing marks?" he asked.

"Only an inscription inside the band that says, 'Alligator Food.'"

Ana's brow furrowed. "Alligator Food? What on earth does that mean?"

Abby shrugged. "I wish I knew."

Isaac's cell phone blared to life, and he looked at the display with a grin. He held it in his hand and let it ring twice more before answering. "Yes?"

"Were you successful?" asked the eager voice on the other end.

"Yes."

"And you have the two Van Goghs from Amsterdam as well?"

"We do," Isaac said, glancing at the six cardboard tubes stacked against the wall.

"Then we will rendezvous at our usual location for the exchange. In the meantime, write down this name."

Isaac scrambled for a pen and paper and scribbled the name he was given: *Dr. Abigail Mitchell. Washington, D.C.*

"She works for the Smithsonian and has access to something I want. I want you to make her acquaintance."

"What's the target?" A malicious smile crept over his face as he listened to their next marching orders. "We'll need some extra time to line up things."

"Good. Contact me when you're ready, and we'll discuss the details."

Isaac closed his phone and met his brother's frigid gaze. "What did he want?" Alex asked.

"Just checking to see if we had the merchandise."

"And what else? I know that smile."

Isaac chose his words carefully. "He's got another job for us."

Alex shook his head. "This was supposed to be our last gig. I'm out. You know that."

Isaac held up a hand. "You may want to reconsider—"

"We've been doing this for ten years," he interrupted. "It's getting old. We agreed this would be the last heist."

"You don't even know what he wants."

"It doesn't matter. We don't need the money, and I'm bored with the work."

The corners of Isaac's mouth quivered as he suppressed a grin. "If that's the way you want it, fine. But I'm not afraid to do this one without you."

Alex stopped short. "What do you mean? Work alone? What does he want?"

Isaac flashed his brother a conniving smile. "The Hope Diamond."

3

NINE MONTHS LATER

SMITHSONIAN INSTITUTION, WASHINGTON, D.C.

THE IMAX THEATER ON THE SECOND FLOOR OF THE SMITHSONIAN'S Museum of Natural History was filled to capacity. Abby stood behind the podium, hands on its sides waiting for the massive screen to grow still. Sporadic flashes of light illuminated faces in the crowd, but not so much that she could make out details. Almost four hundred people fanned out before her in the auditorium to watch the documentary unfold before them.

She wore a simple cream suit, low heels, and reading glasses, and she had pulled her hair back at the nape of her neck.

Slowly, the sound faded, and the short documentary wound to a close. The last image was replaced with a picture of the Hope Diamond as it looked in the special display case on the second floor of the museum.

Abby stood just left of the screen silhouetted by a single spotlight. She took a deep breath and leaned into the microphone.

"On November 10, 1954, the Hope Diamond arrived at the Smithsonian in a brown paper package sent via the U.S. Postal Service. Its courier was none other than my grandfather, James Todd, a thirty-four-year-old postman with a colorful past.

"It was addressed in the flowing script of famous jeweler Harry Winston to Smithsonian Institution, Washington D.C., attention Dr. Leonard Carmichael. Winston insured the package for one million dollars, bringing the postage to a grand total of $145.29, a whopping sum for a parcel that weighed a mere 61 ounces."

Abby lifted her chin and surveyed the audience carefully. "James Todd escorted the Hope Diamond, alone and unarmed, for one mile. He was greeted at the Smithsonian by a crowd of reporters, television cameras, Washington socialites, and top museum brass. Harry Winston was noticeably absent. With great relief Todd delivered the package into the hands of Leonard Carmichael at precisely 11:45 a.m." Abby paused for a moment and glanced at the screen behind her. "The blue-collar postman knew he carried a legendary, cursed jewel, and that he risked his life just by laying hands on it."

———— ∞ ————

Alex Weld watched Dr. Mitchell give her presentation, mesmerized with the famous gem's history. An old thrill tingled his senses. He was eager to get back into the game after months of reconnaissance. Lifting a few paintings from a local museum in Rio was one thing; stealing the Hope Diamond from the Smithsonian was something else entirely. He sat fifteen rows away from Abby, remembering just why he'd chosen this career in the first place. Yet as he listened to the story, a deep sense of caution nagged at his mind. Something about her was familiar. Alex was a genius at remembering faces. It would come.

"The Hope Diamond is the most infamous jewel in the world, and even in 1954 many people in the United States knew about its bloody history. Things are no different today. It is the most viewed museum object in the world, boasting more visitors each year than the *Mona Lisa*."

The picture on the screen behind Abby changed to a breathtaking blue diamond the size of a plum, surrounded by smaller white diamonds.

"Although we can't pinpoint the exact date the jewel was found, it is believed to have been dug from the Kollur Diamond Mine in India sometime in the early sixteen hundreds."

Here the slide changed from the exquisitely cut blue jewel to a crude black-and-white drawing of an uncut, unpolished diamond of somewhat triangular shape.

"This illustration was drawn by the French jewel merchant Jean-Baptiste Tavernier. He acquired the stone in Golconda, India, in 1653. His memoirs were published in 1675, and although he goes into great detail about his voyages to India, he never indicates exactly how he purchased the diamond. This has led many to believe that he did not acquire the jewel by honest means."

Abby swept a strand of loose brown hair off her face and tucked it behind her ear. "Tavernier was a noted jewel merchant who made a fortune buying and selling precious stones in Asia. At the time, India was the only established source of diamonds in the world, and Tavernier spent the majority of his career creating a trade pipeline between the diamond mines of India and the courts of Europe. He traveled extensively, covering more than twenty thousand miles of terrain in thirty years. Both an entrepreneur and an aristocrat, Tavernier used his connections to develop a deep knowledge of customs, taxes, trade, and some might argue, bribery."

───⊗∞⊗───

For the most part Alex was more interested in the logistics involved in pulling off a heist than the value of the object he stole. Yet there was something intriguing about the history lesson offered by Dr. Mitchell. It was as though she knew the diamond, as though she loved it. Alex watched her continue the lecture. He noticed the expressions on her face and listened to the inflection in her voice. It was quite obvious that she was passionate about her subject, but even that hardly explained why she never once looked at her notes on the podium. It was obvious she knew every detail of this story by heart.

───⊗∞⊗───

"In time the diamond passed from Tavernier into the hands of the French monarchy where it became known as the French Blue. Ultimately, it was inherited by Louis XVI. I think we all know how his chapter of history ended on the guillotine, along with his wife Marie Antoinette, during the French Revolution. It is in the middle of that uprising that things get interesting for the diamond and those who would later come to own it. Though many mysteries still surround the story of the Hope Diamond, the history we do know is just as fascinating, if not more so, than any myths that may be attached to the renowned jewel."

Abby paused for a moment and took a deep breath. "But let's be honest, shall we? We are all interested in the darker parts of its history." She smiled as the audience seemed to lean forward, collectively.

"According to legend, the diamond was originally stolen from the Hindu idol Rama Sita, which is said to have cursed the jewel so that all of its future owners would suffer tragedy. Indeed, its victims are infamous. King George IV, Napoleon, Caroline of Brunswick, May Yohe, Henry Hope, Evalyn Walsh McLean, Harry Winston, and Jackie Kennedy, are just a few of those who crossed paths with the diamond.

"Even our postman James Todd endured his share of tragedy. Just a year after delivering the Hope Diamond into the hands of Leonard Carmichael, Todd was crushed by a truck, lost his wife to a sudden heart attack, and watched his home burn to the ground. Some would argue those events were just a string of unfortunate coincidences in the life of an ordinary postman. But it is no wonder so many believe the diamond is cursed. That legendary curse is part of what makes it so valuable today. Currently on display right here at the Smithsonian, it would fetch as much as two hundred million dollars at auction."

An appreciative gasp rippled through the audience.

"The Smithsonian will celebrate the fiftieth anniversary of the diamond's arrival next week with a huge extravaganza in its honor. Please join us as we continue the story of the Hope Diamond with a presentation you will never forget. I would be delighted to see each and every one of you there. Have a wonderful evening and feel free to visit the Hope on your way out."

With that, Abby gave the audience a polite nod and stepped from the podium as they sat in stunned silence.

She knew the power of story to draw people in, and she knew just when to stop. They wanted to hear more, and that was exactly what she intended. Abby would wager her next paycheck that every person present would be at the celebration next week.

It took a few seconds for the audience to realize she was finished. As she made her way toward the exit, they erupted in applause as if trying to draw her back to the stage. Abby slipped into the hallway and made her way down the gallery to pay respects to the diamond on her way out. It was a tradition she started many years earlier when working on her dissertation.

The Hope Diamond had its own display room inside the Janet Annenberg Hooker Hall of Geology, Gems and Minerals. The wing was large and sprawling, inset every few feet with glass displays filled with the world's most renowned geological formations. At the center of that wing, and the first room to the left, was the Harry Winston Gallery, which featured five attractions, all revolving around the Hope Diamond. In the middle of the room stood a raised marble platform, flanked on five sides by thick columns. Directly in the center sat a square pedestal of matching marble, topped by a glass display case. The Smithsonian's main attraction, a cursed blue diamond that had captured the imagination of king and commoner for thousands of years, nestled inside the glass case.

As part of the National Gem Collection, it was by far the most popular jewel on display. Because of the notoriety and immense value of the diamond, it sat on a rotating pedestal inside a three-inch thick bullet-proof glass cylinder. The renovations to the gems exhibit were completed in 1997, and along with them came state-of-the-art security and surveillance systems.

Abby stood before the display case, arms crossed in front of her, eyes locked on the deep blue stone that had given her so much grief lately.

"Focus," her father had always told her. "Focus on what you want and nothing else. It will take you anywhere you want to go." So she focused on the diamond and its history. She immersed herself in it. She studied and traveled and wrote, eventually establishing herself as the authority on the Hope Diamond. Her father's colleagues at the Smithsonian welcomed her with open arms, and it was here that she carved a niche for herself.

Abby took off her reading glasses and rubbed her eyes with the back of her hand. She pulled her hair from the tight knot at the nape of her neck and let it fall around her shoulders, her scalp aching from the tension.

She stood before the diamond. It was their ritual. Silence. Speculation. Angst. They were in a battle of wills. The irony of fighting with an inanimate object was not lost on her. Abby often found it humorous. It seemed she had a history of giving herself to things that could not love her back.

"Dr. Mitchell?"

The voice shocked her out of her reverie and she spun around to find a man standing behind her with a sheepish look on his face.

"Yes," she asked, flustered.

"My name is Alex Weld," he said, offering his hand. "I'm a journalist with *National Geographic*."

The smile he offered threatened to make Abby blush. Laugh lines crinkled the corners of his bright blue eyes and matched the ease of his smile. He was a few inches taller than she, with sandy brown hair and a solid build.

She took his hand. "Abigail Mitchell. Nice to meet you."

"I was in the theater listening to your lecture. You left before I could get down there to introduce myself."

"Sorry. It's been a long week."

"Nothing serious I hope?"

"Oh, just getting ready for the celebration, that's all," she said with a wave of her hand.

"Well, I won't take much of your time. I was just wondering if I could set up an interview to talk about the Hope Diamond." Alex nodded toward the display case where it sat glistening under the lights.

"An interview?"

"Yeah. I'm doing a piece on the diamond for *National Geographic*. It seems you're doing quite a job with your publicity efforts. Everyone is talking about the diamond, so we thought it would be a great idea to run a piece in our next issue."

Uncertain, Abby paused for a moment. "Sure, that sounds great," she finally said. "When did you want to set up something?"

Alex grinned. "Honestly, I was hoping to get some of your time today, but I didn't realize you were leaving work early."

Abby glanced at her watch. "I'd love to, but I'm starving. I didn't eat lunch. Would sometime next week work?"

Alex gnawed on his bottom lip for a moment, but never broke eye contact with Abby. "I tell you what. I haven't eaten either. If your dinner is on *National Geographic*, would you give me an hour of your time so I can get started?"

Abby hesitated for a moment, but just then her stomach rumbled and she relented. "Why not. If you want to follow me, I know a great café several blocks away that serves a killer panini."

"Consider it done. Lead the way."

"Great," Abby said, glancing one last time at the diamond. She turned and began walking toward the exit.

———❧———

Alex followed Abby out of the Smithsonian parking lot and into the flow of traffic. The mental files in his mind began to fall into place. He remembered the hair, the ear, the neck. And he remembered the ring. Alex Weld knew where he had seen her. He scrambled for his phone.

———❧———

Isaac sat in a dimly lit office with the shades drawn, a set of Smithsonian blueprints spread on the desk. He traced the pale blue lines with a fingertip, mentally working his way through the building.

A stack of black-and-white photographs sat on the corner of the desk. Among them were snapshots of Abby at work, at home, and in her car.

Newspaper clippings were pinned haphazardly to the wall behind him. The most recent was an article about the heist in Rio. Another proclaimed that two Van Gogh paintings had been stolen from the Van Gogh Museum in Amsterdam. A third described the theft of Edvard Munch's classic *The Scream*, known to many as the most frequently stolen piece of art in the world.

The phone rang. Isaac picked it up and asked, "Did you make contact?"

"Yes," replied Alex. "But we have a problem."

"What problem?"

"It seems we've met our mark before."

Isaac snatched a picture from the pile and glared at Abby's face. "What do you mean?"

"In Rio. She was wearing the ring."

"Where are you now?"

"Following her to a café. We're having dinner."

"Get to the bottom of it," Isaac hissed.

"I intend to."

Isaac set the phone down and studied the picture.

<hr />

Alex and Abby sat at a small bistro table on the sidewalk, sipping coffee and eating sandwiches. The smell of autumn leaves suggested that winter was not far off.

"What's the craziest thing that's ever happened to you on the job?" Alex asked, taking a sip of coffee.

Abby grunted and curled her upper lip. "You don't want to know."

"Oh, come on, what can be so distressing about the life of a museum director?"

"Are you insinuating that my life is boring?" Abby grinned.

"Yes." He chuckled.

"You wouldn't believe me if I told you."

"Try me."

Abby shrugged. "How about a theft at gunpoint and the loss of four of the most valuable paintings in the world?"

"At the Smithsonian?"

Abby shook her head and finished the last bite of her sandwich. "No. In Rio de Janeiro. I was on a business trip and found myself in the wrong place at the wrong time."

"Sounds harrowing."

"It was pretty bad." Abby paused and then looked at Alex apologetically. "I'm sorry. You asked me for an interview and I've been babbling on about my problems. All that time I spend around *boring* inanimate objects must have left me hungry for human interaction."

"*Touché*," Alex said, offering a genuine laugh. He pulled a legal pad from the bag at his side and flipped back through the notes he had made during her lecture. "Sooo . . . take me back to the beginning. What happened to Tavernier once he got his hands on the diamond?"

"He held onto it for fifteen years. It's the only stone he kept for any length of time. He later sold it for the equivalent of $3.6 million dollars."

Alex whistled. "Not a bad profit!"

"Perhaps, but I'm sure he soon came to wish he had never laid eyes on the thing."

"How so?"

Abby turned a wistful gaze toward the park across the street. The tree limbs swayed in the gentle breeze. Loose strands of hair swirled across her cheek as she told Alex the story.

4

DECCAN PLATEAU, CENTRAL INDIA, 1655

HAUTES MONTAGNES QUI FONT UNE FORME DE CROISSANT,
Jean-Baptiste Tavernier scratched into the pages of his
journal as he looked at the great stone outcropping atop
Medusala Mountain. Although he had heard many travel-
ers refer to the mountain being shaped in the form of a
cross, he disagreed.

It looks more like a crescent to me, he thought, digging
through his bag for a pouch of dried fruit. *But it could be
the hunger talking.*

The oxen cart jolted along the dirt road, narrowly
avoiding ditches on either side. Tavernier perched atop
the shaky wooden loft like a corpulent bird on a swaying branch. The guide he hired to take him to the Kollur
mines walked beside the mangy beast, carrying a whip in
one hand and a dirty water skin in the other.

"How much farther?" Tavernier asked, aching from
the journey.

"Just over that rise," the guide responded, cracking
a whip upon the malnourished haunches of the old ox.
What was meant as an effort to spur the beast into action

resulted in nothing more than an aggravated grunt. The ox plowed ahead slowly, putting one arthritic hoof in front of another, same as before.

Tavernier sat up and craned his neck to see over the ridge, balancing his weight carefully to avoid falling off the cart.

Within a few moments, the wobbly ensemble of ox, cart, rider, and guide crested the ridge and beheld the largest excavation on the continent. A great plateau spread before them, swarming with tens of thousands of workers.

Europeans dug their mines into the sides of mountains and tunneled deep within, supporting their quarries with elaborate engineering and timber frames. The Indians preferred instead to dig their holes directly into the ground, leaving wide but relatively shallow pock marks throughout their mining areas. Most holes were abandoned after a few feet if no diamonds were discovered. Others plummeted fathoms into the rocky soil and were virtual beehives of activity.

Although Tavernier bought thousands of diamonds from the region during his career, he had never been to the source of their bounty until now. He watched the frenzied activity below with interest. It was not long, however, before their presence was noted, and they were approached by an officer wearing the white turban and golden sash of the sultan.

"You are trespassing," he said, without taking note of name or rank.

"I am here on official business," Tavernier retorted, lumbering off the cart with minor difficulty. "I am here to see Prime Minister Jumla."

At his full height, the Frenchman stood over six feet tall, a great contrast to the short, slender officer. The excess of one hundred extra pounds made Tavernier seem even larger.

"Are you a friend?"

"A business associate."

"I see," the officer said with a slight nod. "Please come with me."

Tavernier followed the officer through the midst of the camp where thirty thousand slaves—men, women, and children—hauled dirt from the pits and carried it away to be sifted for diamonds. On a small rise in the midst of the vast camp rose a large mound of earth, topped by an ornate wooden pergola. The sides of the structure were hung with tapestries, blocking its occupant from sight.

The soldier led Tavernier to the entrance, motioned for the guards to let him in, and then slipped away without a word.

As he parted the heavy curtains, Tavernier stopped short, clenching his jaw. Seated on the plush cushions was not Mir Jumla, but a man that Tavernier had grown to detest during his many travels to Golconda.

The old Brahmin sat cross-legged on a cushion, looking deceptively frail. The swath of red fabric wrapped around his waist was hiked up to the knees, pooling around his thin legs. A yellow sash hung over his bare chest, and his long, oily hair was tied back with a strip of leather. The beard that had once been thick and black was almost completely gray and came to a scraggly point a few inches beneath his chin.

"Rai Rao," Tavernier growled.

"That is hardly a way to address a Brahmin," Rai said, hands folded across his belly.

"Where is Mir Jumla?"

"I govern these mines for the sultan. Why would you expect to find that Persian traitor here?"

"We had an appointment last week, and he never arrived. I assumed he was delayed by business at the mines."

"Would that appointment have involved the sale of diamonds rightly owned by the sultan?" Rai asked. He cocked his head to one side, eyeing Tavernier guardedly. "Perhaps you came looking for another blue diamond to match the one you stole two years ago?"

It took Tavernier only a brief moment to regain his composure, but he feared his expression had confirmed the Brahmin's assumption. "I came to buy diamonds. And I buy them from the prime minister, sanctioned by the sultan to do so. I am a jewel merchant. That is what I do. You know that very well, Rai."

"I prefer to be addressed as Brahmin."

"I prefer to speak with Mir Jumla."

"Indeed," he grunted. "You will need to find a new middleman. prime minister Jumla no longer works for the sultan."

"I find that odd considering I received a dispatch from him a short time ago requesting that I meet him in Golconda."

"Perhaps that was before he decided to find employment with the Mughal emperor, taking over four hundred pounds of the sultan's diamonds with him."

"I know nothing of that," Tavernier answered.

"You are hardly a convincing witness considering you and Mir Jumla have a long history of trading the sultan's jewels."

"Jewels I bought and *paid* for honestly."

41

"Just because you paid for them does not mean they were rightfully for sale."

Tavernier paused, considering a new tactic. "Whether Mir Jumla traded diamonds honestly is not *my* concern, nor is it *my* problem. I bought what he sold. There is no crime in that."

Rai Rao leaned in with a devilish grin. "It will be if you are found to have any diamonds larger than ten carats on your person or in your belongings. My officers are searching your room at the palace as we speak."

Tavernier began sweating long before he entered the Brahmin's pergola, so the cold beads that dripped down his brow did not belie the sudden panic that gripped him. His concern was not for the hundreds of diamonds that sat in his quarters on the palace grounds, but for the 112-carat blue diamond that rested in the buckskin pouch next to his heart.

"You look worried Jean-Baptiste. Is there something that you need to tell me before I have my soldiers strip you?"

The color rose in his cheeks, and he leaned forward until he was but a few inches from Rai's face. "Do *not* mistake my anger for fear. You are forward, indeed, if you believe for a moment that you can treat the sultan's ambassador to France with such disdain. There is not a man in the sultan's court that would dare accuse me of dishonest dealings, and I would greatly caution you from becoming the first."

A self-satisfied grin spread across Rai's face, and he brought his palms together in a series of three loud claps. The curtains were instantly parted by two guards who moved forward and took Tavernier by the arms.

"We will see if you have anything to fear or not," Rai said as he leaned back into the cushions. "Take him back to Golconda and throw him in the dungeon."

———— ⋙⋘ ————

Tavernier sat on the rough stone bench inside the sultan's prison with his chin clenched in defiance. The stench of urine and unwashed bodies smelled rank to his refined nostrils. Although he desperately wanted to breathe fresh air, he resisted the urge to pace the floor and shake the iron bars that covered the narrow doorway.

The distant light of a flickering oil torch cast long shadows on the floor at his feet, illuminating the occasional rat or cockroach as it scurried to safety. The buzz of flies, feasting on excrement, was a constant irritant that deprived him of silence.

Rai Rao was at least possessed of enough sense to put Tavernier in an empty cell. The maddened, half-starved slaves who occupied the dungeon would have made short work of the wealthy Frenchman dressed in luxurious robes. For that Tavernier found room to be grateful, even while suppressing his immense rage.

The Brahmin had at his disposal a number of horse-drawn chariots that he eagerly employed to usher Tavernier back to the city, making quick work of the return journey. Though certainly a fool, Rao wisely chose not to follow through on his threat of a strip search.

The buckskin pouch that rested against Tavernier's skin had never seemed heavier. As the hours slipped away, he pondered his risk of losing the precious blue diamond. Should it be discovered, he had a variety of resources at his disposal for buying his way out of the situation, yet he was all too aware that the value of the diamond out-weighed them all. His life would no doubt be forfeit the moment it was discovered.

I could have sold it a hundred times, he thought. *Had I sold it, I would not be in this situation, perhaps; but I also would not have as much advantage for a future sale. The right buyer has yet to come along. There will be someone willing to offer a great fortune for this diamond, and I will not part with it until then.*

His reverie was broken by the distant barrage of foot-steps descending into the dungeon. They were purposeful and swift. He knew they were coming for him.

Tavernier rose to greet his captors.

The sickly yellow light began to brighten as three sol-diers drew closer, carrying torches and long wooden spears with hammered steel tips. He did his best not to blink in the face of the sudden glow.

"I assume you have come to release me," Tavernier said to the captain of the guard.

Their eyes locked for a moment, testing one another's nerve. "We are on orders from the sultan," he said. "You are to come with us."

One of the soldiers unlocked the door with a long metal key and swung open the wrought iron gate to his cell.

Tavernier walked into the corridor with composure, despite the fact that his legs felt like tree trunks.

"Please follow," the captain said. He turned and marched back down the tunnel.

When the iron gate slammed shut, the sound of clang-ing metal thundered through the stone corridor, vibrating the walls and settling dirt onto the floor.

Tavernier fought the instinct to clutch the leather pouch above his heart. Instead, he confidently followed the guards into a patch of blinding sunlight that flooded the courtyard. He raised a hand to shield his eyes and waited.

The captain turned and said, "You are free to go. The sultan sends his deepest apologies that you were treated with such disrespect. He hopes that you understand the Brahmin was attempting to act on his behalf. He was, nonetheless, overzealous."

Tavernier parted his lips, allowing the great sigh of relief to exit slowly.

"The sultan also wishes us to inform you that you are most welcome to trade for diamonds in this city any time you wish. Is there anywhere you wish us to take you, Ambassador Tavernier?"

"Have my belongings sent from my quarters and arrange for transportation to the shipyards. I will be catching the next vessel to France."

The guards nodded politely, put their hands together, and said "*Vanakkam*" in unison.

Thus Tavernier found himself a free man. His only concern was that of getting the jewel to safety. The possibility of losing his head bothered him a great deal less than the thought of losing his diamond.

I never did like ships. Seems an unnatural way to travel.

Tavernier clutched the rails on the starboard side of the merchant vessel until his knuckles turned white. He could see the coastline in the distance, lurching violently as though the earth rocked uncontrollably on its axis. Up. Down. Up. Down. Up. Down.

Oh no, here it comes again.

Yet another wave of nausea rose in his stomach, and he heaved the last remaining evidence of an unsatisfactory dinner into the swirling mass of foam and water below. It was an odd feeling, indeed, when it seemed as though he stood still and everything around him spun like a drunken sailor attempting to waltz. The opposite could not be more true, however, as the small ship pitched to and fro across the choppy water.

Somewhere behind him, the petrified crew frantically scampered across the deck, yanking at the rigging and bellowing orders that could barely be heard above the squall.

The rain had begun to fall several hours earlier when they left the fathomless depths behind and headed toward shore for the last leg of their journey. The winds hounded them from the rear. The effect was both a blessing and a curse, as the gales pushed them to the shore with great speed, and the rain bit into their faces like stinging hail. Ultimately, the biggest dilemma facing the crew was the fact that they had no control over the ship's direction. Wheel and rudder were of little use when the devil was at your back, pushing with the speed of Hermes.

Normally, they charted a delicate course through the rocky shoals into the port of Tondi, but tonight they were cast directly into the jagged path that made the waters off the small trading town infamous as many a sailor's final resting place.

Between retches, Tavernier could hear the crew give orders to abandon ship. The teeth-like black rocks rose from the waves before them, eager to grind the vessel to splinters.

Weak and pale, Tavernier saw the deck hands throw empty wine casks overboard, lashed with rigging. One by one they timed the waves splashing onto the sideboards and dove in as they receded.

The rocks loomed ever closer. The frigid water poured onto the deck, swirling at his feet and knocking him further off balance.

"Get off this ship, you fool, before we run aground," a deckhand screamed, grabbing him by the arm and trying to tug him away from the rail.

Tavernier scowled at him, aghast that he actually believed they had any better chances in the water than they did on the ship.

The cracking, splitting sound of breaking wood caused his insides to boil and lurch again. Somewhere beneath the surface, the bottom of the boat had scraped along the ever nearing shoals.

"I'm coming!" he shouted, as he waded his way through the knee-deep water that coursed across the deck. The sailor led him to the other side of the ship where the waves receded with greater frequency.

"If you toss the barrels overboard and time it just right, you won't be sucked under the ship," the sailor shouted.

What a comfort. And here I thought drowning was the worst death we could endure tonight.

Tavernier edged closer to the rail, feeling the rhythm of the rocking boat. He steadied his breathing, in and out, with the thrust of the ship. As he prepared himself, Tavernier grabbed for the leather pouch around his neck. He would hold it between his teeth while he jumped.

He grabbed a second time and then a third. The pouch was gone. He frantically dug his hand inside his robe and scraped across his bare chest, searching for the worn buckskin.

Panic-stricken he scanned the waterlogged deck in search of the pouch. And then with a sickening feeling he remembered that he had taken it off before coming up on deck for fear he would lose it in the commotion. In his mind's eye he could see the pouch resting atop his clothing inside the trunk next to his cot.

Without a word to the sailor, Tavernier turned and waded through the water, desperately trying to reach the hatch that led to the quarters below.

"You fool!" the sailor screamed. "What are you doing?"

Tavernier did not respond, but rather slowly descended the steps into the bowels of the ship.

"Go to your death then! See if I care!" The deckhand jumped overboard.

The Frenchman paused halfway down the steps, staring into the blackness below. The single lantern that hung in the hallway had long since been put out by the waves pouring through the hatch.

Tavernier was alarmed to see that the water came not only from the deck above but also from the hull below. The rocks had obviously gouged a sizeable hole in the bottom of the ship. The water rose quickly. He turned for a moment to look back through the rain at the pale gray patch of sky. In that direction lay escape and *possible* death. But below was his beloved diamond and almost *certain* death. The choice was obvious.

I have not carried that diamond with me for ten years to lose it now.

The Frenchman descended the steps into the icy water. By the time he set foot on the hall floor, the water swirled around his waist, and he could see little more than vague shadows. His only advantage was the fact that his small chamber was the first door on the right. Four paces and he would be there. Though he pushed forward with all his strength, the force of the water pressed against him. He lost a step for every two he took.

Hands waving before him like a blind man, Tavernier felt for the door opening. Though only a matter of seconds, he felt as though he had lost all grasp of time. Finally, his hands hovered over emptiness, and he pulled himself into his chamber. Little more than eight feet by eight feet, he thought it should take no time at all to find his trunk in the tiny room. However, everything that had not been bolted to the floor now floated in the chest-deep water. Complete darkness surrounded him, and he blindly splashed through black seawater, desperately searching for the wooden trunk.

The gold. The gold is in the bottom of the trunk. It can't float because of the weight.

Tavernier took a deep breath and dove beneath the water, pulling himself to the floor. He spun around, arms waving frantically, unable to find the trunk. When he came up for air, he could not remember which direction the door lay. He filled his lungs with air and descended into the water again.

This time his hands brushed against the steamer trunk. He flipped the latch and pulled on the lid until his forearms burned. The pressure of the water pushed against the heavy mahogany. Tavernier planted his feet on the floor and pulled again, using the strength in his legs. The lid rose just enough for him to slide an arm into the trunk. He grabbed the soft buckskin and rose to the surface.

The water rested just beneath his chin, and his toes barely scraped the floor of the cabin. Tavernier pressed himself forward and grasped for the wall. No door. He moved along the rough boards, searching for an opening. No door. He moved along the next wall. No door. The water danced at his lips, and he had to lift his chin in an effort to feed his shallow breaths.

He found the opening on the fourth wall, but the mantle of the door rested below the water line. Tavernier gripped the leather with his teeth and pushed himself beneath the doorway. It took every ounce of self-restraint he possessed to pause and remember which direction led to the stairwell.

Left. Go left.

He could no longer walk, so he swam with clumsy strokes toward the staircase. His knee banged against the wood, forcing hot, stinging tears to the corners of his eyes. But with much relief he scrambled up the waterlogged steps onto the deck. Just then the sea gurgled up from below, fully submerging the cabins. Only the rails, mast, and sail remained above water now.

Tavernier could not jump for there was nothing to jump from. Instead, he pushed himself over the rail and desperately swam away from the ship before it sucked him beneath the water in its wake.

His jaw ached from the pressure of biting into the leather; he could feel his teeth meet.

Neither rain nor wind let up as Jean-Baptiste Tavernier half swam, half floated toward the projecting black rocks. All he could think of was that he had managed to rescue his blue diamond from the greedy sea that had tried to claim it.

5

ABBY TOOK A SIP OF HER COFFEE, PRIVATELY ENJOYING THE HORRIFIED look on Alex's face.

"A shipwreck?" he said, draining his cup. "*Really?*"

"Everyone who takes the diamond suffers something tragic," she said with a shrug.

Alex choked, spraying the table with coffee.

"You all right?" Abby asked.

"Yeah," he said, pounding his chest. "Just went down the wrong pipe." Alex looked at his watch. "Wow! Looks like my hour is up, and we've barely started the interview. I've got a meeting to run to." He caught Abby's glance and offered her an impish grin. "Could I get a rain check on the rest of the story?"

She returned his grin. "Sure."

"It was a pleasure to meet you, Dr. Mitchell," he said, reaching for her hand. Alex held onto it for a few seconds longer than the shake required.

"Call me Abby. Everyone does."

"I look really forward to continuing our interview, Abby."

"Likewise."

"Now if you'll excuse me, I have to get going." Alex rose, paid the tab, and hurried to his car.

━━━ ⋙⋘ ━━━

Isaac sat with his feet propped up on the desk, deep in thought. Thick, sweet-smelling clouds of pipe smoke hung around him, making the dark room even more oppressive.

Once again the phone buzzed, and he answered on the first ring.

"Yeah?" He paused, listening. "I'll be there in thirty minutes."

━━━ ⋙⋘ ━━━

Abby parked her Land Rover in front of a renovated brick warehouse that had been turned into a loft apartment building. She climbed the few short steps and pressed a buzzer beneath a pair of familiar names.

"Who is it?" a man growled into the receiver on the other end.

"It's just me."

"Come on up."

The door clicked, and Abby walked into the dark hallway toward an old freight elevator at the end. She pulled the grate down and pushed the button for the third floor. The elevator clinked loudly as it rose at a snail's pace. It jolted to a stop, and Abby stepped from the cage, thankful that once again it had made it to her destination without plummeting to the bottom.

A woman in her early fifties swung the door open before Abby could even knock and pulled her into the loft with a warm hug.

"Welcome, deary," she said.

Abby leaned into her embrace. "It's good to see you again, DeDe."

"It's been too long." DeDe's salt-and-pepper curls, thin frame, and bohemian aura revealed her sense of personal style. It had found its way into the home and made it a comfortable if somewhat messy retreat. Black-and-white photographs, artwork, wall hangings, and stacks of old newspapers were scattered at random.

"Dow!" Abby beamed as her friend wandered in from the kitchen holding a glass of murky green liquid. Older than DeDe, Dow's wild-looking gray hair was held loosely in a ponytail. He chugged the contents of his glass with a grimace.

"Good Lord, what on earth are you drinking?" Abby asked, eyeing the glass suspiciously.

"Barley green," he said, wiping the green moustache on his shirtsleeve. "Wretched stuff. Tastes like grass clippings."

"Then why are you drinking it?"

"Because I'm old, I'm ugly, and I smoke too much. I figure I ought to do something that's good for my body."

Abby laughed with affection and gave him a big hug. "I hate to be the one to tell you this, but barley green won't change any of that."

"You're probably right. But it keeps my wife happy."

Abby surveyed the apartment, resting her eyes on a recent stack of newspapers. "Looks like you've been busy."

"Busy yes . . . productive no. The Collectors have pulled off three major heists this year." He dug frantically through a stack of newspapers in the corner. After searching for a moment, he found what he was looking for and shoved it in Abby's face. "The heist in Rio . . . the Dali . . . and the others."

"Ugh," she said, waving the paper away. "You don't have to remind me. I was there."

"Yes. Yes. Remarkably lucky you were able to witness them firsthand."

"Not exactly the word I would use to describe it."

DeDe shook her head. "Most men take up golf, or fishing, or welding. My husband spends his spare time documenting art thefts."

"So you're sure it was the Collectors in Rio?"

"Without a doubt." He dove into another stack of newspaper clippings and continued. "Fascinating, absolutely fascinating, how they work. It's a competition among them you see. They're in a race to acquire priceless works of art. We have yet to see a piece resurface. From what I can gather, it doesn't seem to be a business, but rather a pastime."

"I'm sure Interpol would be interested to hear that."

Dow snorted and waved an accusatory finger in her face. "Interpol isn't doing half of what they should to catch these guys."

She shook her head and suppressed a laugh. "So it's up to you then? You're going to catch them on your own?"

"If I have to," he said with a curt nod.

Abby lifted the top paper from the stack in Dow's arms and read the headline:

EDVARD MUNCH'S *THE SCREAM* STOLEN AGAIN

"What is that, like the twentieth time?"

"Mark my words," said Dow. "It will be the last. You'll never see that painting again. The Collectors took it. It's gone."

"But it always surfaces. Surely, it's just a matter of time."

"I'm telling you, these men don't sell what they steal."

DeDe bustled in from the kitchen, carrying a tray of food. "Enough of that. Let's eat."

Abby eyed the tray. "Sorry, DeDe, but I've already had dinner."

"With whom?" her friend asked.

"A reporter from *National Geographic*."

"A *date*?" Dow and DeDe questioned in unison.

"Hardly," Abby said. "It was an interview."

Eagerly, Dow took her elbow and led her to the table. He could not hide the excitement brimming in his eyes. "Now tell me everything what happened in Rio. And I mean *everything*."

Isaac pushed through the revolving door of Driscoll's, an upscale watering hole in D.C.'s financial district, and headed toward a private room at the back where Alex and the man they knew only as the Broker were waiting.

"Have a seat," the Broker said, motioning toward a plush leather chair. He was an attractive, brown-eyed gentleman, somewhere in his late fifties, with flecks of gray at his temples. He rarely smiled, and he never laughed. He would have been a great deal more handsome if he did.

"Let's get down to business," Isaac said, wasting no time.

The Broker took a small sip of his dry martini and brushed an invisible piece of lint from his pant leg. "Have you made contact with the woman?"

"I have," replied Alex.

"And you can use her to get the diamond?"

"Yes, I believe so."

"Good. Then we just need to make payment arrangements."

"Not so fast," Isaac interrupted. "We still need to negotiate a price."

"Negotiate? I think not. Our standing fee should be more than sufficient."

Isaac laughed. "Twenty million dollars may be adequate to secure a few paintings, but it hardly scratches the surface on this job."

The Broker leaned forward in his chair, lips drawn into a tight line. "Twenty million *dollars* is—"

"Not enough to draw me out of retirement," Alex interrupted.

"Retirement?"

Alex cast a sideways glance at Isaac, but spoke to the Broker. "You were well aware that I stepped down from your employment after our last contract."

"Your brother assured me—"

"My brother doesn't speak for me," Alex said. "So if you want your diamond, and you want me to participate, then I'd suggest you up the ante."

The Broker narrowed his eyes. "I doubt that your commission warrants such a drastic change in terms."

"I beg to differ," Isaac said. "After many months of reconnaissance, we've concluded that we cannot do the job for what you've offered. Our price is fifty million dollars."

"That's ridiculous!" The Broker pounded his fist on the table. The door to their private lounge opened, preventing him from bursting into a full tirade.

The blonde waitress who entered the room was adept at distracting men from their business. She wore a form-fitting black dress, three-inch heels, and a smile that instantly diffused the tension in the room.

"Crown and Coke for you," she said, handing the first glass on her tray to Alex and the second to Isaac. "And Scotch and soda for you. Your friend ordered." She met Alex's appreciative gaze, curled her lips into a seductive smile, and left the room.

It took Alex a few seconds to regain his train of thought. He lifted the tumbler from the mahogany table and took a long swig of his drink. "You remembered. How thoughtful."

"You must be out of your mind," the Broker said.

Isaac shrugged. "You know how this works. The price is never fully settled until we've completed the background work and determined the difficulty of the job. This heist is a logistical nightmare. The price is fifty million dollars."

"Absolutely not."

Isaac wiped the sweat from his glass and met the Broker's steely gaze without flinching. "The Smithsonian is a fortress, unlike any facility we have ever penetrated, and the odds of us succeeding are almost nonexistent. If we're going to risk our lives and almost certain prison time, we will be well compensated."

"I have never paid such a ridiculous amount, and I won't do it now."

The brothers exchanged a glance and rose from the table. They left the room without another word. Alex could not help but scan the bar for their waitress on the way out. It was not until they had exited the building that they dared look at one another.

"He'll come," Alex said, sticking his hands deep in his pockets.

"Of course he will," Isaac agreed.

"He wants it bad enough. I give him thirty seconds."

They began to walk toward the parking garage.

The Broker stumbled out the revolving door, the fury evident on his face. He struggled to hide it. "Wait!" he shouted. "I need more time to consider the price."

Alex pulled a slip of paper from his pocket and handed it to him. "Twenty-five million dollars will be wired to this account by midnight tonight as a down payment if you are serious about enlisting our services. If not, we don't ever want to hear from you again."

The Broker took the paper with a trembling hand and slid into the back seat of a silver BMW that waited at the curb.

Alex's eyes narrowed as he watched the car pull away. "Call me when he makes the transfer."

"Where are you going?"

A mischievous grin crept across his face. "I think I'd like to make the acquaintance of a certain waitress."

Three hours later, Alex lay in bed wide awake, watching the clock. Beside him slept a naked woman, wrapped in sheets. Her blonde hair spilled across the pillow.

As soon as the numbers on his digital alarm clock changed to 12:01, the phone rang. He grabbed it from the cradle before it could ring a second time.

The pleasure in Isaac's voice was evident. "He was serious."

"I thought he might be."

6

ABBY PULLED THE COVERS OVER HER HEAD AND TRIED TO GO BACK TO sleep. Sounds of Sunday morning traffic echoed through the walls of her apartment, and despite her best efforts, she could not ignore them. So she lay motionless under the rumpled covers, letting the sleep drain from her body.

Finally, she pulled the blankets down just enough to see a promise of sunrise hug her bedroom window. The clock on her nightstand read 7:30. She had hoped to sleep until at least nine. Abby sat up and tossed her legs over the side of the bed, digging her toes into the thick carpet.

"Coffee," she mumbled, making her way to the kitchen. "I *really* need coffee."

She flicked the switch on the coffee pot and poured a great deal of creamer into her empty cup. She was not a coffee purist and had never been able to drink it black. The water began to hiss and bubble as it streamed through the machine. The hot, pungent smell floated through the kitchen.

A few moments later, cup in hand, she pulled an old red blanket around her shoulders and waited for the sun to rise above a small chapel across the street. It was a beckoning of sorts, one that went unheeded, but one she looked for each morning nonetheless.

Something about the small church comforted her. The warm wooden doors, the stones worn smooth, and the softly chiming bell reminded her of a church on a street corner in Massachusetts that she had entered as a child. Mother had taken her there to kneel before the altar the day her father left them. Her memories of that day were filled with tears and sadness, an ache that drew them into the small chapel. She remembered her bare knees pressing against the smooth wood floor and the feeling of quiet, not just in the church but in her heart as well. She did not know Jesus then, but for the first time she wanted to. Many years had passed since then.

Abby brought the cup of coffee to her lips, parting just enough for a sip of warmth, and waited for her favorite part of every sunrise. The little chapel was plain and unadorned except for two brilliant stained-glass windows, one behind the pulpit and one at the front above the arched wooden doors. Both were circular, and no more than six feet in diameter. The one above the entry was a simple blue sky with a white dove carrying an olive branch in its mouth. The window above the pulpit was a deep crimson, broken only by a cross.

Abby leaned forward, expectantly. Slowly, the burning disk of orange sunlight rose, bathing the chapel in light, and bright beams drifted through the empty church, first illuminating the window of red stained glass, and then drifting to the blue. For a few glorious moments the colors combined, bathing her line of sight in majestic purple.

She watched until it passed, and as the color faded, she felt a pang of loss. The beauty lasted for such a short time, and then once again she sat staring at the cold stones of a church she'd never entered.

Abby sighed and shuffled into the kitchen to refill her coffee cup. On her way back to the sofa she noticed the glaring empty space on the desk where her laptop usually sat. She froze, and her heart began to pound. Her briefcase was missing as well. It always sat next to her chair under the desk.

Oh no! This is bad. This is very bad.

Abby bolted through her apartment, checking all her doors and windows. They were locked from the inside.

Think, think. She pressed the heel of her hand on her forehead. *Where did you have them last?* Then she closed her eyes and grimaced.

She had forgotten to bring them home from work. She was in such a hurry to leave that she hadn't returned to her office after yesterday's presentation. The sinking feeling in the pit of her stomach doubled when she realized that she had not locked her office door either.

Abby quickly changed into a pair of jeans, old tennis shoes, and a sweatshirt. She twisted her hair into a loose ponytail, grabbed her reading glasses, and bolted from the apartment without applying makeup.

"How could I have been so stupid?" she moaned. Abby threw her billfold into the car, pulled into traffic, and hit the accelerator.

⤜⟋⟋⟍⤛

To the casual observer it looked like an average, if not obscenely expensive, digital camera. However, what Isaac saw when he looked through the lens was not just the main gallery of the National Gem and Mineral Collection inside the Smithsonian, but also a series of intersecting infrared beams. Yet the display before him showed not where the beams were, but where they *had been* in the last twenty-four hours. He saved the image to disk and changed his angle, methodically recording the entire grid of light.

Every exit, camera, security guard, and museum staffer was photographed as he wandered through the gallery, like any other tourist.

He spent the majority of his time in the room housing the Hope Diamond. The ebb and flow of tourists was constant, and he went unnoticed. Tour guides paraded through, telling the story over and over to snap-happy tourists. The diamond was a favorite attraction, so it was easy for Isaac to mill with the crowds, listening intently and taking detailed pictures of every inch of the room.

The glass cylinder encasing the diamond was three inches thick and bulletproof. Inside the case itself, the diamond sat on a rotating column, taking one minute to come full circle. With each rotation, the light bounced off every facet, giving the appearance that it glowed from within. The lighting system itself was a fiber-optic marvel, created by Absolute Action Ltd. of London, the world's most renowned lighting firm. It had taken a team of lighting engineers five months to complete the display in 1997 at a cost of thirteen million dollars to the Smithsonian. Included in the renovations were the new display case and a security vault directly below the jewel that was so heavy the museum floor had to be structurally reinforced.

Isaac circled his prey like a hungry animal. The diamond taunted him from within, forbidden, impossible. The challenge was intoxicating.

⎯⎯∞⎯⎯

Harsh beams of sunlight fell across Alex's face, burning red behind his eyelids. He squinted into the glare and rolled over in search of his previous night's companion.

Empty sheets met his eager grasp, and he sat up to discover he was alone. Alex didn't bother searching the small penthouse. Her purse and the trail of clothes she'd left on his bedroom floor were gone. An uneasy sigh escaped his lips. He had planned on making her breakfast . . . and asking her name.

———∞∞∞———

Abby's office sat tucked away on the second floor of the Smithsonian Institution Building, a short distance away from the Museum of Natural History. The red sandstone edifice, constructed in an early Gothic motif, complete with turrets, spires, and arched windows, was appropriately dubbed The Castle. Although it held the main visitor center for the Institution and had a number of maps and displays, The Castle's main function was to house administrative offices and security operations.

Abby made it to the office in record time. At eight o'clock she charged through the employee entrance and jogged to the elevator. As soon as the doors slid open on the next floor she rushed to her office. The door was slightly cracked, and she pushed it gently, allowing it to swing open. The lights were off, and the room appeared empty. Abby hit the switch, locked the door, and went straight for her computer. It was sitting on the desk, exactly where she'd left it, scrolling through pictures on her screensaver.

The cursor blinked rhythmically in an open Word document, the last paragraph of which read:

> *Jean-Baptiste Tavernier built a lucrative career on the sale of precious stones he acquired in Asia. An accomplished and shrewd businessman, it was in his best interest to resell his acquisitions as soon as he returned to Europe. Records indicate that is exactly what he did, with one exception: the 112-carat blue diamond purchased from Mir Jumla.*

For reasons he did not record, Jean-Baptiste
Tavernier kept the great blue diamond in his pos-
session for fifteen years. It was the largest and rar-
est diamond he had ever owned, and ultimately,
the one that profited him the most. In 1668, it was
purchased by King Louis XIV for the astounding
sum of 400,000 livres, or the equivalent of 3.6
million dollars in today's currency...

Abby saved the document and went to her control panel. She hastily typed in her password and pulled up a list of recently used programs. Nothing out of the ordinary. She was not fully satisfied, however, and ran *KeyLogger*, a program that showed every keystroke made within the last seventy-two hours.

She had only intended to stay at the office long enough to make sure that her computer and briefcase had gone untouched. But as soon as her mind was put at ease, the piles of paper on her desk drew her attention. Almost three hours later, she was still engrossed in a stack of release forms. The abrasive buzzing of the telephone startled her. Abby glanced at it, but didn't answer.

Her answering machine picked up on the fourth ring, "Hi, you've reached the office of Dr. Abigail Mitchell. I'm out of the office at the moment, but if you leave your name and number I'll get back with you."

"Hi Dr. Mitchell . . . I mean Abby. This is Alex Weld from *National Geographic*—"

She turned and stared at the recording light on her machine and debated whether to pick up.

"I was calling to see if I could set up a time to finish that interview we started. Just let me know when is best for you. My number is—"

She hesitated for just a moment and then grabbed the receiver, "Hello?"

"Hey, I didn't think you would be in the office today."

"I really shouldn't be."

"Do you usually come in on your days off?"

Abby looked at the program running on her computer. "No, I just forgot something yesterday, and I swung by to pick it up."

"So can I cash that rain check you gave me last night? I cracked open my computer this morning only to find that I hardly got any information out of you."

"Sorry about that. My fault."

"Don't apologize. The company was great."

Abby smiled and dug her iPhone from the briefcase. "But to answer your question, I'd be more than happy to pencil something in. Let me see what I've got available." She opened her calendar and groaned. "I have nothing during the day for the next two weeks. How pathetic is that?"

"Popular lady."

"No. Just overwhelmed. It's that celebration I'm planning for the Hope Diamond."

"Surely it can't be that bad?"

"You have no idea."

"Well, would it be too presumptuous of me to ask if we could meet at night? Maybe for dinner again?" Alex asked.

Abby detected a note of hopefulness in his voice and couldn't help but grin. "I think that will work."

"Good," Alex said. "How does tomorrow night sound?"

"Perfect. Why don't you come by my office around five?"

"It's a date then . . . I mean, like a work date . . . thing."

"Sounds good. I'll see you then." Abby laughed and hung up the phone.

Her spirits were a great deal lighter as she stacked the papers neatly on her desk and tucked the laptop into her briefcase. She left the office and locked the door behind her.

———∞∞∞———

Isaac had just taken his final photo when his cell phone rang. "Yeah?"

"She's at work this morning. I wasn't counting on that. You'll have to steer clear of her office," Alex said. "I thought she wasn't coming in today."

"So did I. But I just called her office, and she picked up. You'll have to go back later."

"Okay." Isaac tucked the camera into his front pocket. He was just about to leave the Gem and Mineral Collection when he looked up and saw Abby walking toward him, with keys in one hand and a briefcase in the other. "Hey Al?" he said.

"Yeah?"

"You were holding out on me."

"What do you mean?"

"Well, you told me she was pretty, but you failed to mention how great she looks in jeans."

"What do you mean?"

"She's walking straight toward me."

"Really? What's she doing there?" Alex asked.

"We'll talk later," Isaac said.

"Hey, don't go messing with my territory."

"Don't worry, little brother. I know what my job is. I trust you do as well."

"That's why I love my job," Alex said. "I get to mix business with pleasure."

Isaac stuck the phone into his pocket and pulled out his camera. He wandered around the gallery as unobtrusively as possible, taking pictures of Abby as she stared at the Hope Diamond.

She stayed in the gallery for just a couple of moments, gazing silently at the deep blue stone. Abby brushed her fingers against the display case, her face unreadable, and then turned on her heel and left. A thought occurred to Isaac, and he looked at the thick glass display case for a moment. It was in the direct view of at least six different security cameras. He had an idea.

Isaac stepped into the hallway and walked toward a security guard a few yards away.

Once back at her apartment, Abby drank two more cups of coffee and let the cobwebs clear from her mind. Door and windows locked tight, she climbed in the shower and let the hot water pour over her until her fingertips puckered and turned white. Dow and DeDe, efficient people that they were, would consider it a pure waste of water to take such a long shower, but that was where Abby did her best thinking.

Thirty minutes later she emerged from the bathroom wearing a towel on her head, an old tee shirt, and a pair of sweats. She gathered her laptop, clicked on the TV, and plopped on the sofa. The sound of the morning news faded into background as she checked her email. Her face went pale.

There was only one message in her inbox, but it was enough to make her heart skip a beat. The sender was Douglas Mitchell.

"Dad," Abby muttered.

She waited a moment before clicking on the message and then read:

> Abby,
>> I'm going to be in town next Friday, and wondered if you wanted to have lunch.
> Dad

"Hello to you too," she snapped. She stared at the screen for a few minutes and then tentatively hit the reply key.

Dad,

> *Friday is crazy for me. What do you say we have breakfast?*

Abby

She let the cursor hover over the send button for an uncomfortable length of time, debating whether to reply at all. She squeezed her eyes shut, let out a sigh, and sent the message.

Why do you do this to yourself, Abby? It never ends well.

⊷∞⊷

The security badge declared his name was Randy Jacobs, Smithsonian Physical Security Specialist, and that his clearance level was A5. The picture had obviously been taken several years ago and showed a thinner, happier version of the disgruntled employee. However, it was the magnetic strip on the back that captured Isaac's interest. The badge hung from a nylon pulley attached to a clip at Randy's waist.

Isaac approached the guard, transforming into a friendly tourist. "Excuse me, sir," he said.

"Yes?"

"I seem to have misplaced my wife." Isaac looked sheepish. "She left about thirty minutes ago to take a picture of the Hooker Emerald Brooch. I think she said she was going that way." He pointed down the hall, drawing the guard's attention with his outstretched right hand. "But I've gotten all turned around, and now I can't find her."

As Randy looked down the hallway, Isaac slowly raised his left hand and carefully unclipped the badge with the skill of a veteran pickpocket.

"No, no," Randy said, shaking his head. "You're looking in the wrong place. That wing of the collection houses all the minerals. You're looking for gems."

As Isaac maintained eye contact, listening to his directions and nodding emphatically, he pulled the camera from his pocket and slid the security badge into an empty slot that would normally hold the camera's battery. He waited three seconds while it read the information on the magnetic strip and then removed it, waiting for his opportunity to return the badge.

"Yeah," Isaac said, offering an appreciative smile. "I see where I've gone wrong." He gave Randy a good natured slap on the back, while clipping the badge back in place with his free hand. "Thanks, man," he said, offering a genuine smile. "I appreciate it."

"No problem, sir. I hope you find your wife."

"I'm sure I will. She just won't want to leave. You know women and jewelry!"

───── ❧ ─────

Dow juggled the tottering stack of newspapers in his arms so he could answer the phone. DeDe sat in front of her easel carefully blending colors in preparation to paint. On her left was a print of Edvard Munch's classic, *The Scream*. She took a deep breath, swirled her brush on the pallet, and swept it across the empty canvas.

Dow managed to grab the receiver just before it went to voice mail. "Hello?"

"Dad emailed," Abby said. Her voice sounded shaky.

"No phone call?"

"He never calls. You know that. Phone calls are too personal."

Dow carefully set down his stack of papers and tugged at his earlobe. "What did he want?"

"Lunch. Next Friday."

"The day before the event? He couldn't have picked a worse day. What did you tell him?"

"I asked for breakfast instead. Honestly, I don't even know if I'll have time for that."

"Do you want to see him?"

She hesitated. "Yes . . . and no. You know how it is."

"Abby," Dow said carefully. "I don't know if this is such a good idea."

"When has it ever been a good idea? It's just that, you know, he's my dad. He's the only one I've got."

"I'd be more than happy to interview for the position," Dow offered.

Abby laughed. "And if the position were open you would get the job. But I can't pretend he isn't my father."

"Okay, deary, but be careful. He isn't good to you."

"I know. And thanks. I just thought you'd want to know."

Dow shook his head. *This is bad.*

He moved a stack of newspapers to a long narrow desk on the other side of the room and sat on a wooden stool, sorting them into stacks.

7

THE SILVER BMW FOLLOWED ALEX'S MERCEDES AT A COMFORTABLE
distance. The windows were tinted an impenetrable black,
rendering its passengers invisible. The driver was a non-
descript man of European descent, quiet, yet formidable.
He served many roles for his employer, the least of which
was chauffeur. On more than one occasion he had quietly
dispatched enemies for the man in the backseat. Although
he preferred not to, when needed he was capable of flying
small aircraft. Kidnap, blackmail, arson, and torture were
things he could have added to his professional resume, had
he the need for one. He didn't. The man driving had never
been in want of a job. He had gone by several names during his career, each of them adopted for the necessary task.
Mikál was the name uttered at his baptism in a Roman
Orthodox church in Slovakia, but Wülf was what the
Broker used on the rare occasions that they conversed.

The Broker sat directly behind his driver, eyes on the
red taillights of the Mercedes ahead of them. Neither man
was bothered by the dense quiet in the car, undisturbed by
radio or conversation. Both preferred it that way. So it was
with almost palpable shock that the silence was broken.

"You have been following him for the last week?" the Broker asked.

Wülf nodded.

"Has he gone anywhere out of the ordinary?"

"What is *ordinary*, sir?"

"Anywhere that I wouldn't approve."

Silence.

"And the girl? You've been tailing her as well?"

Silence again. Words were tools used sparingly for Wülf.

"Where has she been?"

"Work. Home. She has been out with Mr. Weld once. Occasionally she visits friends in a loft apartment on the other side of town. Nowhere else."

The Broker nodded, pleased. "Good."

There was a full ten car lengths between the BMW and the Mercedes. In the space between them were two other cars. Once they entered heavier traffic, Wülf navigated the streets, a safe distance away, and followed the car into the Smithsonian parking lot.

"Park and wait," the Broker ordered, leaning forward to watch Alex hurry toward the entrance.

Wülf nodded and slipped into an empty parking spot fifty feet away.

Alex purposefully arrived at Abby's office five minutes early. The door was half open, and he watched as she carried on two conversations at once. Abby wore a pair of black slacks and a red v-neck sweater. Her hair was loose, and she had kicked off her black stilettos. Her bare feet played with the carpet while she held her iPhone in one hand and a diet Coke in the other. Her office phone was cradled in her neck. The desk was littered with stacks of paper waiting to be signed and an untouched Chinese takeout box from lunch, which she either didn't like or didn't have time to eat.

"Yes. That's right," she said. "At least three hundred people. I should be able to get you a final head count in the morning. . . . Yes, the menu is finalized. The suggestions you gave me helped tremendously. Well, you know how the D.C. social circle is. They have pretty high expectations. . . . Okay. Thanks. Bye."

She set down her Coke and hung up the office phone, took a deep breath, and pressed the iPhone to her ear. "So sorry, Mr. Trent, it's been a little crazy around here today. . . . Yes I received the security information. I've got a meeting with Daniel Wallace tomorrow, and we'll be going over all that. . . . Yes, I know. You don't have to remind me how serious this is."

Abby turned in her swivel chair and saw Alex leaning against the doorway. She grinned and motioned him to have a seat. Alex settled into a leather armchair across from her desk and waited.

Several minutes later Abby hung up the phone. "I'm so sorry," she said, scribbling her name on a stack of release forms. "I lost track of time."

"No problem. I'm a little early."

"Give me three more minutes, and I'll be done."

"Take your time."

"You know what," she said, rubbing a cramp in her hand. "These can wait until tomorrow. Let's get out of here."

———— ❧ ————

Abby studied her reflection in the bathroom mirror. Dark hair. Dark eyes. A trace of freckles left over from childhood. Her mother's cheekbones. Her father's jaw.

Her face clouded at the thought, and she busied herself by smoothing the wrinkles from her slacks.

She had excused herself as soon as they arrived at the restaurant. Alex's early arrival hadn't given her a chance to freshen up. She fluffed her hair, powdered the oily spots on her face, and applied a fresh coat of lip gloss. As Abby fussed over her reflection, it occurred to her that she couldn't remember the last time she was concerned about how she looked in the presence of a man. The realization brought a little color to her cheeks.

Oh, come on. It's not like this is a real date.

———— ❧ ————

Alex's cell phone beeped, indicating a text message.

When and where, it read.

Bluefish Grill. Table at the back. His thumbs flew across the tiny keyboard.

"Did you miss a call?" Abby asked, sliding into her chair.

"No. Just putting my phone on silent. This thing usually rings off the hook."

Abby looked over her menu. "I've never been here before. What's good?"

"I like the stuffed grouper. But the steaks are great too."

"Do you come here often?"

"Often enough. I'm a pretty rotten cook, so I go out for something edible most every night."

———— ❧ ————

The Broker stood at the hostess station and watched Alex and the woman sitting across the table from him. She was beautiful, which wasn't necessary, but it certainly helped. The thief preferred beautiful women. However, he'd been known to seduce women of all shapes and sizes to suit his purposes. The Broker was quite sure that Alex was pleased with her hourglass figure and large brown eyes. Her intellect was an added bonus. Stupid women bored Alex. Yet this time, as always, he would do what was required. And those two even looked good together. It would have been impossible to find a better match, not that they were actually supposed to fall in love. Well, Alex wasn't at least. The Broker was not concerned about her emotional stake in the relationship. He wanted her to trust Alex, but even more than that, he wanted her to please him.

The Broker scanned the menu with one eye, and Alex's table with the other. A hand-painted Japanese screen blocked the couple's direct view of him. A few feet away, Koi fish swam in an indoor water feature, surrounded by bamboo, which offered him even more coverage.

A strange pulse of excitement ran through him. This was the first time he had spied on Alex. Typically, he just phoned in his orders, wired the money, and met the brothers at the rendezvous point to retrieve the merchandise and make the final payments. Being on location was fascinating. But then again, he'd never agreed to such a price before. This heist was the most important of his career, and he needed to make sure everything went as planned.

"A table for one, sir?" the hostess asked.

"No, thank you. Nothing here interests me." He handed her the menu and left. The Broker had gotten what he came for, confirmation that Alex was manipulating Dr. Abigail Mitchell.

Isaac waited patiently as his computer scanned the disk he removed from the back of the digital camera. One by one, the pictures he'd taken at the Smithsonian appeared on his screen. He moved them to a file for later use and began working on the scan he'd taken of the magnetic strip on Randy Jacobs's security badge. It took only a few seconds to copy the information and transfer it to a second computer across the room. Then Isaac went to work with a vengeance.

An image of the security card was placed on the screen. Randy's picture was replaced with his own, but everything else remained the same. Isaac inserted the electronic code on the new magnetic strip and printed the badge. Slightly warm to the touch, it was a perfect copy. He would be able to go anywhere inside the Museum of Natural History that Randy Jacobs could.

Isaac looked at the clock. It was ten past eight, and Alex was waiting. He grabbed a duffel bag from the closet and filled it with an assortment of mechanical gear, the newly copied badge, a small black case, and a grey uniform identical to those worn by Smithsonian security staff.

Before leaving the apartment, he sent a text message.

Men's room in 30 minutes

—————∞—————

Alex's phone vibrated just as he flipped open the notepad. He moved it to his lap and glanced at the text as if he were adjusting his napkin.

"So," he said, swallowing a bite of filet mignon. "I'm assuming that Jean-Baptiste Tavernier survived the shipwreck?"

"He did."

"Is that where the legend of the curse started then, with him?"

"Not officially, no. That concept grew over the course of many hundreds of years, although Tavernier certainly played his part in advancing the notion."

Alex took a sip of wine and dabbed the corners of his mouth with the black linen napkin. "You really like this stuff, don't you?" he asked.

"What do you mean?"

"Well, I've been watching you. It's like you've got the whole thing memorized. You must really love this story."

"You've been watching me?" she asked, a playful note in her voice.

Alex laughed. "Aside from the *obvious* reasons, I couldn't help but see that you really know your stuff."

"I did my doctoral work on the Hope Diamond. You spend all those years researching and writing, it better stay with you."

"Impressive. A Ph.D. at what . . . " he paused, not wanting to assume her age.

"Thirty. Two years ago."

"I must say *Dr.* Mitchell. You are one fascinating woman." Alex forced his eyes away from her and redirected them to the notepad on the table. He paused, gathering his thoughts. "So, this curse, help me understand it. Did something tragic happen to everyone who owned the diamond?"

"Well," she said. "This is where staunch proponents of the diamond's curse run into trouble. If you take a quick glance at history, it certainly seems that its owners all suffered something terrible, but when you dig into the confirmed facts, you find that it often skips a generation or two."

"So where did the idea of the curse come from?"

"Good question and one that's hard to answer. In reality it comes partly from legend, partly from religious belief, partly from superstition, and partly from the famous jeweler Pierre Cartier." Abby slowly worked on her fish while she told Alex the story. "What you have to understand is that the diamond originated in India, a country steeped in Hindu mysticism. Everything means something in Hinduism. And diamonds are no exception. Even the color of a diamond has meaning."

"For instance?"

"Well, each color is associated with a different Hindu god. White diamonds belong to Varuna, god of the sea; yellow diamonds to Shakra, goddess of learning; and *blue* diamonds are associated with Yama, the god of death. So right from the start Mir Jumla connected the huge blue diamond with death, and he passed that idea on to Tavernier."

Alex scribbled furiously on his legal pad as he tried to keep up with Abby.

"As a matter of fact," she continued. "The mystical quality of diamonds was so ingrained in Hindu culture that archeologists have found Sanskrit texts, which describe the belief that any diamond that had spots, crow's feet, lines, cracks, or blue color should be avoided because they were a source of sorrow."

"So how do you separate fact from fiction? Because it seems that a lot of the people who came in contact with the diamond really have led tragic lives."

"Ah, therein lies the rub. There actually is a great deal of truth in the legends surrounding the diamond. It has to go back to what we know for sure. There are large gaps in the diamond's history that no one can verify with any certainty. But what we *can* confirm is that Tavernier bought the diamond, in Golconda, India, and that he held onto it longer than he did any other jewel he owned. The question we have to ask ourselves is *why*," Abby said.

"Interesting. Why not sell it immediately and make a profit?"

"Exactly."

"Any ideas?" Alex asked.

"A few. Maybe he couldn't find a buyer, but I doubt that. Tavernier dealt with the upper echelon of European aristocracy. They would have gobbled up the diamond immediately had he put it on the market. Maybe it wasn't safe to sell the stone so soon after purchase because technically it shouldn't have been offered to him in the first place. Yet that doesn't seem likely either. The Indian sultan would have no means of knowing what stones Tavernier possessed or when he sold them."

"So what's your theory then?"

"I think he kept it for himself because he loved the stone, had grown deeply attached to it, and didn't part with it until it would have been financially ludicrous not to."

"Are you saying he was *possessed* with the stone?"

Abby stared deep into her wine glass. "Or by it."

"The curse?"

"Just an opinion and—"

"—completely unverifiable," Alex finished for her.

"Exactly."

They sat in silence for a moment. "It does make one wonder," Alex finally said.

"Which is why the Hope Diamond has captivated the imaginations of so many people for hundreds of years. There is something compelling about a mystery we just can't solve."

Alex scratched a few words on his notepad and then asked, "So he held on to the diamond for fifteen years. Who finally bought it?"

"King Louis XIV, and he paid *dearly* for it."

Isaac passed through the doors of the Bluefish Grill unnoticed. A quick scan of the room revealed his brother sitting at a small table in the corner with Abby. They appeared to be deeply engaged in conversation. Alex had always possessed a gift for connecting relationally, and it had come in quite handy over the years. Yet there was something about the look on his face that bothered Isaac. Alex enjoyed his work, but at the moment it appeared as though he was enjoying the company as well.

Isaac kept his distance from Alex's table. Soon he made eye contact and strolled toward the men's room.

"Would you excuse me for a moment?" Alex said, rising from the table.

"Of course."

He pushed open the men's room door and quickly checked out the small room. Two men in their late fifties stood at the urinals, discussing a disappointing round of golf they had played that day. Only one of the three stalls was occupied, and Alex entered the one next to it. A contact lens case dropped to the floor beneath the partition, and Alex picked it up and put it in his pocket. He waited a couple of moments, flushed the toilet, and exited the stall. He ran water over his fingertips, dried them on a paper towel, and returned to the table without a word to Isaac.

"Sorry for dominating the conversation tonight," Abby said.

Alex smiled. "This is an interview after all. You're supposed to do all the talking."

"My throat is parched." She sipped her wine. "Why don't you tell me a little about yourself?"

"There isn't much to tell. I'm a journalist. I live in the city. And I travel a lot. So much of my time is spent living out of a suitcase that I wonder why I even bother paying rent."

"Everyone needs a place to come home to."

"Home is a concept I lost a long time ago," Alex said.

"That's pretty sad. Don't you ever find yourself wanting to slow down?"

Alex stroked the stem of his glass. "I can't say that I actually know how to slow down. I fear it would be tremendously boring."

"But living at breakneck speed can't give you much time to establish . . . friendships." Abby winced. She had almost said *relationships*.

"Ah, yet another thing I'm not good at."

Abby leaned back in her chair and studied him for a moment. "You don't strike me as the kind of guy who is bad at anything."

"What do you mean?"

"Oh, just that you're confident and intelligent and successful. I can't imagine you have a lot of insecurities."

His eyes glinted as he studied her. "I'm afraid you have me pegged. One of my worst character traits is that I don't often find myself in need of confidence. Some people find it quite annoying."

"On the contrary, I admire people who are confident. It's not something I come by naturally."

"Could've fooled me."

"Yes, well, I've spent a lifetime trying to prove myself."

"The art community doesn't strike me as being an exclusive men's club."

"It isn't really. But establishing myself as an expert among my father's colleagues is another matter. He's brilliant, so I'm expected to be brilliant, and differentiating myself as an individual has been difficult."

Alex shrugged. "They've entrusted you with the Hope Diamond event. That's a pretty big deal."

"More like a disaster in the making. That thing is going to be the death of me."

"How so?"

Abby tapped her finger on the white linen tablecloth as she decided how much to share. "Well, the truth is I'm not sure I'm up to the task."

"You're being a bit hard on yourself, aren't you? You earned a doctorate from Cambridge at the age of thirty. That's pretty impressive."

"Cambridge?" Abby grinned. "Somebody has been doing his research."

"Busted. I Googled you."

"Funny, I tried to Google you, but I didn't find anything."

Alex dropped his gaze. "That could either be a sign of a dismal career, or the fact that I often write under another name."

"Really? What name?"

He met her gaze and offered a sinister smile. "If I told you I'd have to kill you."

Abby laughed. "Isn't it a little early in our relationship to be keeping secrets from one another?" There it was again, that word. *Relationship.* She'd used it unintentionally, but a blush of red crept across her face nonetheless.

Alex pulled away from the table and leaned back in his chair. "When the article comes out, you can meet my alter ego."

"I can't wait."

"Now," he said. "Back to this Tavernier fellow. He eventually sold the diamond to King Louis XIV. How did he manage that?"

"Tavernier acquired a reputation throughout Europe as not only the premier jewel merchant, but a top-notch storyteller as well. He learned early on that if he could weave a story around a particular gem, it increased the value. So the king invited him to Versailles on December 16, 1668, to present his current jewel collection and tell stories of his travels."

"I'm assuming he did an outstanding job because the king bought the jewel."

"He didn't just buy the diamond, he incurred the wrath of his Minister of Finance, Jean-Baptiste Colbert, because he spent such an extravagant amount."

"What was the purchase price?" Alex asked.

"Four hundred thousand livres. Or the equivalent of $3.6 million in today's currency."

Alex let out a low whistle. "A shrewd businessman."

"One of history's most notorious. When you study Jean-Baptiste Tavernier, he makes Donald Trump look like a carpet salesman."

"So do you think it bothered Tavernier to let go of the stone?"

"I imagine there must have been some remorse. But whatever twinge of regret he had was easily soothed by the gross fortune he made."

"I must say, this is turning out to be one fascinating interview." Alex took a sip of his wine. "For more than one reason."

An hour later Alex walked Abby to her apartment, making sure to stay a few steps behind. He unscrewed the cap to the contact lens case and took out what appeared to be a penny. As Abby fiddled with her keys, he slipped it into her purse.

"Thank you for dinner," she said. "I really enjoyed it."

"The dinner or the company?" he asked, tilting his head to one side.

Abby's cheeks colored and she laughed. "Both, actually."

"Likewise. And thank you for letting me pick your brain."

"Any time," she smiled.

Alex looked at her for a moment, noticing that her eyes were the same reddish brown as her hair. Warm. Comforting. Soft.

"Do you mean it?" he asked.

"Mean what?"

"Any time?"

The corners of her mouth turned up into a smile. "Yes, I guess I do."

"Good. Then I'm going to take you up on that offer."

"Please do," she said. Her voice hovered just above a whisper.

Alex took a step closer. "You know, for all the talking we did, I still only have a fraction of my story. May I call you again?"

She grinned. "About the story I presume?"

"Yes," he said with a mischievous grin. "And no."

They looked at one another for a moment, not quite sure what to do. Finally, Alex leaned in and brushed his lips against her temple. "Goodnight, Abby."

"Goodnight," she replied, suddenly nervous.

He ran his thumb over her fingers for a moment and then left.

❧

Abby entered her apartment in a daze. Alex had left her with an unfamiliar flutter in her stomach. She walked to the window and watched as he left the building and made his way to his car. She stood there in the dark and felt the color rise in her cheeks once more when he turned to look up at her apartment. He stared for several seconds, and Abby felt quite sure that a smile spread across his face.

Turning toward her bedroom, Abby peeled off her work clothes and tossed them in the hamper. For a moment she considered taking a shower and then decided she was too tired. Instead, she brushed her teeth, washed her face, and put on an old tee shirt. No sooner had she climbed into bed than the phone rang.

"Surely not," she said, looking at the clock. She grabbed the phone. "Hello?"

"You said I could call."

Something began to flip uncontrollably in her abdomen as a smile spread across her face. "That I did."

"Did you mean it?" His voice was deep on the other end of the phone—intense.

"Yes."

"Good. Because there's something I wanted to say."

"And what would that be?"

"Just that I really had a great time tonight."

"And here I thought you were calling me to get the rest of the story, Mr. Weld."

He laughed pleasantly. "I've got time. Why don't you tell it to me?"

She sat up in bed and crunched her eyebrows. "Really?"

His voice shifted from flirtatious to serious, and he said, "Yeah, why not? I've got a deadline, remember? Unless, of course, you've got other plans tonight."

"Like sleep?"

"You can do that anytime."

Abby looked at the clock, its minute hand inching toward midnight.

"What do you say, Dr. Mitchell? I could use a bedtime story."

She hesitated, feeling somewhat adolescent. Wasn't this the kind of thing she did in high school? Yet she only debated for a moment, considering that the alternative was hanging up the phone. "Sure, why not?" Abby pulled the covers up to her chest and lay down her head on her pillow.

"So good old Tavernier kept his greedy little hands on the diamond for nearly two decades. What could have possibly convinced him to part with it?"

"Oh, surely you've figured that out by now, Alex."

"What do you mean?"

"He wanted the same thing every thief wants—money."

There was a prolonged silence on the other line that Abby took for interest. She leaned over, switched off her bedside lamp, and told Alex exactly how Jean-Baptiste Tavernier sold his soul to the cursed diamond.

8

VERSAILLES, FRANCE, DECEMBER 6, 1668

RARELY HAD JEAN-BAPTISTE TAVERNIER TRAVELED IN SUCH LUXURY AS HE did now. It was not the king's personal coach that carried him through the cobblestone streets of Versailles, but one sent by Louis the XIV nonetheless. It was for moments like this that he endured such hardship during his career.

Only a month before, Tavernier received the summons for which he had been waiting patiently for fifteen years. Though he could have sold his precious blue diamond any number of times, he chose instead to keep it until presented with the right opportunity.

It was no small honor to be invited to the king's court, but Tavernier was specifically asked to tell of his travels and to bring the king any jewels he thought worthy of the Crown. The lust of a wealthy aristocracy for precious gems was a never-ending thirst that Jean-Baptist Tavernier was uniquely equipped to satisfy.

The carriage moved closer to the Château Versailles, home to King Louis XIV, as it rolled through a tree-lined park on the outskirts of the estate. As the carriage rounded a bend, the palace came into view, its heavy stone buildings sprawling out over acres of pristine gardens.

"Monsieur, nous approchons le palais," the driver shouted, announcing their approach to the palace.

Tavernier took a deep breath and caressed the leather pouch hidden beneath his robes.

Today we part, my beautiful.

The king's court was a complicated place for such a man as Tavernier. He fell somewhere between the ranks of nobility and commoner. He was not important enough to command the king's respect, nor was he simply an afterthought. Tavernier was a curiosity in the eyes of Louis XIV, and today he would play that to his full advantage.

The carriage pulled to a stop before the palace steps, and Tavernier took a moment to prepare himself before stepping down. In order for things to go as planned, he must proceed carefully.

The coachman swung open the carriage door, and Tavernier descended into the gravel courtyard. A great expanse of manicured lawn, speckled with fountains and ornate topiaries, surrounded him. He savored this royal moment. On the steps leading to the massive palace doors stood Jean-Baptiste Colbert, the Controller General of Finance.

"Good afternoon, Minister," Tavernier said. He bowed as expected.

Colbert returned the greeting with a slight nod, guardedly eyeing Tavernier's odd attire. Colbert was a tall man with a pencil-thin mustache and mounds of curly black hair. Unlike so many of the king's courtier's he had no need for a wig. Nature had supplied him in abundance with the required mane. Over his breeches and coattails, Colbert wore a heavy black velvet cloak and white lace collar indicating his status as officer in the royal court. The wrinkles around his eyes and the tight lines embedded at the corners of his mouth belied his age and his natural bent toward stoicism.

"*Heureux pour vous rencontrer, Monsieur Tavernier,*" said Colbert after careful observation.

"I'm pleased to finally meet you as well, Minister Colbert."

"I have heard much about you, *monsieur*. Your travels are as legendary as your diamonds."

"No doubt blown largely out of proportion," Tavernier said. "I fear you may find yourself horribly bored by my company."

"Nonsense. His Majesty assures me that you have many a grand tale to tell. Now please follow me. The king awaits you in his private apartment."

"I am eager to make his acquaintance."

"I will order one of the butlers to take your valise to your suite. His Majesty requested an audience with you the moment you arrived."

"I am humbled," Tavernier said with another short bow, forcing the smile from his face. The king must be eager, indeed, to see his blue beauty.

"If you will follow me?"

Colbert turned and walked up the steps, the heavy fringe of his cape barely dusting the ground.

The court of King Louis XIV was deeply immersed in ritual, dictating the dress, behavior, and mannerisms of all who came before him. Etiquette was a carefully observed art form by which courtiers advanced in royal society. It was therefore no surprise that Tavernier's arrival in the royal court caused such a stir. He presented himself not in the required attire of britches, vest, and coat, but in his elaborately embroidered Oriental robes. On his head he wore a silk turban popular in the Far East, not the heavy coifed wig of French nobility. Although he drew gasps and stares as he followed Colbert through the palace, Tavernier was fully aware that this marked departure from accepted protocol would ultimately work to his advantage. King Louis's interest had set the gem merchant apart from every other member of the royal court. All eyes were on him.

Colbert escorted Tavernier to the king's antechamber where the highest ranks of French nobility gathered. Most would have stood in awe of the fifteen-foot ceilings trimmed in elaborate gilded crown molding and the deep crimson walls along which hung massive portraits of past and present monarchs. A chandelier of Austrian crystal dangled above the travertine tile floor below. Courtiers sat scattered ceremonially around the room on a series of red velvet divans. It appeared that their single purpose in life was to attend the comings and goings of the king.

Although Tavernier considered this to be a life wasted and dismally boring, it was an honor of the highest degree to those seated in the room. What was most notable to Tavernier, however, was not the extravagant apparel or ornate fixtures in the room, but the overwhelming stench of unkempt bodies poorly masked by oily perfume. Tavernier steeled himself not to wrinkle his nose in distaste. He knew it was not unheard of for French courtiers to go months without bathing, resulting in agonizing outbreaks of head lice. It made his scalp itch just to think about it. Many of the women seated around the room held in their laps thin mahogany sticks for those moments when the itching became unbearable. The odor was quite offensive to the delicate sensibilities of Tavernier, a man used to lavish living, but also wide open spaces and clean air.

A murmur ran through the antechamber as Colbert led him toward the intricately carved mahogany doors that opened into the king's private chamber. The courtiers regarded how this turbaned stranger could be given an honor few of them would ever receive.

"The king has requested that you dine with him this evening, and he is also arranging a lengthy tour of the palace grounds tomorrow. But for now he requests that you join him immediately."

"I am more than pleased to oblige His Majesty," Tavernier said.

It was considered improper to knock on the king's door. Instead, those wishing to speak with Louis XIV were required to gently scratch the door with their left little finger. Most of the court, including Colbert, had grown the nail on that finger longer than the rest to accommodate the command. Most, however, would never dare so bold a move. Colbert on the other hand got much use out of that fingernail.

A series of swipes across the heavy wooden panel produced a loud enough sound to be heard within. Tavernier noted the courtiers waited patiently to see if he and Colbert would be admitted.

"*Entrez*," came the reply.

Colbert swung open the massive doors and ushered Tavernier into the sitting room, closing the doors behind him. The king lounged at a long oval table covered in an intricately woven blue silk tablecloth. The parquet wood floors were polished to a mirror shine, and a bright fire glowed in the fireplace at one end of the room.

Tavernier and Colbert approached the king and knelt before him with bowed heads.

"Your Majesty," they said in unison.

"Jean-Baptiste Tavernier, your reputation precedes you," said the king with a curt nod.

He waved them forward and invited them to join him at the table. King Louis sat in an ornately carved high-backed chair covered with blue and gold brocade. Draped around his shoulders was a thick winter cloak of heavy silk, lined with fur, and embroidered with hundreds of gold *fluer-de-lis*. His wig of black curls fell in preposterous mounds below his shoulders.

"I have worked hard on my reputation," Tavernier said. "I hope you have heard only the good things."

The polite bantering continued. "I hear that you are the most noted jewel merchant not only in Europe but also in the Far East," King Louis said. "I hear that you have traveled hundreds of thousands of miles in every kind of weather. I hear that you have been arrested, that you have escaped armed conflict, and that you even survived a shipwreck."

"It was a mere squall, Your Majesty. Not worth telling."

"No need to feign modesty in my presence. I am not impressed by it. I invited you here because you have extraordinary stories to tell and because you have exceptional jewels to offer. And it will come as no surprise to you, Monsieur Tavernier, that I only buy the best. My finance minister here can assure you that price is no issue."

The muscles around Colbert's mouth twitched. "His Majesty is known for an elaborate lifestyle."

"And it is your job, Colbert, to orchestrate ways for me to pay for that lifestyle."

"Meaning I must convince the French people that taxes are not only necessary but a joy as well."

Louis threw his head back and laughed. "And Minister Colbert is a genius at taxing the people. Versailles is financed entirely by an elaborate set of taxes he created."

"And the people have not howled?"

Colbert smiled for the first time since Tavernier arrived. "The art of taxation consists in so plucking the goose as to obtain the largest amount of feathers with the least possible amount of hissing."

Tavernier regarded Colbert for a moment, gauging whether he would be foe or ally in his business with the king.

"I have heard much about Versailles, Your Majesty," Tavernier said, turning his attention back to Louis. "I understand it is quite a marvel."

"It rivals anything built in the world."

"Something of a bet was it?"

"Not so much a bet as an illustration. My last minister of finance, Nicolas Fouquet, had the audacity to build a palace grander than mine in Paris. As if a mere courtier should live in greater abundance than the king!"

"Was I right in hearing that Fouquet built his chateau with monies embezzled from the royal purse?"

"Indeed," Louis said, nodding with great disapproval. "It simply couldn't be tolerated."

"And where is this Fouquet now?"

"Imprisoned. For life. I couldn't very well let him be executed now could I? An example must be made of those who betray the king."

"And execution is not sufficient punishment?"

"Sufficient perhaps. But far too quick. I wanted something a little . . . longer," Louis said. "But enough of that. I am anxious to see what you have brought me, Monsieur Tavernier."

"I am pleased to hear that you have such a high regard for my merchandise. I have long felt that Indian diamonds are the largest available and of the utmost quality, a perfect fit for royalty."

The king gave a short clap, and one of his many butlers stepped into the room from a side chamber. "Have Monsieur Tavernier's merchandise brought from his chambers immediately," he ordered.

"Yes, Your Majesty," the butler replied and scurried from the room.

"Now," said Louis. "I would like to hear of your travels."

Tavernier settled in his chair, running a finger casually over the intricate upholstery. "I have bought and sold precious gems from the time I was fifteen. It was in the writings of Marco Polo that I first heard wondrous tales of Indian diamonds. Polo believed that diamonds sprung from the ground at the bottom of fathomless valleys and could only be extracted by throwing dead animals to the depths, where eagles would then swoop in and recover the carcasses. Diamond hunters then climbed to their nests and picked diamonds from the eagle droppings."

Tavernier gauged the king's expression for a response, and when he felt as though he maintained interest, continued. "These legends are of course absurd, but you can understand how as a young man I became entranced by the lure of diamonds in the Orient. Over the course of my career I have traveled to many countries, and I believe that Marco Polo was right. There are no diamonds that compare to those found in India.

"They are mined in a way I find very peculiar. Instead of tunneling into the sides of mountains, they dig pits straight into the ground. Each shovelful of earth is carefully sifted for gems. Those larger than ten carats are appropriated for the sultan's personal use. The rest are available for sale."

The king frowned. "I was hoping that you were bringing me jewels of note, Tavernier. Not pebbles to be used as a child's plaything."

Tavernier smiled. "It is certainly difficult to escape with a large diamond, but it is not impossible. Let's just say that I have my ways, and you will not be disappointed with what I offer. The greater part of my life has been spent trading in gems, gaining allies, and negotiating customs. I doubt you will find another merchant in France, or all of Europe for that matter, who can deliver jewels of the quality that I have brought."

"Pray tell, Monsieur Tavernier, how could a man such as yourself, obviously of European descent, escape India without suspicion?"

For a moment Tavernier's thoughts drifted back to Rai Rao and his short imprisonment in the sultan's dungeon. "Suspicion is one thing, detection is another."

The king appeared quite pleased. "Ah, intrigue. Do continue."

"For many years my liaison in Golconda was a man named Mir Jumla. Officially he was prime minister. Unofficially he acted as a small-time diamond smuggler. Those individuals with fewer scruples than myself were known to approach him with jewels that far exceeded the sultan's requirements for sale. Jumla would then purchase those jewels for a measly sum only to resell them later for an exorbitant profit. It was not my concern how he acquired the diamonds or what he paid for them."

"And this Mir Jumla is still in Golconda?"

Tavernier shook his head. "Two years after I made my final purchase, Mir defected to the Mughal Empire, taking with him over four hundred pounds of diamonds, including a 780-carat diamond that you may know by its current name, the Great Mughal."

It was at that moment that Louis's butler returned, pushing a cart on which sat a small wooden trunk.

"Perfect timing," Tavernier said, rising to his feet. "Would you care to see what I have brought, Your Majesty?"

Louis was practically salivating at the prospect.

With great fanfare Tavernier lifted the ornately carved chest and set it on the table before the king. From deep within a pocket of his robe he drew a small gold key, which he inserted into the lock. Three rotations brought a click and then Tavernier stepped back. He turned the chest to face the king and slowly lifted the lid.

King Louis's gasp of awe produced a deeply satisfied smile from Tavernier.

Inside the chest were more than one thousand polished diamonds of various colors, shapes, and sizes. The king of France slid a hand into the trunk, letting the smooth stones slide between his fingers. He said nothing for a long while, but instead gazed upon the treasure, occasionally holding one up to the light.

Instead of revealing the jewels individually or in small groups, Tavernier purposely had presented them together for maximum effect. He learned long ago that those with wealth and prestige were easily bored, even with things as spectacular as diamonds.

The king stirred Tavernier's diamonds with his bejeweled hand as resolve steadily covered his countenance. "I want them," he finally said, looking at Tavernier for the first time since opening the trunk. "All of them."

"I thought you might," he grinned.

Colbert watched the exchange in guarded silence. "We will, of course, need to present these to the court jeweler Monsieur Pitau to check for clarity and irregularities."

"Of course," said Tavernier. "You are more than welcome to do so. I think he will find it an easy task, for I only brought those diamonds that are of the clearest grade and largest size. I did not want to waste Your Majesty's time with the rest."

"There were more?" Louis said with raised eyebrow.

"Thousands more, Your Majesty, but none fit for a king such as yourself."

"I see." The king's hand once again slid into the chest and fondled the diamonds.

"And your price, Monsieur Tavernier?" asked Colbert. Hedging in the king's purse was a challenge not for the faint of heart.

Tavernier leaned forward, his face devoid of expression. "For this collection I require 490,000 livres and a title."

At first the king and his finance minister stared blankly at him, and then they laughed. It was only when Tavernier did not return the mirth that they realized he was quite serious.

"Impressive though your collection may be, it hardly merits advancement in rank. I hardly think you could argue that, Monsieur Tavernier," Colbert stated coldly.

"That is a pity." Tavernier looked boldly at the king. "Because you have not yet seen everything I have to offer."

He reached beneath his robe and pulled the worn buckskin pouch from around his neck. There was a slight moment of hesitation before he gently placed the pouch into the king's outstretched hand.

Louis grinned as he felt the full weight of the leather pouch. The two men locked eyes in a moment of understanding before he opened the drawstrings and slid the large blue diamond into his palm.

Colbert leaned forward and stared at the diamond. "I have never seen such a thing," he muttered.

"Nor had I," Tavernier replied, his voice cracking with unexpected emotion. "And Mir Jumla insisted there was something unique about this diamond."

"How so?" Louis asked, his eyes still wide.

"When I purchased this stone from him, he told me it had been chiseled from the eye of a large Hindu statue. It comes with quite a tale of theft and mystery. Mir Jumla insisted that the stone was cursed. At first I did not believe him, but over the last fifteen years I have come to wonder if his tale does, in fact, bear some truth."

The king heard little of what Tavernier said, for his gaze was still arrested by the deep blue diamond in his hand.

"Yet I have always intended that stone to be the means by which I receive a title. And if that is too great a price for you to pay, I know of monarchs in both India and Spain who would be more than willing to accommodate me."

Louis' fingers instinctively closed over the diamond. "A title you say?"

"I have had my heart set on a baronet for quite some time."

"And 490,000 livres is your price?"

"Yes, for the chest of stones. The great blue is an additional four hundred thousand livres," he said. "Plus the title."

Colbert gasped in anger, but the king dismissed his objection. "I feel certain that we can make arrangements,

Monsieur Tavernier. It is not every day that I am presented with a stone such as this."

Tavernier cast a longing glace at his precious blue stone. "Indeed," he said. "Diamonds such as that one are most rare."

"So are titles," Colbert growled.

"A worthwhile trade in my opinion."

"You drive a tough bargain, Monsieur Tavernier," Louis said, his fingers still tightly wrapped around the diamond.

"I work in a tough business, Your Majesty. Diamonds do not find themselves." All the while, Tavernier's eyes were on the jewel in Louis' hand. He suddenly felt naked without the familiar weight around his neck.

"And yet, what you request in exchange is simply preposterous," Colbert argued, pulling at the stiff lace collar around his neck. Red blotches covered his cheeks, and his lips were drawn tight.

"Perhaps," Tavernier nodded. "But I also know that the French monarchy has never had a jewel such as this. The crown jewels would benefit immensely from its addition."

Louis snapped his fingers, ending their discussion. "I have made up my mind. I will have this jewel, along with the rest. And you shall have your title."

"I am most honored, Your Majesty."

"Colbert," Louis ordered. "See that Monsieur Tavernier is compensated for these jewels."

Jean-Baptiste Colbert looked at Tavernier with an icy resolve. "Yes, Your Majesty," he said through clenched teeth. "I will ensure that Monsieur Tavernier gets exactly what he deserves."

9

ALEX WELD DROVE WITH ONE HAND ON THE STEERING WHEEL AND THE other pressing his cell phone to his ear. "You do know how to tell a story, Dr. Mitchell."

"Well, I have to make sure you call me again, don't I?" She sounded tired.

"Have no fear of that."

"Good night, Alex."

"I'll talk to you soon, Abby."

Alex folded shut his phone and tossed it onto the passenger seat. He smiled at the windshield as he navigated traffic.

"Well, well, well, this is going to be more fun than usual," he said to no one in particular.

Daniel Wallace, head of security, loomed inside the Smithsonian Office of Protection, glaring at a blinking red light on the console before him. "That can't be right."

He sat before a row of closed-circuit television screens inside the computer terminus on the second floor of The Castle. The building rested like a slumbering giant in the early morning hours, undisturbed by the usual frenetic activity. He should have been home hours ago, but he had no one to go home to and little need for sleep.

"Marshall, did the motion detectors just go off in the basement?" He asked a bleary-eyed security guard working another console.

"I doubt it. Who would be in the basement at nearly one o'clock in the morning?"

"Run a check for me," Daniel ordered. He pulled a pen from his coat pocket and clicked it with his thumb.

Blake Marshall glanced nervously at the blinking light and shook his head. He changed the video feed on the screen before him to basement footage and ran a security check on the motion sensors. "Well, I'll be," he muttered. "Someone is in the basement."

Daniel glanced at the clock. "When did the cleaning crew finish?"

"They coded out at midnight, and shift change isn't for another ten minutes."

"The entire basement requires security clearance. Run the pass codes and tell me who just scanned their card."

Marshall's fingers flew over the keyboard. "Looks like Randy Jacobs's, sir. He ran his card two minutes ago."

A copy of Randy Jacobs's security badge appeared on the screen before them, looking just slightly less tired and overweight than he did in person. Daniel looked at it suspiciously for a moment and then unlocked a drawer beneath his desk.

"Where is he now?" he asked, rummaging through the contents.

"Let's see," Marshall said, dragging and dropping information with his mouse. "He came in the ground-level employee entrance and took the service elevator to the basement. As far as I can tell he's in the Server Room now."

"What do you mean as far as you can tell?"

"We have motion detectors in there but no cameras. Cards are required to enter a room, but not to exit. I can verify that he went in, but I don't know if he's still there."

"Why don't we have video feed in that room?"

"It's just information technology. No need, sir."

"What do you mean no need? Someone is down there right now, and I need to know who it is?"

Marshall frowned. "Randy Jacobs, sir?"

"That's not possible. Randy Jacobs left for Mexico this morning, and according to procedure, left his security badge with me at the end of his shift last night." Daniel held up the security badge that was displayed on the monitor before them.

The copied badge easily gained Isaac access through the employee entrance and into the bowels of The Castle. The maze of corridors was empty as he traveled beneath the near-deserted building. Had he run into anyone, it would not have mattered. Not only did he have the proper clearance, but he wore the gray uniform of a Smithsonian guard. Although his initial breach of security had gone off smoothly, Isaac knew he had no time to relax.

His footsteps echoed on the sterile concrete floor as he walked through the information technology storage room. Dozens of fluorescent lights flickered above the sea of computer processors. Row after row of stainless steel shelving held hundreds of black boxes, each sprouting wires, cables, and plugs. The room hummed with the whirring of computers and the rush of air-conditioning. In a colossal effort to keep the machinery from overheating, the temperature inside the room was easily twenty degrees colder than in the hallway.

Isaac pulled a small flat black box from inside his uniform and made his way down the center aisle, stopping occasionally to check the numbered rows. Fifteen rows in, he turned left and knelt before a processor halfway up the shelf. It was labeled: Museum of Natural History, Floor Two, Janet Annenberg Hooker Hall of Gems.

—◦◦◦—

Daniel Wallace had spent the majority of his career working security management as a naval officer assigned to the State Department. After retiring from the Navy at the age of thirty-eight, he took a job as head of the Smithsonian Office of Protection and was charged with the oversight of security for all Smithsonian facilities. Twenty years of wiretapping, terrorist surveillance, and special operations had piqued his appetite for adventure, and he was pleasantly surprised with the level of intensity in this government position. So it was with keen anticipation that he leaned over Marshall's shoulder and attempted to discover the identity of the stranger on his turf.

"Which security team is closest to the Server Room?" Daniel asked, running a finger over the master list of teams on duty.

"That would be Security One. They're on the first floor, but on the other side of the wing."

"Send them to check it out. Now."

Marshall tapped into the security communications system. "Control to Security One."

A few seconds later came the reply. "Security One."

"We have a disturbance in the Server Room. How close are you?"

"Less than five minutes away."

"Check it out and report back."

"Yes, sir."

—⦵⦵⦵—

Isaac's black box contained a flash drive, a small keypad, and a six-inch video display. He pulled a smaller black pouch from his pocket that held a razor blade, a pair of wire strippers, plastic ties, and black electrical tape. He used the razor blade to cut the tie binding the mass of wires coming from the processor and let them dangle until he located a thick black cable that ran to the input plug. He stripped the plastic casing, exposing raw copper wire beneath. Isaac spliced the recorder to the exposed input wire and began typing on the small keypad. He inserted the flash drive into the recorder, pulled up the needed information on the video display, and recorded two years' worth of video surveillance. It only took three minutes. Then Isaac covered the exposed section with electrical tape and bound the loose wires with a plastic tie, just like he found it. Pleased with his work, Isaac slid the black box inside his uniform, turned off the lights, and left the room.

—⦵⦵⦵—

"There, sir." Marshall pointed at the closed-circuit screen as it showed someone leaving the Server Room.

"Zoom in," Daniel directed.

"It's just one of us," Marshall said, looking at the gray uniform.

Daniel let out a disgusted snort. "If it were one of us, Marshall, he would have his own security badge and wouldn't have used Jacobs's. Now please do me a favor and zoom in on his face."

The closed-circuit TV kept track of the stranger as he navigated the basement labyrinth. "I'm trying to get a close-up, sir, but he's got a cap on and keeps his head down."

"He's a pro. Follow him. And alert all security teams. I want to know who this guy is."

Marshall pressed his earpiece and spoke into the communications system. "Control to all security teams. We have a level one breach."

―――∞∞∞――――

Isaac headed for the service elevator, his window of opportunity shrinking with every second. He rounded a corner and saw the double steel doors before him. He swiped the security card through the scanner and waited for the elevator to descend from the floor above. The doors opened with a ping, and Isaac stepped inside.

―――∞∞∞――――

"Okay, he's in the elevator now," Marshall said. "We've got him. That elevator only goes back to ground level."

"Get him on the cameras," Daniel demanded. He leaned over the back of Marshall's chair and stared at the screen expectantly.

Marshall pounded his keyboard, directing the screens before him to register video feed from the service elevator on the ground floor. Five seconds later the doors slid open, revealing an empty elevator.

"What happened? Where'd he go?"

"I don't know, sir. We both saw him get in."

"Well he obviously isn't there now," Daniel shouted. "Find him!"

"I'm trying, sir, but he disappeared off the grid."

"Okay, okay," Daniel said, clicking his pen with increasing intensity. "He can't exit the building without using that card. Let me know when he scans it again."

―――∞∞∞――――

It took little effort for Isaac to raise the panel in the ceiling of the elevator and pull himself onto the roof as it rose. Just as the plans had shown, the service elevator only went to the ground floor, but the shaft above ran all the way to the second to allow room for maintenance. He steadied his balance as the elevator came to a stop, and then swung on to the metal service ladder. He scampered up the rungs and scanned his card on the security console next to a steel door. The moment he slipped through, he bolted across the hall and into the stairwell.

⸺⸙⸺

"There!" shouted Marshall. "He used it. Looks like he's on the second floor outside the elevator maintenance shaft."

"Clever," Daniel hissed. "Get him on the screens now!"

"There's no one there," Marshall said, frantically searching the area around the maintenance shaft.

"Pull back. Show me everyone within three hundred feet of that door."

Marshall's fingers raced over the keyboard, as he utilized both motion sensors and video cameras to find three security guards in the vicinity. All three guards were of similar height and build. All were male, and all freely showed their faces to the security cameras as they patrolled the halls.

Daniel pressed his earpiece and leaned into the console. "Control to security three, second floor." Both men stared at the screens as all three guards stopped. "Stop all security personnel on sight and apprehend Randy Jacobs."

⸺⸙⸺

Due to fire codes the stairwell remained unlocked at all times. Isaac ran down one flight of stairs and then leaped over the rail, dropping ten feet to the floor below. He emerged on the first floor, near the employee entrance just as two guards were headed toward the exit.

"Heading home?" one guard asked as he heard Isaac approach from behind.

"Yeah. Long shift."

The guard pulled his security badge and swiped it through the console. He swung open the door leading to the employee parking lot and motioned to Isaac. "After you."

Isaac stepped through. "Thanks, man. Have a great night."

"You, too."

"We've lost him, Mr. Wallace."

"How could we lose him? We just had three guys on the screen!"

"I know, sir, but they've all been crossed checked. The three on screen were Brian Petak, James Chavez, and Jason Randolph. We've lost our suspect."

"Control to all security teams. We've had a level one breach. Lockdown will commence in three seconds. No one goes in or out." He punched a code in the main terminal, locking all windows and exterior doors.

"But, sir, we're in the middle of a shift change."

Daniel closed his eyes and shook his head. "Yes, we are, and he knows it." He stepped back and regarded the screens before him. "We've got the footage. We can find him."

"Footage, yes. Real time feed, no. He could be out of the building by now."

Daniel stuck the pen in his mouth and gnawed on the end. "We'll find him."

"We don't even know if he took anything, sir."

"He took something. He was in my building with a stolen ID, and he didn't come here to play hide-and-seek."

Marshall turned his attention from the closed circuit TVs for the first time since the motion detector went off and looked at Daniel. "What do you think he was doing down there?"

"Gathering information."

"On what?"

"That's what I want you to find out. What do we keep on those servers?"

Marshall pulled up a security grid of the building and located the room where the motion detectors had gone off. "That room is ITS three. It's where we store all the video footage from the security cameras. How could that information possibly be important to anyone but Smithsonian staff?"

"I don't know yet, but we're going to find out. Can you tell me what he accessed while he was in there?"

"No, sir. I'm not showing that any of the video feed was interrupted. If there had been a disconnect we could have traced it. But if he just tapped into the source without disrupting the flow, there's no way to know what he accessed."

Daniel Wallace settled into his chair. "I want to know what he was after. This is going to hit the fan tomorrow." He tapped the pen on the console and then stuck it back in his mouth.

10

Dr. Peter Trent was tempted not to answer the phone. He sat at the antique wooden table in his kitchen, stirring a fifth spoonful of sugar into his coffee.

Senator Baker, no doubt, calling to harass me about the event again. I swear that woman could strip the paint off a barn door with her barbed-wire tongue.

The phone stopped ringing, and Peter sighed in relief. He unfolded the *Washington Times* and opened it to the Arts section. Just as he reached for his cup, the phone rang again, and he tipped over his coffee, soaking the paper with the dark French roast.

"Peter Trent," he snapped into the receiver, shaking coffee off his paper.

"Daniel Wallace, sir. Sorry to call you so early."

Peter looked at the clock. Six-thirty. "Early, indeed. How can I help you?"

There was a long pause on the other end. "Sir, we've had a level one security breach at The Castle."

"When?" Peter dropped into his chair.

"Early this morning, sir."

"What happened?"

"An unidentified man snuck into the basement using a stolen security badge."

Peter rubbed a hand across his forehead. "Was anything stolen? Accessed?"

"Not that we can verify, sir. We suspect he tapped into our surveillance storage system, but we don't know for sure."

"Did you at least retrieve the stolen security badge?"

"I use the term *stolen* loosely. Somehow he managed to obtain a badge used by one of our guards on vacation."

"But all security personnel are required to hand in their access cards when they take leave."

"True."

"Did you not have the card of this officer?" Dr. Trent rose from his chair and paced across the kitchen floor.

"That's just it, Dr. Trent. I did have the card. As soon as we detected the intruder and verified the card scan I retrieved it from my desk. I was looking at it while he was in the building."

"Then how did this intruder manage to get his hands on a security badge? Much less the very one you had in your possession."

"That has yet to be determined, sir."

"When he's questioned by police I want them to find out."

Daniel cleared his throat. "That's just it, sir, we didn't apprehend him."

"Excuse me?"

"He got away. Just before we put the building on lockdown."

Peter pinched the bridge of his nose and squeezed his eyes shut. "Just how exactly do you presume I will explain this to the Board of Regents?"

Silence on the other end. And then a faint clicking sound.

"What is that?"

"What is what, sir?"

"That clicking?"

"Oh. My pen, sir."

"Well, stop it!"

Daniel cleared his throat, and Peter knew he was working up the courage to say something else.

"Daniel, please don't tell me there's more bad news."

"No more news, sir, it's just that—"

"*What?!*"

"I think we should reconsider the Hope Diamond celebration this weekend."

The face of Senator Elizabeth Baker loomed in Peter's mind—her expectations and her threats. She had made it perfectly clear on more than one occasion that this event was high on her priority list. "Daniel," he said, "I don't think we need to be rash."

"This was a major security breach."

Peter Trent closed his eyes and exhaled slowly. "I understand. We'll discuss this later."

"But—"

"Good-bye, Daniel."

"Dr. Trent—"

"Listen, Daniel," he snapped. "You are one of the most hard-working employees I have. No one doubts your devotion. But we have no reason to believe the breach is connected to the event."

"You think I'm overreacting? I have security footage! Ask Blake Marshall. He was with me in the security terminus."

Dr. Trent clenched his fist. "We can talk about this when I come into the office. But for now, everything will move forward as planned."

ARIEL ALLISON

Abby took a seat at the round mahogany conference table and set her purse on the floor. Daniel Wallace and Henry Blackman, vice president of Diebold, Inc., were already seated and engrossed in small talk.

"Sorry I'm late, gentlemen," she said. "Things are a little crazy around my office these days."

Abby gave the conference room a cursory look while she pulled files from her briefcase. The conference room was on the eighth floor of the Tower Building in downtown Washington, D.C., and looked out on the bustling activity of afternoon traffic. The clean, sparse room held nothing but the mahogany table, eight leather chairs, and two black-and-white photographs of famous architect Aldo Rossi's buildings. Efficient, just like the company it represented.

As usual, Daniel Wallace wore a three-piece suit, polished dress shoes, and the perpetual crew cut of a former military officer who hadn't quite adjusted to civilian life.

"You look tired, Daniel," she said.

"Late night."

"You shouldn't work so much."

Daniel opened his mouth to reply, but turned away and cleared his throat instead.

Abby glanced between the two men seated at the large polished table and tried to order her thoughts. "Thank you for taking the time to meet with us, Mr. Blackman," she finally said, offering her hand and a pleasant smile.

Henry Blackman drifted somewhere in his mid-fifties and waged a losing battle against baldness. "The pleasure is all mine, Dr. Mitchell. It's nice to finally meet you in person" he said. Blackman took her hand and held it for just a little longer than she was comfortable with.

112

"This is our head of security, Daniel Wallace." Abby pulled her hand free and motioned toward him. "He's assisting me on this project to ensure that the Hope Diamond is fully secure for our upcoming gala."

Daniel leaned forward. "As you know, Mr. Blackman, we have a major event coming up, and we need your full assurance that the Hope Diamond will be secure."

Blackman offered a toothy grin. "To the best of my knowledge, the Smithsonian has never reported an attempt to steal the diamond. When we engineered the current security systems in 1997, we made even the possibility of theft obsolete."

Abby seemed less convinced. "I'm not sure that I share your confidence, Mr. Blackman. The Hope Diamond is a tempting challenge, and I believe there are those out there who would be willing to try."

"Try, yes. Succeed, no," he said. "You are familiar with the parameters we have in place?"

Daniel grunted. "Unfortunately, our records give us the bare minimum of information on the security features you designed."

"Exactly," Blackman said, leaning forward and placing his elbows on the table. He tapped his fingers together lightly. "When we were contracted to design the state-of-the-art system housing the diamond, we separated the various aspects among several different engineers. There is no one organization who understands how the system was put together, myself included. The design documents are kept in our vaults, and as you know, our burglar-resistant vaults have earned us the reputation of being the industry standard. I assure you, your diamond is safe."

To eliminate feedback noise, Isaac adjusted the audio coming from the bug in Abby's purse. He and Alex watched the voice patterns of Henry Blackman fluctuate on the computer screen before them. Isaac looked at his brother with a malicious grin. "Looks like we've got ourselves a little challenge."

Alex didn't respond. He sat with his feet propped up on the leather sofa. Abby's voice transmitted cleanly through the receiver, and as he listened to her talk he recalled the look of surprised pleasure that crossed her face when he kissed her temple the night before. She was responding just like he wanted.

———◦◦◦———

"The diamond's display case is three inches thick and bulletproof," Blackman continued, pride evident on his face. "If that is not enough of a deterrent, and someone actually tries to smash their way into the case, the jewel will immediately drop through the floor and into a specially designed vault below. When the remodel was done, the contractors reinforced the floor due to the weight of the vault. It cannot be broken into or lifted out without heavy machinery. And don't forget that even if a thief were able to bypass all those security features, which is technically impossible, he would still have to get out of the museum. Along with those hard security features, there is an intricate web of soft features such as containment security, electronic monitoring, and state-of-the-art alarm systems. We have created a total protective solution. Besides, our reputation is on the line. Not only do we protect the world's most precious gem, but also the foundation of America's history. In 2003 we were commissioned to build three customized high-tech vaults for the National Archives that store the U.S. Constitution, the Declaration of Independence, and the Bill of Rights. In addition to the vaults that hold those documents at night, we also created the permanent displays that encase them during the day at the Rotunda."

Abby listened to Blackman's spiel, running the odds in her mind that anyone would be bold enough to try and steal the diamond. As much as she'd like to believe his declaration of total security was gospel truth, she knew better.

Blackman looked at Daniel. "I hear you spent a good portion of your career at the State Department?"

Daniel nodded. "Ten of the twenty years I spent in the service."

"Then I think you'll understand that there are no more sophisticated measures than the ones we have taken at the Smithsonian."

Daniel flinched as he leaned back in his chair and crossed his arms. "What I'm concerned about is the fact that your systems are so renowned. It's like dangling a carrot before an eager thief. And believe me, there are people in this world who can crack your security measures. We don't know if they *will*, but we do know that they *can*."

Blackman forced a strangled laugh. "You may be a bit too pessimistic, Mr. Wallace. If someone can crack our security measures, then there are more important things than your diamond at risk. We are the primary supplier of vaults for the Federal Reserve, and we service seven bank sites and more than twenty vault doors. I suspect they would be a much greater target."

"In theory perhaps, but it's not my job to protect the Federal Reserve. I've been given the task of protecting the Hope Diamond. Part of that job is due diligence to ensure that we have all taken the appropriate measures."

"Our systems aside, it is my understanding that the Smithsonian itself is an impregnable fortress. I don't think you have anything to worry about."

Abby listened to most of their conversation in silence, but felt that the egos of the two talented men were about to clash. "That is why we are here, gentlemen," she said. "I believe that if we work together we can cover all of our bases and protect the diamond."

Her voice had a soothing effect on the men, and they regarded each other quietly. Blackman offered Abby a smile. "I'm sure you're right, Dr. Mitchell. And if you feel the need to discuss matters more thoroughly, you are more that welcome to call me any time. This is the number to my personal line." He slid his business card across the table to Abby.

She waited until he withdrew his hand before taking it.

Alex rolled his eyes. "Slimeball."

"Sounds like someone has a crush on your girlfriend."

"I think you mean my *target*, and she is way too smart for him."

"I don't know. He sounds like he's got it together."

"He sounds old. And fat."

"You sound jealous."

Alex leveled his gaze at Isaac. "This is work. My *job* is to seduce Abby and get her to trust me. This guy is a putz."

Isaac shrugged and changed the subject. "Any suggestions on where we go from here? It certainly appears they've covered their bases. A direct heist is out of the question. The infrastructure is too tight."

"We'll never get it out of that case. And even if the stars lined up just right and we did, we would never get it out of the museum. What do you give our chances now?" Alex asked.

"Bleak at best. Utterly impossible at worst."

"Think we should back out? That's why we always secure a down payment, in case something like this comes up."

"I have no intention of quitting. We'll get that diamond," a confident smile spread across Isaac's face.

"What are you thinking?"

He tapped Alex on the chest. "That seduction is a very powerful thing."

"We need to talk," Daniel said. He hailed a cab outside the Diebold offices.

"About what?" Abby asked.

"There's been a breach in security."

"What?" she gasped. "When?"

"Last night. At the Castle. An intruder gained access to the ITS room with a stolen security card."

"Did you catch him?"

Daniel stepped back from the curb as a yellow cab pulled to a stop three feet away. He opened the door for Abby and slid in next to her. "No. We lost him on the security grid."

"Did he take anything?"

"We don't have any way of knowing for sure."

Abby leaned over the seat and spoke to the driver. "Smithsonian Institution, please." The cab pulled into the flow of traffic, and she looked back at Daniel; worry etched her face. "What did Trent say?"

"I called him first thing this morning. He wasn't happy," he paused for a second, looking out the window. "I suggested we cancel the Hope event."

Abby shook her head. "*Why?*"

"It's a major breach of security, Abby, and it happened on my watch."

"I get that," she said. "But it happened at The Castle, not the Museum of Natural History."

"Better safe than sorry."

Abby pursed her lips and glanced at Daniel from the corners of her eyes. "Let me talk to Dr. Trent."

"What did you do?" Alex demanded of Isaac.

The conversation between Abby and Wallace was breaking up as they navigated through traffic, but Alex had caught just enough to arouse his suspicions.

"I was gathering information."

"You almost got caught."

Isaac's lip twitched as he faced his younger brother. All the warmth drained from his voice. "I can assure you that I most certainly did not."

"They know you were there."

"Someone. They know that *someone* was there."

"Well, apparently, it's got them up in arms. What were you thinking?"

"I was doing my job."

He stuck a finger in Isaac's face. "You were reckless."

Isaac grabbed him by the wrist and twisted his hand away. "Watch it. I know what I'm doing."

Alex took a step back. "Don't think I won't walk."

Isaac just laughed. "Sure."

Alex grabbed his jacket and walked toward the door. "Apparently, you don't know me that well," he said over his shoulder. "I don't need this. One more stunt like that and I'm gone."

⸻⸺⸻

DeDe sat before her easel, paintbrush in one hand, pallet in the other. She swept the brush across her canvas, swirling the ruddy color of burnt umber into what was now an angry red sky. To the untrained eye it was a perfect copy of Edvard Munch's *The Scream*: the deformed face with hands on its cheeks, mouth open in a scream, messy sunset sky, brackish water swirling beneath a bridge and drifting off toward the horizon. Simple. Ugly. Worth untold millions.

Yet all DeDe saw were the imperfections, the blurred lines on the wooden railing, the robe that was more gray than brown, the too long chin.

"They're getting better," Dow said as he stood over her shoulder. He nodded at the corner of the room where a stack of discarded canvases were piled, each bearing an attempt to reproduce the painting.

"Hmmm," she murmured, noncommittally.

"Well, that's your problem."

"What?" She looked at her husband and brushed a wiry curl from her cheek.

"You're not concentrating."

DeDe waved her paintbrush in the air randomly. "This whole thing is bothering me."

"But you've been doing this for years."

"Not the painting." She tossed her pallet on the floor. "Abby. And her father. It just doesn't seem right, you

119

know? I realize you put a lot of faith in that girl, but I think this is a lot to expect of her."

Dow rested an arm across his wife's shoulder. "The girl is tough," he said. "And we both learned a long time ago that she doesn't do anything she doesn't want to do."

"I know. It's just that her father isn't . . . safe."

⟶ ∞ ⟵

"How'd it go?" Marshall asked as soon as Daniel returned to the main security terminus at The Castle.

He shrugged and loosened his tie. "Not well."

Marshall turned and studied his boss with a questioning glance. "What did he say?"

"I told Dr. Trent we need to cancel the event."

"Because of one security breach?"

"One is enough."

Marshall shook his head. "But we have no suspect, no missing information, and no proof. All we know for sure is that Randy Jacobs accessed the basement last night at one o'clock."

"Randy Jacobs was in Mexico."

"Can we prove that definitively?"

Daniel squinted his narrow brown eyes and shook his head.

"So what are we going to do about it?"

"Nothing . . . for now."

"How do we find out what information he took?"

Daniel leaned back in his chair and pulled the pen from his coat pocket. "I think I've got an idea."

11

ABBY SWUNG OPEN THE DOOR TO HER APARTMENT AND LONGINGLY eyed the worn leather couch. Her jacket, keys, and laptop landed on a side table, and she went straight to the bedroom to change. The heavy, starched pant suit was swapped for a faded pair of jeans, one size too big, and an old Boston College sweatshirt that most likely would not survive another washing. Her outfit was completed with a pair of hideous blue-and-orange toe socks. Before heading for the living room, she caught up her hair in a loose ponytail.

Abby threw herself onto the couch and sank into the worn cushions. The old red blanket beneath her head made for a lumpy pillow. On the far wall hung a photograph collection of old churches, mostly in sepia tones, but a few in black and white. Captivating her with the beauty of stone and spire and cross, she had taken the photos on her travels. Yet she had never found the courage to set foot in any of them.

Weariness settled over her, and she buried her face in the blanket, eager to forget the chaos that surrounded her at work. But now that she was home, the stillness was even more disturbing than ringing phones, instant messages, and endless interruptions at the office. She resolved the situation by throwing her windows open and letting in the cool breeze and sounds of traffic below.

Much to Abby's chagrin, the clash of egos between Daniel Wallace and Henry Blackman had not ended at Diebold, Inc. Daniel popped into her office twice that day, trying to convince her to cancel the event. Although certain he was overreacting, she did her best to reassure him. In all the time she had known him, Daniel operated with a level of energy that could only be surmised as a coffee buzz gone terribly wrong. No other human being could work so much, sleep so little, and still manage to maintain what appeared to be perfect health. This man of few words must have used a three-week quota during his assorted visits to her office that day.

"You can't be overly cautious, Abby," he'd retorted on her fifth attempt to reassure him.

"I agree. I'm simply suggesting that there is the possibility that we are humanly incapable of taking more precautions that we have."

"We could always do more."

"Such as?"

"Armed guards. Lockdown—"

"What's next? Martial law?" He shrugged. "I've never seen you this agitated."

He folded his hands behind his back as though standing at parade rest. "I'm just trying to do my job."

Abby leaned forward with a smile. "Do you believe that I am trying to do mine as well?"

Hesitating a moment, he finally nodded.

"At the moment my job is to organize this celebration in honor of the Hope Diamond. It needs to be the biggest event in the history of the Smithsonian. It is by and large one of the most difficult undertakings of my career thus far. The logistics are beyond description, and the ultimate success or failure lands squarely on my shoulders. I must balance the needs of our guests, who expect to be entertained, with the need of the Smithsonian to raise ungodly amounts of money in a single night. Plus I'm responsible for the safety of the most viewed museum object in the world. I appreciate your help, Daniel. I really do. But I need you to make my job easier, not harder. We have to move forward with our plans."

He seemed to relax a little and sat down in her guest chair, perhaps for the first time since he'd taken the job at the Smithsonian. Normally, he always stood just inside her door with hands folded behind his back. He looked so uncomfortable and out of place sitting in the chair that she felt sorry for him.

"I just don't feel good about this whole thing," he said.

"I know, Daniel, but I'm very confident in your abilities. Our little diamond could not be in better hands."

After Daniel left her office, Henry Blackman called, but the aging security expert's reasons for interrupting her day were far more personal. After trying to impress her with the stats on a new vault they had in production, he asked her to dinner. She almost laughed. It took her nearly fifteen minutes to get rid of him, and then she avoided his calls for the rest of day.

As Abby's mind left work and returned to her comfy position at home, a more pleasant memory rose up.

Alex. He almost kissed me last night. A peck really. But he did ask to see me again.

123

Abby grinned, climbed off the couch, and slid into the kitchen in her sock feet. With hands on her hips, she stood for a moment, staring at an assortment of takeout menus. Nothing sounded good. She opened the fridge, only to slam it shut a few seconds later in disgust and peruse the menus again. Unable to make up her mind, she clasped a hand over her eyes, waved her finger, and pointed randomly.

"Tofu burger. No thanks."

Her finger landed on grilled chicken caesar salad on the second attempt. Nah. The lettuce would be soggy by the time it arrived. Best outta three.

It took six more tries before she settled on beef fajitas from a nearby Mexican restaurant. Just as she was about to pick up the phone and call in her order, the doorbell rang.

Although tempted not to answer, she changed her mind. Occasionally, the elderly Italian couple from two floors below felt sorry for her and brought up homemade spaghetti and meatballs. Of course, the home-cooked meal always came with a lecture, insisting that she needed to meet a nice man and settle down and have *molti bambini*.

One look through the peephole left her wishing she had chosen anything in her closet but the dirty sweatshirt and ugly socks. Alex stood outside her door, holding a large brown paper bag that she highly suspected contained food.

For a brief moment she considered bolting to the bedroom for a quick change, but she didn't want him to think she wasn't home. And she didn't want to tell him she needed to change for fear he would stand on the other side of the door and picture her naked, or worse, assume she was high maintenance. Instead, she cracked open the door, mortified at how she was dressed.

"Hi," he said. His eyes twinkled.

"Hi." She tried to hide behind the door.

"I realize it's not exactly proper to show up unannounced, but I thought you might be a little hungry and want some company. I can tell by the look on your face that you're starving, and I can see by those ghastly socks that you're most certainly spending your evening alone."

"You don't like my socks?" Abby asked, feigning offense. She swung open the door.

"They're hideous," he answered, bending slightly to brush her forehead with his lips.

Her stomach dipped somewhere near her knees, and she wondered if she would be able to eat a bite.

"Cute," she retorted. "They're cute."

"No. *You* are cute. The socks should be burned."

Abby could not help but rise up on her tiptoes and peek into the brown paper bag.

"Spaghetti, meatballs, hot bread, and salad," he said, finding his own way to the kitchen. "And if you're good, there may even be a little *tiramisu* somewhere in the bottom."

"How could you have possibly known that was the very thing I wanted tonight?"

He smiled. "Just a hunch, Dr. Mitchell. I thought you might need a little warm food and some good company to wind down."

She winced. "Do I look that strung out?"

"You look tired . . . and just a little tense."

"Long day."

"The event?"

"Ah, the event. It's just *the* defining moment of my career."

"How's that?"

"My colleagues believe I can inspire the attendees to write obscenely large checks to the Smithsonian. Our notoriously wealthy and snobbish patrons only care that

I divert their boredom for an evening. And together they have assumed that I am the world's leading expert on the Hope Diamond. I dare not disappoint them, or I will most surely hear from both sides."

"Well," Alex said, searching a cabinet and pulling out two plates. "What does success look like?"

She stood for a moment, gnawing gently on her bottom lip. "That's a great question, and I can honestly say, in all my planning, I have not asked myself."

"From what I'm hearing, you need to raise gobs of money while simultaneously putting on a show to remember. Is that right?"

"Spot on."

"So what's the plan?"

"Live music. Dancing. Lots of bejeweled women wearing dresses that are just a little too small and revealing. Bored men sipping champagne when they'd rather have whiskey. A little caviar. An ice sculpture." She sighed. "Basically, an event doomed to failure."

"And you planned all of that because?" he asked, spooning heaps of steaming food on the plates.

"I'm supposed to."

Alex looked at her with a mischievous smirk. "Do you always do what you're supposed to, Dr. Mitchell?"

She smiled. "Pretty much."

Without giving her the opportunity to protest, Alex leaned in and kissed her. It only took her a moment to return his kiss.

He pulled away with a broad grin. "Well, you shouldn't have done that."

"Done what?" she asked, slightly bewildered. "*You* kissed *me*."

"True. But you returned the kiss . . . and quite well I might add. We simply don't know one another well enough to be kissing like that." He carried the plates into the living room and sat on the couch.

Abby followed and sat down next to him, somewhat bewildered. "We don't?"

Alex shook his head. "Not nearly well enough. We shouldn't be kissing like that for at least another three days."

"What should we be kissing like now?"

"Like this," he said, tipping her chin up with a finger, and lightly brushing his lips against hers.

"I think I like the other way better."

"You'll just have to keep me around for three more days," he said.

"Deal."

"Now," Alex said, turning his attention to the food before him. "Let's eat."

"Where did you get this?" she asked, wiping sauce from her chin with a napkin. "It's incredible."

"A little hole in the wall near Georgetown called Bella Sera."

"Beautiful evening."

"What?"

"*Bella sera* means beautiful evening in Italian."

"Don't tell me you speak Italian? It's not enough that you have your doctorate and are much smarter than I am, but now you must show me up with linguistics as well?"

Abby set her fork on her plate and raised an eyebrow. "Say what you like, Alex Weld, neither of us is fooled into thinking I'm smarter than you."

He paused for a moment, his expression undecipherable. "I'm not the one with a *Dr.* before my name."

"A string of letters that doesn't mean squat to most people."

"And the Italian?"

"A few words here and there, but nothing fluent."

Alex nodded and stuffed another forkful of spaghetti in his mouth. "May this be a *bella sera* then."

"Hear! Hear!" she said, tapping a chunk of bread against his.

They ate in silence for a moment, sprawled casually on the couch.

After wiping out three-quarters of the food on his plate, Alex furrowed his eyebrows and turned to her. "Back to this event. What's proving to be your biggest hassle?"

"That would be security."

"How come?"

"First, I have an overzealous ex-military head of security who feels the need to batten the hatches and not let anyone within three hundred feel of the diamond."

"And that's a problem because the diamond is the main attraction."

"Exactly. People want to get up close and personal. They want to touch the display case. These are women who could easily own this diamond were it not locked away in a museum."

"They want to be enticed," Alex said.

"Yes."

"They want to be impressed."

"Yes."

His eyes flashed as though stumbling upon a clever idea. "The question is do you want them to be jealous?"

"*Jealous?*"

"Yes, jealous of the fact that they can't have that diamond no matter what they do. Jealous enough that they will donate with no regard to the balance in their checkbook."

She considered it for a moment. "Yes, I suppose I do."

"Then those are the women you need to appeal to, because the truth is that the vast majority of men in that room won't care. They are being dragged there by their wives, and the only interest they have is one-upping the boys from the country club. The women will have the motivation, but the men will have the checkbook. Pit them against one another, and you'll have solved the first of your dilemmas. And you may just get yourself a raise in the process."

Abby leaned back and regarded Alex with genuine interest. "You are brilliant."

He grinned. "I know. Food good?"

"Yes. Very."

"Now," he said. "On to your second problem."

"The event itself."

"Yes, the event, which brings us back to the jealous little socialites."

"Indeed."

"They will all be dressed in designer gowns I presume?"

"To the point of vulgarity."

"Then you need to one-up them."

Her pasta-laden fork paused halfway to her mouth. "What?"

Alex leaned back on the couch, his plate resting precariously on his knees, and fixed his gaze on the far wall. He was about to say something, but stopped, head cocked to the side. "Did you take those pictures?"

"I did."

"They're really good."

"Thanks. It's a hobby."

"Why churches?"

Abby tugged at her ponytail and dropped her gaze to the floor. "Just drawn to them I suppose."

He gave her a sideways glance. "I didn't take you for the religious type."

"What did you take me for?"

"For granted, apparently."

"What was it you were saying?" she asked, not wanting the conversation to continue down this path.

He seemed to search for his lost train of thought. "They're coming to see a diamond they can't have. And you're the means by which they can get close to it."

"I don't follow."

"Since they won't actually be allowed to stick their hands inside the case and scoop up the diamond, they'll hang on your every word." Alex stopped for a second and looked at her. "You will be giving a speech?" She nodded. "Good. Then use your words to entice their desire and use your appearance to make them feel like they're not the prettiest girls at the dance. They'll trip all over themselves to compensate."

"I don't think I could pull off something like that."

Alex looked not at her body, but deep into her eyes. "You could pull it off. Believe me."

Abby felt heat flood her cheeks.

"I embarrassed you?"

She answered by shoving a mouthful of bread into her mouth.

"Sorry," he said with a shrug. "But it's true."

"Alex, we're talking about some of the wealthiest women in the country. Some of their gowns will cost more than I make in a year. And the jewels! I think I might own a pair of real diamond earrings. *Maybe*."

He twirled his fork in the pile of spaghetti. "Jewels," he murmured, deep in thought. He looked at her, eyes alight. "But Abby, you *do* have a jewel to beat them all."

It took only a second for her to realize where he was heading. "You can't possibly mean—"

"Yes," he said, nodding emphatically. "Yes. *You* should wear the Hope Diamond."

"Not going to happen."

Abby shook her head no, while Alex polished off the rest of his dinner.

"Impossible. They'd never go for it."

He shrugged.

"You're really serious, aren't you?" she asked.

"Why not?"

"You're insane."

"Hey, just a minute ago you called me brilliant."

"It's a fine line, and I think you just teetered over the edge."

"But it was a good idea, wasn't it?"

"No," she retorted stubbornly. "It was a *great* idea, and I can't do anything about it."

He took their plates to the kitchen and rinsed them off in the sink. "Don't worry. You can just continue with your boring little party and you'll raise a decent amount of money. Everyone will be reasonably satisfied, and the event will go down as just another thing they attended once. Your career will survive, quite nicely I'm sure."

Abby groaned. "Well, when you say it like *that*—"

Alex returned from the kitchen with two movies in hand. "Your pick. *Rambo* or *Marie Antoinette*?"

She laughed. "How could I possibly choose between such classics?"

He held up *Rambo* in one hand. "Lots of stuff gets blown up in this one."

"Let's go with that."

"*But*," he said, waving *Marie Antoinette* in her face, "If we watch this one you can teach me something."

"How so?"

He tapped her lightly on the forehead with a finger. "Well, Miss Historian, I believe that Marie Antoinette was married to Louis XVI, and it's my understanding that he once owned the Hope Diamond. I mean you're cute and all, but I still have to write that article you know."

"I guess it's settled. *Marie Antoinette* it is. And to think, I was so looking forward to watching *Rambo*."

"One more thing. You have to take off those socks, or I can't take you seriously."

Abby settled in and stretched her arms out on the back of the couch. An impish grin stretched across her face. "We don't know each other well enough to start taking our clothes off."

He gave her a mischievous sideways glance. "Will that start happening in three days?"

"Don't count on it."

Alex rose from the couch and popped in the DVD. After flipping off the lights he rejoined her on the couch. They spent the next 120 minutes deeply engrossed in the bizarre lives of King Louis XVI and Marie Antoinette.

After sitting through the entire movie, credits and all, Alex reluctantly rose to go. He led her to the door with fingers lightly entwined.

"Hey." Abby looked up at him, brown eyes curious. "I was wondering something."

"What would that be?"

"Would you be interested in being my date for the big event? I'll be working, but I'd really like you to be there. Who knows, you might even learn something."

Alex wrapped his arms around her waist and pulled her close. He buried his face in her neck, inhaling the sweet scent of shampoo and floral lotion. "I'd be honored," he whispered.

Abby tilted her head back and looked at him. "So how is this possible?"

"What?

"*This*. Last I checked all you wanted was an interview, and now every time I turn around you're kissing me."

"Life is full of surprises," he said with a shrug, avoiding eye contact.

"Apparently so."

"Can I call you tomorrow?"

"Please."

His lips met hers with the lightest touch, giving the barest impression of a kiss. She pressed in deeper, but he pulled back and whispered, "Three days."

"*Three days?*" she groaned.

"Three days." He stepped out the door, and she closed it behind him, watching him through the peephole as he disappeared down the hall. Abby Mitchell bathed her apartment in a very satisfied grin.

Abby stood at her front door for some time, cheek pressed against the wood, deep in thought. She shook her head and laughed, not believing he had actually seen her ghastly socks. She wrenched herself away from the door and yawned. For a moment she pondered the comfort of her warm bed but then went to the kitchen and pulled cleaning supplies from under the sink.

He wants me to wear the diamond, she thought, first cleaning the dishes in her sink and then scouting her apartment for dirty surfaces. She chewed on her bottom lip, pondering the idea and what it meant.

Two hours later, once her mind was fuzzy and her fingers pruned, she brushed her teeth and crawled between the Egyptian cotton sheets. As Abby slipped into the world of sleep, a dog began to bark in the darkness outside her apartment, the harbinger of uneasy dreams.

12

MESHERA FOREST, RUSSIA, FEBRUARY, 1689

JEAN-BAPTISTE TAVERNIER STRUGGLED THROUGH THE DEEP UNDERGROWTH of the towering pine trees, encumbered by his weight and the heavy Oriental robes. His breathing was labored; he was unaccustomed to such physical exertion. The hands that usually sold crown jewels were ripped and bleeding from deep cuts. He stumbled again and fell face first into musty pine needles.

"Forêt stupide!" he cursed, pulling himself to his feet. He paused for a second, a stitch burning in his side.

Then he heard the barking again, and the beads of sweat on his forehead turned cold.

The dogs. They were closer now. Much closer.

Tavernier bolted, and in his fright lost all sense of direction. He could not tell if he was running from the dogs or toward them. He scrambled desperately over fallen logs and under low-hanging branches. The wild animals were but a few paces behind him now, growling, barking, hungry.

He desperately scanned the trees, looking for one to climb. But with his eyes off the ground, he tripped again, this time crashing to the forest floor and knocking the breath from his lungs. The blood rushed through his head, pounding against his eardrums. He could hear the dogs behind him, tearing at the forest floor as they ran.

Tavernier turned, and as he did, saw the first of seven dogs leap through the air. Finally, able to draw a breath, all he could do was scream. Instinctively, he covered his face with his hands as they descended upon him.

13

ABBY WOKE WITH A START, SCREAMS STILL ECHOING IN HER MIND AS the dream of Tavernier faded. The clock on her nightstand read 5:00, so she slid out of bed and shuffled to her shower. She turned the water on full blast, as hot as she could stand it. It stung her skin like searing needles and chased away the remainder of a troubled night's sleep. When she stepped out of the shower her skin was beet red and her bathroom filled with steam.

Abby rejected her usual slacks and sweater in favor of a black pencil skirt and fitted white blouse. The three-inch black stilettos added just the right amount of sex appeal without overdoing it. She kept an eye on the clock as she dressed, paying special attention to her hair and makeup.

A long day of work loomed before her, and she still needed to go by Dow and DeDe's apartment. Abby took a step back from the mirror, eyeing her handiwork.

If this doesn't get their attention, nothing will.

———

Isaac ran still shots of Abby's face through Identix, the facial recognition software used by the U.S. government and Interpol to track criminals. The 3D analysis captured distinctive features on the surface of a face that most programs missed, such as eye-socket depth and the contour of the nose and chin. However, Isaac's concern was not whether she had a criminal background but rather her fascination with the Hope Diamond. He saw something in Abby's face during his initial reconnaissance that troubled him. It was something he recognized immediately: obsession. She looked at the diamond like a jealous woman watching her lover seduce a stranger.

He slid the flash drive into his computer and typed in a date, scanning through the footage until the approximate time that Abby arrived at the Hope display. It was only a matter of seconds before he found an image of Abby, with all the needed recognition points. Isaac froze the frame and copied it to Identix. He then added the complete section of video and had the program check her face against the full length of tape. The computer hummed beneath the desk, occasionally offering faint clicking sounds as it checked her face. A few seconds later, the program beeped and a number appeared on the screen before Isaac.

"No way," he murmured.

Over the last two years, Abby Mitchell had gone to see the diamond nearly six hundred times.

Isaac had felt a deep, lingering suspicion about Abby from the moment that Alex recognized her from the heist in Rio. It was only now that his suspicion turned to fear. Isaac Weld was not a man accustomed to that emotion.

⤝✺⤞

DeDe answered on the first buzz, and Abby made her way into the building and rode up in the rickety elevator to their apartment. When the door swung open, DeDe did not give her the usual hug, but instead stood in the doorway with her brow furrowed and lips pursed.

"Good morning to you too," Abby said, somewhat disconcerted.

DeDe smiled and pulled her into a hug.

"Is something wrong?" Abby asked.

"Why don't you tell me?"

"What do you mean?"

"I can see it on your face."

"See what?"

"I'm not sure."

Abby shook her head. "I don't follow DeDe, what are you saying?"

The older woman offered the charming smile that Abby had grown to love, the corners of her eyes crinkling like paper, and led her to the small living room. Dede's curly salt-and-pepper hair was swept back into a French twist, and she wore a black knit dress, silhouetting a figure much slimmer than one would expect for her age.

"Let me guess. The journalist?" DeDe asked. "Is it the same man from the interview?"

Abby nodded. "Alex Weld."

Dow sorted newspapers at his usual spot by the window. At this announcement he rose and joined them in the living room, deeply interested in the conversation.

"So it's official then?" Dow asked.

Abby chewed on her bottom lip. "Well," she finally answered. "I don't know if you would call it *dating*. We haven't exactly known each other very long. But we have been spending time together."

"Romantic time?" DeDe tried to hide the glimmer of a smile.

"Yes," Abby laughed. "I would definitely call it romantic."

"Good," Dow and DeDe said in unison.

"Good?" she asked.

"Yes, good," DeDe said, breaking into a full smile.

"Yes, I suppose it is."

Dow clapped his hands, startling both women. "Now, do tell how things are going with that little event you're in charge of?"

"That's actually why I'm here." Abby turned to DeDe with an imploring look. "I was hoping I could borrow your diamond stud earrings."

DeDe raised her eyebrows. "My earrings?"

"I know Dow gave them to you, and I wouldn't normally ask for something like that, but I'd like to wear them Saturday night."

"Is it really that soon?" Dow asked.

"Unfortunately, yes. I'm running out of time to get everything ready."

DeDe offered her a gentle pat on the back. "Oh, I've no doubt you'll get it all done."

"That's just it. I think the plan may change."

Dow's blue eyes narrowed. "What do you mean the plan may change?"

Abby shook her head. "There is no way the Smithsonian will go for it."

"Go for what?"

Abby tried to find a way to explain Alex's suggestion. While scrubbing floors the night before she had written the idea off as ridiculous, but after a night of fitful dreams, she woke this morning with second thoughts. She always cleaned when she had a lot on her mind, which was a trait she was particularly grateful for. Her mother had sat and stared out the window when thinking, and as a result, little or nothing had ever been done around their home. Angela Mitchell's mental illness had rendered her nearly catatonic by the time Abby was seven, and Abby had to leave her mother and go live with her father.

Although she no longer lived in a pigsty, she had in many ways lost both parents. Instead of caring for her himself, her father had sent her off to one boarding school after another, spending only the required school breaks with her. Even then, she was attended to mostly by servants and nannies. Some would have considered her life privileged and pampered. To Abby it was an aching lesson in loneliness. When it came time for college, her father wanted her to attend Cambridge. She chose Boston College, both to spite him and to be near the memory of her mother. What little relationship she maintained with her father through the years fractured after she graduated, despite the fact that she chose Cambridge for her doctoral work. Neither of them had made much of an attempt to restore it since. With the exception of a rare bribe given in place of affection, Abby had little contact with him. Yet, even though she tried to ignore it, there was a latent desire to know her father.

"Abby?" Dow asked, looking at her quizzically.

"Yes? What?"

"You just zoned out on us there. What were you going to say?"

"Sorry." She shook her head. "I was trying to figure out how to explain it without giving you a stroke, and I wandered off on another train of thought."

"Just spit it out, dear," DeDe said.

Abby took a deep breath. "I want to wear the Hope Diamond during my speech at the Smithsonian."

Stunned silence.

"I know. It's crazy. It makes no sense. And there's no chance Dr. Trent will let me do it." She looked at their incredulous expressions. "You don't have to say it. I know it's insane. But just think about it for a moment. This is the Hope Diamond. It hasn't been worn by a single human being since Michelle Pfeiffer modeled it for an article in *Life* magazine in 1995. And this event is a big deal. Hundreds of people are coming to celebrate its anniversary. And—"

There was a twinkle deep within DeDe's black eyes. "I think it's brilliant."

"You *what?*"

"I think it would accomplish the very thing you want."

"But they will never let you do it," Dow said.

"Never." Abby shook her head.

"But it would be brilliant," he added.

Abby gauged her next comment carefully. "It wasn't my idea."

Dow's eyes narrowed. "It wasn't?"

"Alex suggested it."

"That's interesting."

"He thinks it would create an aura of jealousy in the women attending. You know, me wearing something they couldn't buy with all their money. He seems to think they would write bigger checks in an effort to outdo each other."

"Well, first off, you wouldn't need to wear the Hope Diamond to make those women jealous. But he is right about the rest. It would have that very effect."

"But, once again, it will never happen. There is no way they will let me take that diamond out of the case."

"You don't know that," Dow said with a shrug.

"I'm pretty sure."

DeDe grinned maliciously and slid next to Abby on the couch. She rested her hand on Abby's arm. "My dear," she said. "These are *men* we are talking about."

"Yes, exactly. Hardheaded, stubborn, arrogant men."

"Precisely."

"What?"

"There is no surer way to get what you want with a group of men than to pit one ego against another."

"Ego is something they have in great supply. But I still don't see a way to convince Dr. Trent and Daniel Wallace to let me wear the Hope Diamond. It's simply absurd."

"But my dear, you don't have to convince them of any such thing."

"What do you mean?"

DeDe shrugged. "You just need to let them think it's their idea."

Dow laughed. "Do you see why I married this woman? She's ruthless."

"I didn't realize that was a character trait you admired in a woman."

"Always."

Abby turned back to DeDe. "Pray tell, how might I convince those men that it is their idea?"

DeDe draped an arm over Abby's shoulder and led her to the kitchen for a cup of coffee and a strategic planning session.

14

THE CURSOR ON ABBY'S LAPTOP BECKONED. THE CLOCK INCHED TOWARD six o'clock, and she stared at the stack of papers on her desk: release forms, security procedures, invitation lists. They all needed attention hours ago. Yet her thoughts returned to the unfinished speech on her computer screen.

"I don't have time for this," she murmured, trying to squelch the sudden burst of inspiration. "I need to get this paperwork done." But try as she might, Abby could not stifle the train of thought. She shoved the papers to the corner of her desk and pulled her laptop forward.

She reread her last entry, allowing her mind to orient to its point in the story.

> *The diamond, now referred to simply as the French Blue, was placed in King Louis XIV's Cabinet of Curiosities sometime between 1669 and 1673. Apparently, the king was unconcerned with the illicit history surrounding his favored trinket and went about his business with little thought to the supposed curse. The diamond was soon recut by the court jeweler, Sieur Pitau, and*

reduced to just over half its former size. Weighing in at just over 67 carats, it was worn by the king either as a brooch or as a necklace suspended on a pale blue ribbon.

The reign of Louis XIV was marked by a single venture—the building of Versailles. In so doing he acquired the nickname of the Sun King for his belief that, as king, he bathed the common man in his glory. Yet this glory did not come without a price to those same commoners, as the funding for the world-renowned palace fell solely on their shoulders. It was an era of exorbitant taxation and the emergence of divine kingship.

As a monarch, Louis's obsession with jewels grew along with the scope of his elaborate lifestyle. He commissioned an entire room on the south side of Versailles solely for the exhibition of the crown jewels, which he put to regular, personal use. Visiting nobles were often lent the jewels during their stay, and Louis delighted in such ambassadors partaking in the abundance of his generosity. Yet there was one diamond that was never worn by friend or mistress. That sole jewel, deep blue in color, was preserved as the king's favorite adornment, and it was only on occasion that it graced his own person.

Abby followed the story on the screen, mouthing the words as she read them. Then she placed her fingertips on the keyboard and added the thoughts that were bubbling in her mind.

After 72 years of rule, King Louis XIV died. Although it certainly would have brought him satisfaction, the great monarch was unable to

145

take his precious jewel with him into eternity. Instead, it passed to his great-grandson, a five-year-old boy who became King Louis XV. As is often the case during times of peace and great prosperity, those who find themselves with an abundance of time and wealth tend to squander both.

At a mere thirty years of age, King Louis XV was knighted into the Order of the Golden Fleece, a social status with little more significance than a gentlemen's club. Yet to the king, a man obsessed with status and titles, it was an honor that he believed should be recognized by all who laid eyes on him. So it was with no small amount of pomp that he commissioned the design of an elaborate brooch, containing no small number of stunning jewels, the centerpiece of which became the infamous French Blue. Once completed, the Golden Fleece was valued at almost 1.3 million livres, or the equivalent of 7.3 million dollars in today's currency.

Louis XV's reign was marked by self-absorption that left his nation in financial ruin. Lacking the moral fortitude necessary to lead well and endure sacrifice, he died just as he lived—a weakling. King Louis XV succumbed to smallpox in the palace built by his great-grandfather. Bourbon tradition insisted that the ruler's heart be cut out and placed in a special coffer. Yet this king was the first monarch not to have that "honor" bestowed on him. Instead, those preparing the body poured alcohol into his coffin and soaked his body in quicklime. He was given an uneventful late-night burial. It was attended by a single courtier.

Abby typed quickly, her thoughts racing ahead of her fingers. Although she never stopped writing, she often closed her eyes, seeing the picture in her mind. It was a fluid moment, the kind writers strive for in their storytelling, where thought and motion blend without effort. She smiled.

> *Though many who believe the Hope Diamond to be cursed would look at the lives of both Louis XIV and Louis XV and believe them to have led somewhat pleasant, uneventful lives, it can be noted that they possessed a jewel that robbed them of the ability to truly enjoy their lives. It makes one wonder if there is no greater curse to endure that that of a never-ending discontentment. Yet, the saga of the Hope Diamond does not disappoint those who wait for it to strike its victims with cruelty. And a student of the jewel does not have to wait long to see two of the greatest monarchs in history meet a grisly fate at the cold and uncaring whim of the Hope Diamond. For next in line to the throne of France was a man born with the name Louis Auguste. History knows him as King Louis XVI, and his wife bears the renowned and unfortunate name of Marie Antoinette.*

Abby settled back in her chair, satisfied with her words and the abundance of text that preceded them. Even as she told this story, she understood the part she played in it.

The indoor climbing wall at Chimborazo was the first of its kind in Washington, D.C., and as far as Isaac Weld was concerned, the best. Frequented mainly by serious climbers it was free of the usual distractions: youth groups blaring obnoxious Christian music, corporations on team-building events, and amorous couples on the ever pressing third date who would rather be in the darkness somewhere groping one another.

He walked into the upscale training facility in his usual climbing gear: cargo shorts, baseball cap, white tee shirt, and running shoes. Isaac paid the fee at the front desk, but was followed to the four-story wall in the back by an eager attendant wearing a name tag that read Wyatt.

"Hey, sir," he called after Isaac. "Excuse me."

Isaac turned, in no mood to chat with a post-pubescent college student. "Yes?"

"If you're heading to the back wall you gotta pass the belay test," he said apologetically. "Sorry, man, but it's the rules."

Isaac cast a glance at the towering façade, pockmarked by neon-colored foot- and handholds. It swept upward, bulging irregularities in its surface, and was one of the better attempts to imitate a natural surface. "Let's get it over with then."

Wyatt led him to the back and collected a series of harnesses, carabiners, ropes, and rappelling gear. By the time the young man finished and turned around, Isaac had vanished. "Hey, man, I thought you wanted to climb," he shouted through the empty room, his voice echoing off the high ceiling.

"I do," Isaac responded from twenty feet above, dangling like a spider by his fingertips from a three-inch handhold. He swung his legs forward, planting his toes in a small crack, and pushed himself higher, quad muscles straining against his skin.

The young man watched with gaping mouth as Isaac traversed the man-made cliff, swinging lithely from one outcropping to the next with no ropes or rappelling gear. Once he ascended the forty-foot precipice, Isaac maneuvered back and forth across its face, testing his strength against the various handholds and chimney climbs. Finally satisfied with his ability to best the wall, he shimmied down the surface and stood before the stunned attendant.

"You said something about a belay test?"

Wyatt held the ropes in his hand, watching a single bead of sweat roll down Isaac's temple, his breath barely accelerated. "Man, I've never seen anything like that. How long you been climbing?"

Instead of answering, Isaac turned his back and sprang five feet into the air, latching onto the surface of the wall like a spider monkey. Then he climbed the course again, this time with his eyes closed.

———⸺———

Douglas Mitchell maintained his penthouse in Bethesda, Maryland, even though he rarely stayed there. The physical address came in handy, as did the two-story, three-thousand-square-foot apartment with valet service, sauna, and private rooftop pool. Although he originally paid millions for it and enjoyed an obscene rate of appreciation on the property, it was empty except for a bed, a fully stocked liquor cabinet, and a laptop. The walls were devoid of pictures—even of his only daughter.

Tall and clean shaven, Mitchell was unfamiliar with the phrase "business casual." He dressed in a tailored three-piece suit every day and expected those who worked for him to do the same. He removed his jacket, laid it carefully on the bed, and grabbed his laptop. A series of hollow footsteps followed him across the parquet wood floors as he made his way to the spiral staircase and up to the second level.

The French doors leading to his rooftop terrace were unlocked, and he pushed through them, refreshed by the chill of an early evening. A teak patio set rested near the pool, and Douglas Mitchell slid into one of the chairs and opened his computer. It hummed for a moment, warming up, and then he checked his email. There were several messages waiting, but he only opened the one from his daughter.

He read the trepidation behind her sparse words. She requested breakfast. Short. Noncommittal. An easy escape. Just like Abby.

Ripples danced across the swimming pool, but he did not see them. For the first time in weeks, he thought about his daughter.

Dow stood before the large, industrial window that was once part of a steel manufacturing warehouse and watched the sun set on another day. The building now housed his second home, and he and DeDe relished their time spent in the loft apartment. Low, indirect lighting fell in pools across the floor, blurring the lines between light and darkness.

"It's been a slow day," he said over his shoulder, feeling his wife's presence.

"I thought your assistant was going to transfer your calls here?"

"She did. There just weren't many of them."

DeDe joined him at the window, placing her hand in the small of his back and resting her head against his shoulder. "I hate this part."

He nodded. "The calm before the storm."

She slid in front of him and looped her hands around his neck. "Have you ever wondered why we chose this career? I mean, really, normal people don't do this."

"The thrill of the chase, I suppose."

"Perhaps. But we're getting old. The travel takes its toll you know."

"What else are we going to do? Retire to the French Riviera?"

DeDe snorted distastefully. "Gracious no. I just wonder if we'll ever truly be satisfied with what we've accomplished."

"Proud yes. Satisfied no. There is always more to be done."

⸺◦◦◦⸺

In a city of 5.3 million people, it only made sense that Alex would see the same style car on more than one occasion. Yet it wasn't the silver BMW that bothered Alex, it was the driver. He had seen Wülf many times over the years while working for the Broker, and Alex wasn't such a fool as to believe he and Isaac went unsupervised in their work. But he didn't like the increased level of scrutiny that came with this heist. It was all well and good in the early days when he and Isaac were up against a slew of other professionals vying for the job. But they no longer had anything to prove. The other guys were winnowed out or ended up in prison. Hundreds of thefts later, he and Isaac were the only big players left in the game. And that was just the way they liked it, cherry-picking the best jobs from an endless pool of opportunity. Let the little guys fight for the table scraps; Alex Weld wanted to enjoy the feast. But he didn't like being shadowed in the process.

On a whim he crossed over two lanes of traffic and glanced in his rearview mirror. Sure enough, the silver BMW stayed with him, six cars back.

Alex took the next right, drove down one block, and slipped into a parking garage. He steered his Mercedes into the nearest empty spot and turned off the engine. A digital camera rested in the console, so he grabbed it before slipping from the car. The concrete rail hid him as he jogged into the shadows beside a large support column and waited, camera ready. Within a few seconds the BMW came into sight but didn't pull into the parking garage. Alex let it pass and then zoomed in on the license plate.

He got back in his car and looked at the picture, committing the license plate to memory.

Abby's mind was adrift with ideas floating on a sea of improbability. In just a few days she would host the single most important event in Smithsonian history, and she was about to ask the largest museum in the world to disregard every one of its security measures.

So it was with measured determination that she approached the office of Dr. Peter Trent, curator of the Smithsonian Institution, for their scheduled meeting. Behind his door waited not only the man ultimately in charge of every major decision at the museum but also the one who would prove to be her greatest challenge in getting the diamond out of its case—Daniel Wallace.

Abby stopped outside the door and took a deep breath. Juggling an armload of files, with her free hand she smoothed her skirt and combed her fingers through her hair. When she walked through the doors of Dr. Trent's office, she wanted to give the impression that she was a woman worthy of wearing the Hope Diamond. The fitted black pencil skirt, three-inch heels, and tailored blouse were a perfect blend of professionalism and femininity. And they were a marked departure from her typical conservative attire.

"Come in," Dr. Trent replied, his voice muffled.

Abby pushed through the door and found Daniel Wallace already seated in one of the antique chairs facing the oversized mahogany desk. Bookshelves that held rare first editions by such famous authors as Charles Dickens, Ernest Hemingway, and John Steinbeck lined two walls. On either side of the door hung original Ansel Adams photographs, matted in white and framed in black. Yet the most striking feature in the room was the large gothic arched window that rose ten feet behind the desk. Peter Trent's office resided inside the main turret of The Castle and, with this place of honor, enjoyed fifteen-foot ceilings, thick hardwood floors, and a stunning Persian rug. The room was approachable but formal, just like its occupant.

The secretary of the Smithsonian Institution was nearing sixty but retained a head of dark brown hair and a certain youthfulness that came with having a job he loved. His eyes were surrounded by deep creases, exaggerated both by smiles and laughter. Many years spent in the field on archeological digs had given him a permanent ruddy complexion. Yet several years ago he traded his khaki digging garb for a herringbone jacket and bifocals.

"Hello, Daniel." She slid into the chair next to him and crossed her legs.

Daniel's eyes narrowed as they passed from her hair to her heels. He nodded a greeting and returned his glance to the security schematic in his lap.

Peter Trent looked at her over the rim of his glasses and his eyes opened wide in surprise. "Good afternoon, Abby . . . Dr. Mitchell. You look . . . well . . . nice today."

"Thank you."

Dr. Trent tapped his fingers lightly on the desk. "I'm sorry for arranging this meeting so late in the day, but there are some things we need to take care of right away. I have a meeting with the Board of Regents soon, and I need to present them with our plan of action."

"I was working late anyway." Abby placed her files on his desk and pushed them forward. "I have the information you requested."

"Ah, yes," Dr. Trent said. He took the pile and flipped through the pages slowly. "The two of you met with Mr. Blackman?"

Abby nodded. "Yes. The security measures that Diebold has in place are quite impressive." She turned to Daniel and smiled. "Wouldn't you agree?"

He gave her a sharp look and replied, "Impressive, yes. Perfect, no."

Dr. Trent glanced over the file in his hand. "What could possibly be lacking? They are the most renowned security firm in the world."

"Diebold's procedures are solid; I have a problem with the assumptions they've made."

Abby settled into her chair as Daniel climbed aboard his soapbox.

"I don't understand, Mr. Wallace, please enlighten me," Dr. Trent said, the faintest air of condescension in his voice.

Daniel stiffened in his chair and sat up straight. "They assume the Hope Diamond can't be stolen. That assumption is always the first, and greatest, mistake made by a target. The reality is that *anything* can be stolen."

Peter Trent shook his head. "I don't know that I agree with your assessment. I would agree that most things can be stolen, but not all."

"I don't mean this as a form of disrespect, Dr. Trent, but most of my career has been spent outside the walls of a museum. There are people today who, if they want it bad enough, could get that diamond out of its case and walk out the front door."

"I have a deep regard for you, Daniel, which is why I hired you in the first place, but I find that implausible."

"You hired me to think of the things you couldn't." Daniel dropped the words carefully, hitting their mark with measured intensity.

Peter Trent leveled his gaze at Daniel. "Mr. Wallace, I am going to make the assumption that you did not just call me stupid."

"Absolutely not, sir. You are one of the most intelligent people I've ever known. However, I think we both understand that there is a big difference between earning a doctorate and having street smarts. What we need at the moment is a commonsense approach to our security measures. We do not have the luxury of assuming anything."

Peter ground his jaws together as he thought about Daniel's comment. The insinuation was thinly veiled with respect. Instead of answering Daniel, he turned to Abby. "What do you think, Dr. Mitchell?"

"Well," she said, resting a hand on Daniel's arm, "I was in that meeting with Henry Blackman and, to be honest, Dr. Trent, I have to agree with Daniel."

Daniel flashed a triumphant look at Dr. Trent and leaned back in his chair.

"I do think there are people out there who would like nothing better than to steal the Hope Diamond," Abby said. "But in all honesty I don't think they would ever succeed."

Daniel stiffened and watched her with narrowed eyes as she continued.

"The fact remains that Diebold has created a system of groundbreaking measures to protect our diamond. However," she said, with a disarming smile. "I have so much confidence in Daniel and his abilities that even if I were to *wear* that diamond during the celebration, he and his team would be more than capable of protecting it."

"Wear the diamond? Have you lost your mind, Abby?" Daniel perched on the edge of his chair, shaking his head.

"I believe what Abby is saying is that regardless of where the diamond is, you would be up to the task of protecting it," Dr. Trent added, coming to her aid.

Abby nodded. "Exactly."

Daniel's temper hovered at the surface.

"And I find the idea fascinating," said Dr. Trent.

"What idea?"

"Abby wearing the diamond."

Daniel tilted his head to the side. "Excuse me? Have you lost your mind? We've already had a major breach of security and now you want to take the Hope Diamond out of its case?"

"Gentlemen," Abby interrupted, her voice soft. "I don't think there's any need for a heated discussion. I was just illustrating my faith in both Diebold and Mr. Wallace."

Peter Trent nodded slowly. "That may have been your intention, Abby, but I think you may be on to something. I think if you wore the diamond during the celebration it would lend a certain extravagance."

Somewhere behind his bookish glasses, a fire burned in Dr. Trent's eyes.

"I don't follow."

"I think it could work. I think we should consider having you wear the Hope Diamond."

"I can't believe I'm actually hearing this." Daniel shook his head and pressed a thumb into his temple as if trying to suppress a headache.

Dr. Trent grinned. "It's not so unheard of you know. Back in 1995 Michelle Pfeiffer wore the Hope Diamond for a magazine spread in *Life* magazine. And it's been taken out for an occasional cleaning."

"I don't know, sir," Abby said. "This would be—"

"Utterly unexpected." A grin spread across his face. "You do know it would make us the hottest ticket in Washington?"

She chewed thoughtfully on her bottom lip. "If it's donations you want, I could almost guarantee that pulling a stunt like that would get you all the donations you need."

"Yes, yes. You're right." He nodded vehemently. "I think we should do it. When I meet with the Board of Regents I will propose that you wear the Hope Diamond."

"Wait a minute!" Daniel stammered. "You can't be serious. Two minutes ago I told you the diamond isn't safe in its own case and now you want to let her wear it? That's the most absurd thing I've ever heard!"

"I'm sorry to offend your sensibilities, Mr. Wallace, but I hardly care what you think."

"Given the fact that I know more about security than anyone in the tri-state area, I think you may want to consider what I have to say."

"I find that ironic coming from the man who just presided over the largest security breach in Smithsonian history."

Daniel pressed his lips into a thin line. "That illustrates my point. We don't know who has an interest in the diamond, and we can't give them a chance."

"*If* anyone has an interest. We don't have any reason to believe that the diamond is in any danger whatsoever. This entire conversation is pure speculation."

Daniel took a deep breath and then uttered his words carefully, as though speaking to a child. "I can guarantee you that there are parties who would love to get their hands on it. They're just waiting for the right opportunity. I don't want to provide them with one."

"What you are saying, Mr. Wallace, is that those criminals are smarter than you."

"I did not say that."

"Your words imply that you believe it."

"Ridiculous!"

"Then why don't you prove it to me? If you are truly as good at your job as you suggest, then you can prevent another security breach and keep the Hope Diamond safe while it hangs around Abby's neck."

Daniel clenched his jaw as he stared at Dr. Trent. "You don't think I'm up for the challenge?"

"You said it yourself, Mr. Wallace."

"I can do it."

"Then show me."

Daniel stood, his face flushed with anger. "I don't like being challenged, Dr. Trent."

"And I don't like being insulted. So why don't you do your job, and I'll do mine."

"I'm trying, *sir*."

"Then stop worrying about policy and start worrying about keeping dirty little hands off my diamond."

"Guys, I think this is getting out of hand," Abby said. She stood and placed a hand on Daniel's shoulder.

"I appreciate you wanting to be the peacemaker, Abby, but I've made my decision. I want you to wear the diamond during the fund-raiser. It will be the highlight of your presentation."

"I do believe it would be dramatic," she said. Daniel tensed under her hand. "But I also think it would be risky."

"Perhaps. I can't deny that. But it would be groundbreaking as well."

"It would definitely qualify as groundbreaking."

"Do you think you can pull it off, Dr. Mitchell?"

"Pull it off?"

"Wear the diamond, I mean. Do you think you could do that?"

Abby laughed. "I think every woman on this planet has dreamed about wearing that diamond at one time or another."

"Then we're done here," Dr. Trent said. "The two of you make whatever preparations you need to in order to secure this event. I will take this to the Board of Regents. You have my full support."

Scowling, Daniel Wallace left Dr. Trent's office and returned to the security terminus. He had gone into the meeting insisting on higher security for the diamond, and left with it utterly exposed. And somewhere in the middle was Dr. Abigail Mitchell.

Daniel took a seat before the computer consoles, lost in thought.

"I'm guessing the meeting didn't go well," Marshall said.

"That would be an understatement."

"What happened?"

Daniel pulled his pen from his coat pocket and clicked. "The diamond is coming out of the vault during the fundraiser."

"*What?*"

"Abby Mitchell is going to wear it while she delivers her speech."

"That's ludicrous! Whose idea was that?"

Daniel looked at Marshall sharply. "That," he said, "is a great question."

Dr. Trent had certainly insisted on the idea, but as he recalled the conversation, it was Abby who had thrown the idea out there in the first place, casually. Perhaps too casually.

Something occurred to Daniel as he mentally reviewed the meeting. "Marshall. Did you ever track down a visual on that intruder?"

"Yeah, why?"

"Get it up on the screen." He stared at the security feed from the Hope Diamond display.

"I have a hunch, and I just want to confirm it."

15

"CAN I SEE YOU TONIGHT?" ALEX ASKED.

Abby pressed the iPhone to her ear and propped her bare feet on the desk. "I'd like to," she said, "but I can't. I need to work late. Plus I need to get a good night's sleep tonight. Someone has been keeping me up late."

"I was hoping you could help me pick out a tux for this shindig on Saturday."

"Are you going for classic or edgy?"

"What do you think?"

"Classic would be my suggestion."

"Classic it is then."

"In that case, you probably want Bethesda Tailors. They have the best selection."

"Thanks. Sure you can't come?"

"Positive." She murmured good-bye and hung up.

Abby looked out the window and studied the lights of a city brimming with life. For a moment her thoughts drifted to the families gathered together, and she suddenly felt alone. She was tempted to call Alex and say she'd changed her mind, but she resisted. Instead, she pulled a stack of release forms from her desk and set them on her lap.

She went through them one by one, signing her name, pen scratching against paper in the stillness.

Halfway through her signature, her hand paused, as she tried to unravel the emotional knot in her stomach. This entire event—the planning, the extravagance, and now the manipulation—went against her character. How did she get here?

Abby finished signing her name and then dropped her feet to the floor. She stuffed the remaining paperwork, along with her laptop, inside her briefcase and slipped on her heels. She left The Castle, drawn by a familiar urge.

"My wife's gonna kill me," Blake Marshall said, looking at the clock. "I'm already an hour late."

Daniel paced behind him and glanced at the clock. It crept toward nine o'clock. "Just bring up a still shot of the intruder's face, and you can go. I'll do the rest."

Marshall drummed his fingers on the keyboard, and within seconds a picture appeared on the main screen. "It took me a while to track him because he intersected with at least three guards that night. But I managed to follow him through the building, and he never actually scanned the stolen card on his way out. He went down the stairwell and walked out with a group."

"Clever."

"Perhaps, but not a perfect crime," Marshall said. "We got this picture of him."

Daniel stared at the grainy surveillance photo. "Good job. Get on home. I'll handle this."

"Are you sure?"

"Listen, man, a job like this can eat your marriage. Trust me. You don't want that to happen."

"Thanks," Marshall said. "See you in the morning?"

Daniel never took his eyes from the screen. "I'll be here."

It wasn't often in this job that Daniel Wallace got to use the full range of capabilities he honed during his years in the Navy, but as he scanned the intruder's face, he knew that most of them would come into play now.

He studied the intruder: 5'11", 190 pounds, athletic, confident, dangerous. Daniel knew the man had done this before, knew he would do it again. A career thief most likely.

But who is this guy, and how do I find him?

Alex pushed through the door to his apartment and found Isaac on his couch. His brother had propped his feet on the coffee table, and he gnawed on the end of a lit cigar.

"About time you got back," Isaac said.

"What are you doing here?"

Isaac puffed the cigar, cheeks hollow. "Waiting."

"I don't recall asking you to."

"You didn't have to. It's my job."

"Put that thing out."

Isaac took another drag, smoke curling from the corners of his mouth. He crushed the cigar onto the top of the glass coffee table.

"Where's the girl?"

"At work," Alex said. "Why?"

Isaac stood and crossed the room. "You like her," he accused.

Alex pushed past his brother and pulled a glass tumbler from the bar. "I like my job."

"It looks like you're mingling business with pleasure."

"In case you haven't been paying attention for the last ten years, part of my job *is* pleasure."

"This is different. The girl is getting to you."

Alex grabbed a bottle of Crown and poured himself a drink. "What's with you all of a sudden?"

"Just making sure you don't lose focus."

"I don't need a babysitter."

Isaac made his way to the door. "So tell me, is she good in bed or do you just make up for it with your enthusiasm?"

Alex drained his tumbler and slammed it down on the granite counter. It shattered, sending shards of glass skittering across the hardwood floor.

Isaac clicked his tongue. "Temper, temper."

"Get out."

"You mean you've known this broad for almost a week and you haven't done it? Must be a record."

Alex locked the deadbolt after Isaac's smug departure. The acrid smell of smoke hung in the apartment, and he flung open the balcony door to rid himself of the stench. He dropped onto the black leather couch, letting his thoughts settle into the darkness of his apartment.

She's not getting to me.

⌘

Abby parked outside the employee entrance and scanned her card to enter the National Museum of Natural History. The distance between her office and the Hope Diamond was a well-worn path that she could travel in her sleep. She drew a few curious looks from the night staff as her heels clipped along the marble floor, but they dismissed her quickly when she flashed her security badge.

Abby stepped onto the diamond's platform and peered into the display case. "You and I have a sordid history," she said, her voice low but accusing. "I'm ready for this to be over."

⁂

There were two lines of silver print on the black business card. The first said *Munson Financial*. The second was an international number starting with the country code 33 for Saint-Tropez, France. Isaac Weld sat in his car, spying through the windshield at Alex's apartment while he rolled the card between his fingers. It only took a moment for him to reach a decision. He dialed the number from his cell phone.

"*Munson Financier ce qui est votre langue préférée?*" the receptionist answered.

"English," Isaac said, stating his preferred language.

"Very well. Hold please." She switched to perfect, unaccented English.

Isaac waited in silence until the line clicked over. "Munson Financial. Sebastian speaking."

"Sebastian, my name is Isaac Weld, and I find myself in need of unique financial assistance."

"Mr. Weld, if you have my number you know that I specialize in such matters. Yet it is a matter of protocol for me to ask how you were referred."

"That may prove to be an issue. I'm not in the habit of giving out the names of my friends or enemies."

"I see. Then I must insist on at least knowing the nature of your needs before we continue."

Isaac closed his eyes and settled into the darkness of his car, hidden behind smoky black windows. "My business partner and I have a large sum of money in an offshore account. I've been reasonably satisfied with the services we've received. But now I'm in need of more, shall we say, *discretion*, than they are capable of providing. I wish to transfer the full amount elsewhere without going through regular channels."

"Understood. Please know that we can accommodate your request, but first I must know two things."

"And what would they be?"

"First, let's deal with the transaction itself. How large a sum are we talking about?"

"Nine figures."

"Very good. We never deal with less than eight."

"And the second?"

There was a short pause on the other line. "I must be clear up front that our fee is five percent of the total transfer."

"I see," Isaac said, his jaw clenching involuntarily. "I find that obscene."

"As do all my clients. And I remain unapologetic. What I can do for you is untraceable and highly illegal. I don't negotiate my pricing, and if you have issues, as many do, you are welcome to destroy the card in your hand and attempt to find someone else who can help. I can assure you that such help does not exist, and I will not take your call if you ring my offices again."

"It would seem that I find myself in a bit of predicament then."

"I prefer to think of it as a partnership," Sebastian said, his voice level, almost pleasant.

Isaac tapped his fingers on the armrest, doing a mental calculation of what this endeavor would cost. "Very well. We have an agreement."

"Wonderful. Now, why don't you give me the name of your current banking institution, as well as your account number, and I can get the process started."

Isaac rattled off the information from memory. He heard a gentle tapping in the background, and he could not help but cringe as his most vital, personal information was stored on a computer somewhere along the French Riviera.

"Very good, Mr. Weld. I have verified your account information, as well as your balance. Many of my clients request new documents such as passport, credit cards, and birth certificate. Will you be needing those as well?"

"Yes."

"I will have them shipped to you within the next two days. Is there an address you prefer?"

"The one on my account will suffice."

"And when might I expect to hear from you again?"

"I anticipate our next point of contact to be on Sunday."

"Excellent. Is there anything else I can assist you with, Mr. Weld?"

Isaac lifted his eyes to the darkened windows of Alex's apartment. "Yes," he said. "There is one other matter that requires your unique skills."

Daniel shifted the main screen in the security terminus to the video feed coming from the Hope Diamond. His intent was to cross-check the intruder's image against surveillance footage from the Hope display. He never got the chance.

Abby Mitchell stood before the Hope Diamond, speaking to it as though it were an animate object capable of response. He could not hear her words, but he could see the angst on her face. She circled the display case, her arm outstretched and fingers brushing the glass. Her gaze did not leave the diamond as she vented her emotions, which seemed stark and raw.

He leaned forward to watch Abby press her forehead against the glass. She closed her eyes, palms flat on the display case, and mouthed silent words. Daniel was captivated by the pain and obsession that coursed over her face. Before he knew it, his hands were flying across the console, freezing a still shot of her face to a smaller screen. A moment later Abby turned and left the Harry Winston Gallery.

I wonder, he thought, eyes locked on the surveillance feed. He tapped his fingers on the console, thinking. Then the chief security officer for the museum picked up the phone and dialed the number of an old friend.

It only rang twice. "State Department, Wayne Edward."

"Hey, it's Daniel Wallace. I didn't think you'd be at the office."

"What're you doing, man? I haven't heard from you in at least a year."

"Still at the Smithsonian."

Wayne laughed. "Bored out of your gourd, I'm sure."

"You might be surprised. Things get interesting around here. I actually need to call in a favor you owe me."

Wayne hesitated, and Daniel knew his mind coursed over the recorded call and the dozens of security procedures that might be at risk.

"Don't worry," Daniel said. "I just need you to run two people through Identix and check a length of surveillance tape for matches."

"Seems easy enough." Wayne sounded relieved. "But don't you have access to Identix?"

"Not here. And I'm kind of in a hurry."

"Okay, can you give me about thirty minutes?"

"Sure. I'll email the package."

"I'll give you a call when I've got something."

Daniel hung up the phone and emailed the still shots of both Abby and the intruder to Wayne Edward at the State Department. He also included a six-month stretch of surveillance feed. And then he waited.

16

VERSAILLES, FRANCE, JANUARY 24, 1789

A SODDEN RAIN FELL, UNUSUALLY WARM FOR A WINTER'S DAY. THE CLOUDS gathered in great angry heaps, crackling with lightning. Sharp pieces of hail pummeled the ground, bouncing on the hard-packed earth and biting into the ankles of those unfortunate enough to be caught outside the palace. A small group of peasants shielded their eyes and cursed the temperamental weather. Had it been the brightest and warmest of days, they would still have been in a dark, foul mood. But the heavy rain turned their hearts to murder. Cold, wet, and hungry, the crowd of horse carts, rickety wagons, and poorly shod commoners approached the gates of the Versailles Palace. They could not know that three stories above stood the king of France, observing them in stony silence.

King Louis XVI leaned against his bedroom window, watching the crowd of peasants and fingering an ornate brooch that hung from his neck on a scarlet ribbon. Upon his coronation he inherited the *Toison d'or*, along with an induction into the knighthood that the brooch symbolized. Hundreds of the crown jewels were amassed in the making of the five-inch pendant, often referred to as The Golden Fleece, not the least of which was a great blue diamond known as the French Blue.

The queen consort, Marie Antoinette, sprawled lazily on a divan, twirling a loose ringlet of hair. Her skin, caked in white powder, and her blood-red painted lips, gave her the appearance of a corpse dressed for burial. She wore a deep burgundy dress of Dupioni silk, edged with black velvet at the hem and sleeves. The neckline of her gown plunged halfway down her breasts, revealing a greatly exaggerated depth of cleavage. Her waist was cinched to a rib-crushing narrowness, and her eight-foot train draped the floor. On her well-coifed hair sat an elaborate hat of matching silk and velvet, combined with three plumes of white feathers.

The immense heat radiating from the fireplace caused the king's cheeks to flush, and his clammy forehead soaked the black tendrils of wig that dangled above his eyes. His green swallow-tail coat hung to the backs of his knees, swaying like the limp plume of a tired peacock. He stood with arms crossed, scowling at the miserable crowd of commoners who trailed by in meager protest.

"It looks like a barnyard out there," he growled.

"I beg your pardon *Milord?*" asked the king's secretary, Bertrand Laurent. Sitting behind a heavy wooden desk, feather in hand, and inkwell before him, Laurent pursed his lips and waited for Louis to begin a dictation that would most certainly change, not just his own life, but the very future of France. The secretary was ready to begin transcribing for the king when the king's attention was diverted by the protestors.

"Them," Louis said, pointing angrily at the window. "Disgraceful."

A cramp, slow and burning, moved up Laurent's raised forearm, and he exhaled in silent irritation. After several moments, he dared to interrupt the thoughts of his king, "*Milord*, you were about to say?"

Louis turned narrowed eyes upon his secretary . "Is my hesitation irritating you, Monsieur Laurent?"

"Not at all, Your Majesty."

Louis took a step toward the desk, hands neatly folded behind his back. "Perhaps you feel as though I should rush through a dictation that may very well send this country into civil war. Is that it?"

"No, no!" Laurent shook his head adamantly.

No longer bored, Marie Antoinette turned a calculating gaze toward the two men, a smile playing at the corners of her mouth.

A series of capillaries, red and spidery, pressed against the skin of King Louis's forehead as his temper rose. "Maybe you don't believe my words should be careful and well chosen. Maybe I should spit this order out, as though writing to an acquaintance. *Maybe* the king of France should have no concern that his words will be recorded on the pages of history and that he will be held accountable for every single one of them. Is *that* what you're trying to tell me?"

Spittle sprayed from the king's mouth, and it covered the secretary's face. Laurent blinked. Louis stood but a foot or two away and towered over the seated scribe.

"That is not at all what I meant, *Milord*."

Louis leaned in until his nose almost touched the secretary's. "Pray tell then, Monsieur Laurent, what exactly did you mean?"

"Nothing, *Milord*."

"Then why don't your keep your meaningless comments to yourself? I have at my disposal the Privy Council should I need advice. You are but a secretary, and a poor one at that," Louis whispered.

Laurent nodded feverishly and turned back to the desk. His now shaking hand still remained raised, ready to begin writing at a moment's notice.

Louis returned to the window and played with his brooch once again. He slowly passed his thumb over the surface of the blue stone. As he stroked the diamond, he turned to his wife. "Is this truly necessary M'Lady?" he asked, wagging his wrist at Laurent.

Marie looked at her husband and tilted her head to the side. "This?"

"Convening the Estates General. Raising the taxes?"

She rose slowly from the divan, smoothing the wrinkles out of her dress. "Of course," she purred. "It is an unfortunate duty of the king, but a duty nonetheless."

Louis reluctantly turned to his secretary and asked, "Monsieur Laurent, what is the date?"

"The 24th of January in the year of our Lord, 1789."

"Very well then. Let us begin with that."

Laurent nodded blankly, but remained as he was.

"For God's sake, man, are you an imbecile as well as a sluggard? Start writing!"

Laurent quickly bent his head and dipped the quill pen in his inkwell. He scratched at the parchment with elaborate sweeps of his hand.

"Beloved and loyal supporters," Louis began. Laurent kept pace, word for word. "We require the assistance of our faithful subjects to overcome the difficulties in which we find ourselves concerning the current state of our finances, and to establish, as we so wish, a constant and invariable order in all branches of government that concern the happiness of our subjects and the prosperity of the realm."

Louis paused long enough to look at his wife for approval, and when she nodded he continued. "These great motives have induced us to summon the Assembly of the Estates of all Provinces obedient to us, as much to counsel and assist us in all things placed before it, as to inform us of the wishes and grievances of our people; so that, by means of the mutual confidence and reciprocal love between the sovereign and his subjects, an effective remedy may be brought as quickly as possible to the ills of the State, and abuses of all sorts may be averted and corrected by good and solid means which insure public happiness and restore to us in particular the calm and tranquility of which we have so long been deprived."

Laurent stopped writing but a moment or two after the king grew silent. He dared not look at the king as he waited for him to continue.

"The Estates will convene at Versailles on May 5th of this year."

When the king had gone some length of time without speaking, Laurent dared another glance, to which Louis responded, "You may sign it for me and be done."

Bertrand Laurent closed the convocation with a flourish. He then weighted the corners of the parchment down with gilded bookends so that it would not curl as the ink dried.

King Louis XVI turned back to the window as his scribe rose to leave. "I will need copies of that made and sent to all the provinces."

"Yes, *Milord*," Laurent said, bowing deeply as he left the presence of the king and queen of France.

"I fear this will not work" Louis said. His gaze rested on the great mahogany doors leading from his chambers to ensure they were beyond hearing of the courtiers outside.

Marie approached Louis with confidence and stood next to him at the window. Her careful decorum was far less noted when not within earshot of their subjects. "How could it not? You are the king of France."

"Indeed," he muttered.

"You are worried?"

"*Les États-Généraux* has not been convened for 175 years."

"It will comfort the people to know you are convening the Estates General. They will see you are taking steps in the interests of France."

Louis turned toward his wife. "I am not bringing them together for a banquet, Marie. I am bringing them together in order to ask them to pay higher taxes. Taxes that will pay for your jewelry and *petits fours*."

"Necessities of the crown, dearest. It is an honor for them to serve their country."

"You don't seem to understand the brewing crisis."

"Crisis?"

"There is a shortage of food within the land. Many have insinuated that due to recent crop failures, the people may actually starve."

"My dear, why do you trouble yourself with such small matters? The common people are of no concern to us!"

"Common people? Marie, the Estates General is formed of three parts, the clergy, the nobility, and the *bourgeoisie*— the *common people*."

The queen waved her hand in disgust. "The *bourgeoisie*. I have never understood why commoners are given a role in government. Such matters are too important for simpletons to understand."

"Considering the *bourgeoisie* make up ninety-eight percent of the national population, and that clergy and the nobility are exempt from paying taxes, I regret there is no way to exclude them from government."

Disgust contorted her face. "Not everyone can be noble."

"I have but a few moments before I meet with the Privy Council. I fear the *bourgeoisie* is going to create trouble when the Estates convene, and we need a plan for dealing with them. They are already asking for double representation, which would give them the controlling majority."

"But that is outlandish! Who would ever consider giving power to the people? Such a thing is unheard of."

Louis bent slightly and kissed Marie's forehead. "Don't worry, my dear. I have no intention whatsoever of handing over control of France to the common man. I am formulating a plan that will appease them while making them impotent."

Marie wrapped her arms around the king's neck, and then she ran her hands down his chest, slowing to brush her fingers against the Golden Fleece.

"It is a pity," she said, tracing the blue diamond lightly with her finger. "There is a stunning gown of blue organza in my wardrobe that would complement this jewel exquisitely." She dared a glance at her king and asked, "Will you continue your stubbornness and refuse my enjoyment of this trinket?"

Louis grabbed her wrist firmly. "Last I checked you were not the king of France."

She tightened her jaw and yanked her hand free. "That has not stopped you from allowing me use of the other crown jewels. I do not see why you remain so selfish with this one."

"This one," he hissed, "is mine. Will you be demanding use of my crown next?" Louis covered the brooch with his palm and stepped backward.

Marie Antoinette stared at his hand, cheeks flushed. "Of course not, *Milord*. Forgive my indiscretion." She turned on her heel and marched from the room, the train of her gown whipping across the floor.

17

It took longer than thirty minutes for Wayne Edward to call Daniel back. But when he did, Daniel was waiting, wide awake, and The Castle was empty except for a skeleton crew of night security. He monitored the security terminus alone.

"Sorry that took so long," Wayne said when Daniel answered on the first ring.

"Don't worry about it. I'm awake."

"Yeah, what's new? Have you ever slept in the fifteen years I've known you?"

"Rarely."

"Well, here's what I've got. I ran both images through Identix. Neither one has a confirmed criminal history, and believe me, if they did, Identix would find it. As far as that goes, they're both clean."

"And the surveillance footage?"

"That," Wayne said, "is where things get interesting. I got one confirmed hit of the male suspect on that length of tape. He's on camera for almost an hour taking pictures the entire time. My guess is that he's not using a standard digital camera, but I can't confirm it. In one shot he gives the security camera a direct glance for about ten seconds. He knows he's being watched."

Daniel sucked on his front teeth, pondering. "Interesting. What about the girl?"

"Wait till you hear this. According to the time stamps on the footage you provided, I've got about six months worth of tape."

"Yeah, that's about right."

"Well, I was able to get a facial recognition hit of the female suspect's face more than one hundred and twenty times."

"What?"

"From what I can tell, she went to the display every Monday through Friday during that time."

Daniel tilted his head to one side and narrowed his eyes. "I see. Thanks."

"She's not bad looking."

"Don't be deceived. She's a clever one."

Wayne laughed. "They usually are. Well, good luck with that, man. Seems like you've got an issue on your hands."

Daniel glared at the computer screen. "Nothing I can't handle."

<hr>

It was well past midnight when Douglas Mitchell returned to his penthouse in Bethesda, Maryland. He walked through the dark rooms, not bothering to turn on the lights. There was no furniture to maneuver around, and his footsteps echoed from the walls. As usual he went straight for his laptop. Its cold blue light flashed across his face, casting distorted shadows on the blank wall behind.

There was a single message in his inbox from Dr. Peter Trent. Douglas pursed his lips and opened the email immediately.

He sat on the edge of his bed, back straight, and palms flat on his legs as he pondered his next step. He typed a quick message and sent it into cyberspace, indifferent to the consequences.

Somewhere in the early morning hours the murky darkness grew less dense. The change was imperceptible at first, but Abby felt it even when she could not see the difference. She lay in bed, eyes open, and stared into the blackness. A thought tugged for entrance at the fringes of her mind.

Breakfast with my father. Why did I agree to do that?

Out in the living room, her alarm clock broke the silence with a harsh metallic buzz. She jerked into a sitting position and crawled out of bed. She had developed the habit in college of putting her alarm in the living room; it forced her to get up instead of hitting the snooze button.

Abby navigated through the apartment until she found the green numbers flashing 5:00. She turned off the alarm and stood for a moment, longing for the warmth of her bed. Instead, she turned on a lamp and threw open the curtain. Only the faintest hint of dawn broke the darkness along the horizon, and yet the city was already awash with activity.

It took her but a few minutes to fix coffee and curl up in the red blanket on her usual spot on the couch. She looked for traces of sunlight to illuminate the chapel across the street, but it was still shrouded in darkness. She reached for her laptop instead.

Abby intended to spend a few moments putting the finishing touches on her speech before taking a shower, but first, she checked her email. A single message from Douglas Mitchell appeared in her inbox.

Her neck stiffened, and hot tears pressed at her eyes. She didn't need to open it to know what sort of message she would find. Abby felt more of a fool than she cared to admit. She closed her eyes, took a deep breath, and clicked open the email.

Abby,

I got caught up on business and won't be able to make our breakfast date. I'm headed to Paris this afternoon, so I'll catch up with you next time I pass through D.C.

Dad

Abby read the e-mail three times. She pressed her lips together, holding back the all-too-familiar emotion. But she was not strong enough to restrain the tidal wave that broke over her. A moan, deep and primal, clawed at her throat. Abby tried to swallow the tears, but was overcome by the collision of anger and sadness. She pushed her laptop aside and threw herself down face first, sobbing into the pillows.

She lay there for the better part of an hour, with liquid emotion spilling from her eyes. Slowly, the first ray of new sunlight crossed her face. Abby rose, eyes red and swollen, and looked out the window.

As if on cue, the small chapel was bathed in light, a dark silhouette against the sun. She stared at the worn stones and bright stained-glass window, almost daring them to speak, to give her reassurance that she was a daughter wanted by someone. She looked and she longed, but the words on a computer screen a few feet away shouted louder than the gentle beckoning of the church across the street. She was not wanted; she was not loved.

Abby turned her back to the window and walked toward her bedroom, passing the wall of framed photographs on the way.

"Why can't you love me!" she screamed, raking her arm across the wall. Three pictures flew across the room, shattering on the hardwood floor. Abby knelt beside them, picking shards of glass from the sepia photographs. She studied the churches for a moment, hesitated, and then stuffed them in the wastebasket beneath her desk. Abby thought about retrieving them, but instead sought comfort beneath the hot water of her shower, attempting to scour her heart from the outside.

Daniel left The Castle at six in the morning and returned home long enough to eat breakfast, nap for thirty minutes, and take a shower. He was back at work hours before Blake Marshall even considered waking up. Yet when Daniel charged through the employee entrance he was headed not toward the security terminus, but to the office of Peter Trent.

He glanced at his watch, hoping Trent would be at work by eight-fifteen. He took the stairs two at a time and burst into the second floor hallway at a jog.

He knocked on the door, fully expecting to wait on the bench outside until Dr. Trent arrived.

"Who is it?" A voice yawned from within.

Daniel stuck his head in the door, eyebrows raised. "I didn't think you'd be here."

"Then why'd you knock?"

He shut the door behind him and approached the desk. "On the off chance. There's something we need to talk about."

Peter held up his hand, palm toward Daniel. "Please stop right now if this is another diatribe about how lax our security is and how worried you are. I've got a long day ahead of me, and I don't need your speculations. I just need you to do your job."

Daniel stiffened. "Not exactly that, sir."

"If not that, then what *exactly* might you be doing here, Mr. Wallace?"

"How well do you know, Dr. Mitchell?"

"Abby?"

"Yes."

Dr. Trent removed his glasses and rubbed the bridge of his nose. "Very well. Her father is an esteemed colleague of mine, and Miss Mitchell has been a regular presence within the walls of this institution since she was a child."

"And do you trust her?"

"Excuse me?"

"Do you trust her?" Daniel repeated.

"Implicitly," Peter said, stressing each syllable. "I insist you get to the point of all this nonsense. I'm losing patience."

"Sir," Daniel said, struggling to keep his voice level, "part of my due diligence as head of security is to run surveillance on the Hope Diamond."

"And what does that have to do with Dr. Mitchell?"

"She was in the Harry Winston Gallery late last night visiting the Hope Diamond display, and she seemed quite upset."

Dr. Trent leaned back in his chair, playing with his glasses. "A little out of the ordinary, granted, but she's been under a great deal of pressure lately. It's not something that worries me."

"But that's just it. Her visit wasn't out of the ordinary at all."

"I don't follow."

Daniel moved into the room and lowered himself into one of the chairs before Dr. Trent's desk. "I was running a check on the Hope display against the surveillance footage of the intruder, and just as I thought, he was there. But I discovered something else quite startling."

"Okay, I give. Humor me, Daniel. Just what did you find?"

"I checked a section of tape covering the last six months and found that Abby has been to the Hope display well over one hundred times."

Peter's eyebrows rose slightly, but he said nothing.

"So you see, Dr. Trent, I don't know that I feel comfortable allowing her to wear the diamond during the ceremony. Something just doesn't feel right. She seems quite obsessed with it, and our suspect has it under surveillance."

"What are you suggesting?"

He paused, trying to find the right words. "That under no circumstances should Dr. Mitchell be allowed anywhere near that jewel."

"Well," Peter said, placing his reading glasses back on the bridge of his nose. "I'm afraid that is not an option, Mr. Wallace."

"But I just told you—"

"I know what you just told me," he interrupted. "And honestly, I find it somewhat juvenile. Unless you have proof that Dr. Mitchell, an employee and personal friend, is up to criminal activity, you may leave my office."

"You can't let Abby wear that necklace."

"I can. And I will." Peter looked at his watch and then jumped to his feet. "As a matter of fact I'm taking the issue to the Board of Regents right now for their approval."

"Please reconsider," Daniel begged.

Peter grabbed his jacket from the back of his chair and moved toward the door. "I'm leaving now, Daniel, which means you are too."

───❀───

Alex sat on his balcony with a cup of black coffee in one hand and a roll of Smithsonian blueprints in the other. The air was crisp with the hint of fading leaves and coming winter. He inhaled deeply, savoring the change of season. With any luck he would never set foot in Washington, D.C., again when this heist was over. His lease expired in three days, and he had no plans of renewing.

He dialed Abby's number and took a sip of coffee, waiting for her to answer. The call went to voice mail. "Good morning, Dr. Mitchell. I missed you last night," he said with a playful edge in his voice.

Alex tossed his phone aside and spread the blueprints across his lap, mentally tracing the route Isaac would use in a little over forty-eight hours.

───❀───

Abby glanced at her phone but didn't answer even when Alex's name appeared on the display. She stood before her bathroom mirror, eyes bloodshot and jaw set with a look of determination. Her slacks, turtle neck, and high-heeled boots were all black today, a color that matched her mood. She applied minimal makeup and twisted her hair into a fierce knot at the nape of her neck.

Two more days and this will all be over with.

Then Abby Mitchell stuffed her phone in her jacket pocket, grabbed her briefcase, and left for work.

When Peter Trent passed through the double doors of the Reading Room, the other six members of the Board of Regents Strategic Planning and Program Committee were already waiting for him.

Not all members were required to attend each board meeting, nor could they, due to their respective stations in life. Therefore the board was broken down into specific committees that met to discuss certain aspects of the Smithsonian. The particular group of regents assembled for this meeting consisted of Dr. Trent, two Senators, one U.S. Representative, an esteemed artist, a businessman, and a respected scholar.

Dr. Trent walked confidently into the room and took a seat at the head of an antique Brazilian cherrywood table. The edges were beveled, as were the matching chairs. The Reading Room itself was a cavernous rectangle on the second floor of The Castle, used only by the Board of Regents. During its entire history, it had remained stark and formal. Two-hundred-year-old wood floors, white walls, a fireplace with carved wood mantle, and burgundy velvet curtains were the only adornment in the room.

"Thank you for meeting on such short notice," Dr. Trent said, laying a single sheet of paper on the table before him. "I understand that most of you are needed elsewhere, so I will not waste your time. We have a single matter to which we must attend. I presume you were all provided with our agenda?"

"We were," said an older woman with short gray hair and a trim business suit. "But I must say, this proposal is rather ambitious, don't you think, Mr. Secretary?"

"We will address that matter shortly, Senator Baker. And trust me I am conscious of what your initial response must be. But is there anyone present who is unaware of our purpose here today?" He met her glance for a moment and then moved on.

Those present regarded Dr. Trent with stony silence; he had to force a smile. "Very well then, I'll get straight to the point so we can vote and leave. You are all aware that in two days the Smithsonian will celebrate the fiftieth anniversary of the Hope Diamond's arrival. In its honor we will be hosting the largest fund-raiser in our 162-year history. At the center of this event is our own Dr. Abigail Mitchell who will give a presentation on the Hope Diamond, which is not only the single most viewed museum object in our Institution, but in the world. As our staff deliberated further on this point it became obvious that we would engender a spectacular response from our honored guests if Dr. Mitchell wore the diamond during the event. Our purpose in meeting today is to decide whether she will be granted that honor by the Board of Regents. We will vote on this issue momentarily, but first I would like to allow each of you to address the board and express any concerns you may have."

Senator Elizabeth Baker spoke first, which was not uncommon. "Honestly, I was stunned to receive not only the summons for this meeting, but your agenda as well. I'm aghast, Dr. Trent. I cannot fathom where this idea came from or who thought it valid. My vote is no and will remain such regardless of what is said here today."

Dr. Trent nodded, expecting as much. "Very well, Senator. As always your opinion is welcome. Anyone else?"

"It seems the U.S. Senate is adversely against this idea," said John Rubin, a lanky Senator from Idaho, "because I concur wholeheartedly with my colleague, Senator Baker. I vote no as well."

No surprise there, thought Dr. Trent.

"I think it's brilliant," Anna Moore, Smithsonian artist-at-large, gushed, leaning forward with animation. "As someone who's attended these fund-raisers for the last twenty years, I believe this is the sort of detail that will set your event apart. Providing you have made all necessary security arrangements, I will vote wholeheartedly for this proposal."

"Very well, Miss Moore. I'm pleased to have your support."

So the conversation went for the next ten minutes as each board member took a turn, either voicing concern or approval of Peter Trent's radical proposal.

When the room grew silent, Dr. Trent spoke up. "Obviously, I am in favor of Dr. Mitchell wearing the jewel. She's a remarkable young woman with incredible public speaking ability. I believe that if she were to wear the necklace, it would be a spectacular combination. At the moment we have three regents in opposition to the proposed item, and three in favor. Which," he said, turning to a handsome gentleman at the end of the table, "leaves you, Mr. Mitchell. Ironic that you will decide whether your own daughter is allowed the unique privilege of wearing the Hope Diamond."

"I think Mr. Mitchell should be disqualified from this vote," Senator Baker protested, "due to conflict of interest."

Grant Martin, token U.S. Representative chuckled. "Then I propose that you be disqualified from any vote on the Senate floor involving your state, Miss Baker, for conflict of interest."

Young, ambitious, and idealistic, Grant Martin had taken it upon himself to oppose the matriarchal senator both in Congress and at the Smithsonian. It was something Peter Trent counted on. Yet he needed to play the diplomat. "Now, now Mr. Representative, let's not get into politics in the Reading Room. This is a simple decision, and Mr. Mitchell has been on this committee for years. He has the right to vote, as do each of you, regardless of the fact that it pertains to his daughter."

Dr. Trent observed the calm way Abby's father took in the discussion. "What do you say, Douglas? Do you believe it to be in the best interests of the Smithsonian Institution for Abby to wear the Hope Diamond during her presentation?"

Douglas nodded, contemplating the question. "We have yet to discuss what those interests may be, Secretary Trent."

Board members murmured agreement.

"Fantastic point. We have set two goals for this event. The first is to raise publicity for the Museum of Natural History, and the second is to raise money to fund our ongoing programs. We are funded, in large part, by Congress, but we must raise additional monies to further the reach of our initiative. This event will do that."

"And do you believe you will raise more money if my daughter wears the diamond?" Douglas asked.

"I do."

"Why is that?"

"Because when the jewel is taken out of its case, it instantly propels this event to a new level. Our patrons have deep pockets but short attention spans. If we can capture their imaginations, we will meet our financial goals."

"I agree that your bottom line would certainly be inflated, but I'm not sure the security risks are worth that potential."

Dr. Trent nodded in agreement. "That is a concern that has not escaped our attention. We are working closely with the security experts at Diebold International, as well as our in-house team. I have reviewed the security manifest, and I feel certain the measures we have in place will be more than adequate."

"*Adequate* measures are not sufficient, Dr. Trent." Elizabeth Baker said, her voice short and clipped.

Peter held up a hand. "Mr. Mitchell has the floor, Madam Senator."

Douglas Mitchell pressed back into his chair, deep in thought. "I can tell you that I trust my daughter," he said. "And that I know her to be more than capable of delivering what you expect of her. If you can give the committee assurance that you have this event under control, then I will gladly give you my vote."

"You have my full assurance, Mr. Mitchell, and I look forward to Abby's presentation. Now, for the official record, can I get a verbal count on this agenda?"

Dr. Trent's proposal was approved by a margin of four to three, the tie breaker being Abby's own father.

After attending to a handful of business affairs in her office, Abby spent the remainder of the day with the event staff at the National Museum of Natural History. The only space large enough to host a fully catered meal for three hundred and fifty people was the Rotunda, best known to museum goers for the giant taxidermied Great African Bush Elephant on display in the middle of the room. Originally, Abby attempted to find a way to hide the massive pachyderm, but as her plans solidified, she realized it provided the exact centerpiece she needed for her presentation.

The event planning staff from Experiences Unlimited was already at work draping red, blue, and green silk along the walls and around the columns. Thirty-five round tables, were stacked in piles along the wall, each capable of accommodating ten guests. As soon as Abby verified the seating placements, staff members would arrange and set the tables.

"Is it just me or does it seem like two days prior is a bit early to begin setting up for this event?" Jacqueline Dupree, owner of Experiences Unlimited asked.

She and Abby stood beneath the four-story Rotunda, craning their necks to see the elaborate stone medallion that embellished its peak.

"Typically, yes," Abby said, "but this fund-raiser is unique. We've had to jump through endless hoops to make it happen. In this case, forty-eight hours may not be *enough* time."

"I understand that you had to close off this entire wing of the museum?"

"We did. And that was no small undertaking, let me tell you. It was a matter of securing the perimeter."

"I can't imagine," Jacqueline said. "But it looks as though things are coming together beautifully, wouldn't you say?"

Abby surveyed the Rotunda, pride swelling for the first time. Over the next two days, lighting specialists would create a state-of-the-art visual display that would transform the Beaux-Arts style structure into something reminiscent of sixteenth-century India. She was about to answer Jacqueline's question when her phone rang.

"Do you need to get that?"

Abby looked at the display and saw Alex's name for the third time that day. "No," she said, smiling sadly at Jacqueline. "This is the last thing I need."

———— ✤ ————

Alex snapped his phone shut after leaving Abby a second message. He pulled his Mercedes to a stop before the Department of Motor Vehicles. Images of the silver BMW rolled through his mind, and he stiffened with an unfamiliar sense of worry. Wülf tailed him on more than one occasion while he was with Abby, and now, in the wake of her prolonged silence, he grew uneasy. Just as he pondered tracking her down, his phone buzzed, indicating a text message.

He read Abby's text with a scowl: "I'm buried at work. See you on Saturday."

This is a problem, he thought.

But he had other business to attend to. Alex Weld entered the DMV building and picked his target carefully. There were three women behind the counter, but only one of them looked lonely. He chose her line despite the fact that it was the longest.

The name plate read Myra Spencer. She was short, just over five feet, and a little on the heavy side. Divorced most likely. A single mother. At least two children. This should be easy.

"Can I help you?" she asked. Her tired eyes glanced at him from behind her computer screen.

"Most likely not."

"Excuse me?"

He smiled, easy, comfortable.

Myra Spencer blushed and tucked an unruly clump of hair behind her ears.

Alex straightened the nameplate. "You see, Myra, you aren't actually allowed to tell me what I want to know."

The sound of her name on his lips caused a flush of fresh color across her cheeks. "How is that exactly?" she stammered.

He leaned across the counter, voice low, and eyes steady. "I need a name."

"What kind of name?"

Alex grabbed a pen and scratched down the license plate number of the silver BMW that he had committed to memory. "I need to know who this car is registered to."

Myra took the paper. "I can't do that, sir."

He smiled again, devilish. "That's just what I said a moment ago. You can't help me."

The look on her face said that she would very much like to. "I'm sorry. I can't."

"Pity," he whispered. "I had my hopes pinned on you, Myra."

She fingered the paper and tapped her front teeth together. Both of her co-workers were helping other people, oblivious to their conversation. She cast furtive glances in both directions. "You just need a name?"

"Nothing else. No address. And I'll tell you what, Myra," he leaned in closer and lowered his voice. "I don't even need a first name."

Her fingers flew across the keyboard and she licked her lips.

"I can't do any harm with a last name can I?" Alex smiled.

She giggled nervously. "I suppose not." Myra Spencer found what she was looking for and scratched the name on a piece of paper. She slid it across the counter, doing her best to touch Alex's hand in the process.

He graced her with a final mischievous glance as he took the paper. Alex Weld read the name written in spidery handwriting, and the blood drained from his face.

18

ABBY FORCED HER WAY THROUGH A BOWL OF COLD CEREAL FRIDAY morning, trying to forget the breakfast date with her father that never happened. She stood over the kitchen sink chewing stale corn flakes and battling a desire to crawl back into bed.

The last few weeks had been filled with so much activity that the silence of a lonely morning was distracting. Abby regretted sending Alex the text last night, but he would know by the look on her face that something was wrong, and she didn't have the emotional reserves to explain the dysfunctional state of affairs with her dad. She dumped the remainder of her breakfast down the disposal.

Abby gathered her things and headed for the door. Just as she pulled it open, her phone rang. She hesitated, fearing it was Alex, but saw Dow's number on the caller ID.

"How was breakfast?" he asked the moment the receiver touched her ear.

Abby winced. "There was no breakfast."

"What do you mean? I thought—"

"He canceled by email."

"No phone call?"

"Of course not. Phone calls are too—"

"Personal," Dow said.

She squeezed her eyes shut and refused to shed another tear on her father's behalf. "It's my fault really. I should know better. You tried to warn me."

There was silence on the other end for a moment and then, "Why didn't you tell me?" His voice was gentle.

"I didn't want you to feel sorry for me."

"You did nothing wrong, Abby. This is just the way he is . . . the way he's always been."

"Small comfort when I'm the one caught in the crosshairs."

Dow sighed, and Abby knew he was searching for words that would make it better. She loved him for trying. "Are you hungry?" he finally asked. "Can I take you out for breakfast?"

She turned her back on the kitchen where her dirty cereal bowl lay in the bottom of the sink. "That's okay. I've eaten."

"You sure?"

"Yeah. Besides, I need to get to work. I have a few last-minute details to take care of at the Rotunda, and then I need to pick up my dress."

"Abby," he said, his voice wavering with reserve.

"Don't say it, Dow."

"I think we need to reconsider this whole thing."

"No," she shook her head. "No, we don't."

"You're not ready."

She pressed her thumb into her right temple, but her voice stayed remarkably calm. "I have to."

"We can find another way."

"There is no other way, Dow. You know that. We need this."

"I don't know."

"I can do it. I'll be fine."

He relented. "We love you, sweetie. You know that, right?"

"I do," she said. A smile warmed her face for the first time that morning. "I have to go."

"Okay, we'll see you tomorrow night."

Abby set the phone on its cradle and left for work, her will braced with new resolve.

The apartment was stripped bare, except for a leather couch, glass coffee table, and a suitcase. Alex glanced around the small penthouse. Empty. Lonely, even. He filtered the thoughts through an established order of habit. Leaving. This is what he did.

On the coffee table beside his laptop lay a small black notebook. He opened the laptop and began typing the first of 520 lines. Date. Name. Location. Fee. And object. In that order. He spaced down twice and typed the next line of barely legible handwriting. It took him three hours, but he didn't stop until he was finished.

Alex saved the document to a flash drive and tucked it into his wallet. Then he took the small black notebook to the kitchen, turned on the gas burner of his Viking range for the first time, and dipped it into the blue flame. He waited until it was ablaze and then set it in the sink. When only ashes remained, Alex turned on the water and washed the debris down the drain.

Abby popped into her office long enough to check her voice mail and see if there were any emails that needed a quick reply. She hadn't been there more than two minutes when Peter Trent stuck his head in the door, grinning from ear to ear.

"Where were you yesterday?" he asked.

She tucked her phone between her chin and her shoulder. "At the Rotunda with the event coordinator."

"I should have called your cell phone."

"Why? What's up?"

Dr. Trent smiled. "I met with the Board of Regents yesterday to discuss you wearing the Hope Diamond."

The phone slipped from her grasp, and Abby scrambled to catch it before it fell to the floor. "And?"

"It was a tight vote, but they approved." He beamed, pleased with himself. "Oh, and your father was a real lifesaver."

Sudden nausea rose in her throat. "My what?"

"Your dad," he said casually. "It came down to a tie breaker, and he cast the deciding vote. He wants you to wear the diamond. Isn't that great?"

"Of course," she said, short of breath. "He's on the board."

"Yes, he has been for . . . what . . . fifteen years?"

"Twenty," she whispered, her mouth dry and her mind clouded. "The board met yesterday?"

"Yesterday morning. Removing the diamond from its case requires board approval. I tried to get in touch with you all day so I could tell you the great news. Of course, Daniel Wallace will get his boxers in a knot, but it looks as though this little idea of mine is going to work!"

"Great," she said, her voice small and weak.

"I'll let you get back to work. I know you've got a lot to do."

Peter Trent left her alone with the crushing knowledge that her father was in town for at least one full day without making any attempt to see her, or even talk to her for that matter. Abby Mitchell sank into her chair but she didn't cry. Instead, she welcomed the rage that consumed her.

———∞∞———

"Dow!" DeDe called from their bedroom, her head buried inside the closet.

"Yes, dear."

"Where are my diamond earrings? I can't find them." A slight panic pressed beneath her ribs.

"I don't know."

"What do you mean you don't know? I have to find them." DeDe crawled farther into the closet, turning over shoe boxes and baskets.

Dow walked into the bedroom and leaned against the doorframe. "DeDe?"

"Abby needs them." Her voice was frantic as clothes flew over her shoulder. "And I just saw them a couple of days ago. I don't know what I'll do if I've lost them. How could I have been so stupid?"

"DeDe," he said again, but she ignored him.

"Don't just stand there. Help me look!"

"DeDe!" he snapped. "Will you just turn around for one second?"

She faced her husband, ready to give him a verbal lashing, and saw the long flat velvet box in his hands. "You found them." She breathed in relief.

"Right where you left them."

She shook her head. "In the safe?"

He nodded. "In the safe."

DeDe reached for the box with shaking hands, but he took a step back. "Why don't you let me take care of these?"

She nodded, relieved. "Probably best."

———∽∾∞∾∽———

Isaac grabbed the package from the delivery man and took it immediately to his office. There was no return address, but the postage mark indicated it had been sent Priority International Overnight from Saint-Tropez, France.

He exhaled slowly as he took a letter opener and cut open the seams. Inside was a black leather box containing a new passport with an origin of issue indicating Portugal, a birth certificate, driver's license, and four credit cards, all with unlimited balances. Beneath the papers lay a small device, no larger than a laptop battery. Such devices were hard to come by and cost a king's ransom. A rare smile spread across his face. "Now *that* was worth every penny."

19

ABBY STOOD BEFORE THE MIRROR IN HER BEDROOM, SLIGHTLY EMBARRASSED but also pleasantly surprised at her own reflection. The floor-length black dress had little ornamentation, but given her choice of jewelry for the evening, it hardly needed any. The strapless gown hugged her tightly at the waist where the gauzy fabric then flowed out in almost liquid form as she moved.

She increased her already substantial height by another three inches with a pair of strappy black heels. Abby's hair was swept upward, pinned, and tucked into a series of soft, loopy curls. At the last moment she had decided to invest the time and money to have her makeup done, and the woman at the salon did wonders with a series of creams and powders she didn't know even existed. Her dark brown eyes looked sultry instead of swollen—smoky and playful.

Her cheeks colored slightly as she took in the swath of bare skin across her arms and shoulders. It was hardly inappropriate or overly revealing, yet she couldn't help but feel there was nothing sexier than bare skin.

Abby turned around to see the full effect in the mirror. She pulled at a bare earlobe, feeling somewhat naked without DeDe's earrings.

The buzzer rang, announcing Alex's arrival. Abby took a deep breath, grabbed her purse from the bed, and went to let him in, her heels clapping on the bare wood floors. She pulled the door open; her smile stretched ear to ear.

Alex gazed at her with mouth open, but said nothing.

"Well, hello to you too," she said.

"You look . . . I mean . . . wow."

She pulled him into the apartment. In his hand he held a single white rose.

"For me?" she asked.

"I missed you," he whispered, pulling her into his arms and nuzzling her ear.

Abby ran a finger across Alex's cheek and pulled his face to hers. She kissed him, melting into the warmth of his lips.

He pulled back, blue eyes ablaze. "What was that for?"

"It's been three days."

Isaac lay flat on the roof as he watched the crowd of people stream into the Smithsonian's National Museum of Natural History. The Rotunda began filling up half an hour earlier as those Washington socialites unconcerned with arriving fashionably late trickled in. Below him, security guards checked each guest against the invitation list before they entered.

Night had fallen over the city an hour earlier, and as soon as the sun set, Isaac pulled his Mercedes into the parking garage at Union Station on the east end of the National Mall near the Capitol Building. Then he took the Metro to the Smithsonian Station, emerging on Constitution Avenue.

An observer outside the museum would have noticed nothing unusual about the well-dressed businessman in suit and tie who carried a briefcase.

Isaac had chosen his point of entry weeks earlier, after studying aerial photographs of the entire perimeter. On the rear left corner of the museum grounds nestled a grove of thick oak trees near the building. He passed by the clump of trees, stepped off the sidewalk, and disappeared into the shadows. From there, he scaled a fifty-foot oak tree like a cat. In less than thirty seconds he sat comfortably in the highest branches.

Isaac pressed the briefcase against a branch and rolled the combination dial. A dull thud shook the tree as metal anchors jutted from the case and attached to the limb. The lid flipped open, swung down, and created a small work table.

He stripped off his jacket and white button-down dress shirt to reveal a long-sleeved black tee. Pulling a mask over his head, Isaac completed the ensemble with a pair of black gloves. Undetectable from below, he hid in the shadows of the tree.

With deft hands Isaac removed a small compound bow from the case and adjusted its pieces until fully assembled.

Darkness fought for dominance with the floodlights that lit up the building at regular intervals. Yet Isaac was not worried about the ground floor. His eyes were focused on the roof and the security camera less than thirty feet from his location. It rotated slowly, anchored in place to the northeast corner. The old oak tree where he perched hovered over the building by a good ten feet, and from his vantage point he could look down on the security camera.

Only two items remained in the briefcase: a black tool belt containing mechanical equipment and a grappling hook with thirty feet of climbing rope. He strapped the belt to his waist and set the hook in the compound bow.

Isaac crawled along the branch, inching as close to the building as he could without bending the tree limb. He straddled the branch with his knees, raised the bow, and aimed not at the stone ledge jutting out from the museum's roof, but farther in at a row of atrium windows. Steadying himself on the branch, he took a deep breath, placed the crosshairs on his target, and pulled the trigger.

Thwap. The grappling hook launched through the air. No sooner had Isaac pulled the trigger than he knew he had missed the target. Profanity spit from his lips. The grappling hook landed with a metallic clang, not on the ridge atop the atrium windows, but on the main roof line, just two feet above the security camera.

If he were to cross hand over hand as he intended, he would dangle in full view of the camera. Isaac exhaled through clenched teeth, considering his only viable option: a tightrope walk across thirty feet of open air.

———∞∞∞———

Abby placed a hand on Alex's arm as he escorted her up the front steps of the Smithsonian and into the Rotunda. In the hours since she had left work, her staff had transformed the space. Thirty-five tables covered with white tablecloths were scattered beneath the domed ceiling, each surrounded by ten chairs draped in alternating red and gold slipcovers. In the center of each table sat a floral arrangement of palm frond and Indian paintbrush. Paper lanterns hung from the balconies and glowed with yellow light. The lighting firm hired by the Smithsonian had placed dozens of low-wattage floodlights throughout the Rotunda, creating a subtle display of shadow and light, giving the ornate gothic room the appearance of a dimly lit cave. It was not hard to imagine that a jewel such as the Hope Diamond could be found in these surroundings. And in the middle of the room stood the massive African elephant, appearing as though he waited at the beck and call of an Indian sultan.

Abby took in the enormity of the room, delighted with her handiwork.

Alex pulled her to his side and whispered, "You did this?"

She nodded, unable to hide her smile.

"Beautiful," he whispered. His lips brushed her ear. Abby could not decide whether he referred to the room or to her. Either way, she didn't mind.

The prestigious guests had been chosen carefully by Abby and other museum staffers. Deep pockets and a profound interest in the arts were the initial prerequisites, and the selection winnowed from there. By the time the guest list was established, this was the hottest ticket in town.

Alex and Abby steered clear of the meandering guests in their search for Dow and DeDe. They found them seated at a table on the outer perimeter of the room. Dow wore a trim tuxedo, and DeDe, always the renegade, rejected the typical black evening gown in favor of red.

"You look fantastic." Abby admired the upswept hair and trim figure of her friend.

"You know what they say," DeDe said with a wink. "The girl with the red dress gets all the attention."

Dow grinned. "Not tonight, my dear, lovely though you are. I'm quite certain that our Abby will be the belle of the ball." He leaned in and kissed Abby's cheek. "Thank you for the invitation by the way."

DeDe placed her hands on Abby's bare shoulders. "You are breathtaking."

Dow turned to Alex. "So this must be the man I've been hearing so much about?"

"Alex," he said, grabbing Dow's hand firmly.

"Dow. And this is my wife, DeDe."

"Very pleased to meet you."

"Likewise," said Dow.

DeDe pulled a black jewelry case from her purse and handed it to Abby. "Are these what you've been waiting for?" She caught Abby's glance and slid the box into her outstretched hand.

Abby took the case and flipped it open. Inside was a pair of diamond stud earrings, easily two carats each. She breathed a sigh of relief as she slid the studs into her ears. "Thank you, DeDe."

DeDe grabbed Abby's hand; emotion brimmed in her dark brown eyes. "I didn't think you could be any more lovely," she whispered.

Abby returned DeDe's smile, awash in gratitude. Her fist remained clenched even when DeDe let go.

"You better get going, dear," Dow prodded.

"Ah, yes," Abby said, her nerves on edge. "So it begins."

Dow eyed her with special tenderness. "Indeed."

Abby turned to Alex with a nervous smile. "Shall we?"

"My pleasure." He offered Abby his arm, and they moved toward the bank of elevators where Daniel Wallace paced in agitation.

As they left the Rotunda, Abby looked over her shoulder and caught Dow's attention. He nodded at her, lips tightened in a grim line. "You can do this," he mouthed.

Daniel met them in front of the elevators, his face pinched and his nerves raw. "Abby," he said with a stiff nod.

"Daniel, this is Alex Weld," she said.

Daniel offered a begrudging handshake, herded them into the elevator, and pushed the button for the second floor. Silence filled the space between them as they rose, broken only by a soft ping when the doors opened moments later.

Indirect light fell in pools along the carrara marble floors that lined the Janet Annenberg Hooker Hall of Gems. Abby gathered her courage and let Daniel lead them toward the Harry Winston Gallery and the display that housed the Hope Diamond. One fist was still clenched into a ball, and her lips were drawn tight as she focused on the task ahead.

Dr. Peter Trent stood beside the case, deep in conversation with Henry Blackman and the security team from Diebold. Daniel Wallace joined his crew and waited, ready to assist.

Upon Abby's entrance a hush settled over the room. Her face flushed a deep red, uncomfortable with the attention.

"You are beautiful," Alex whispered in her ear, giving her arm a reassuring squeeze. "That's why they're staring."

"Dr. Mitchell, you look ravishing tonight," Henry Blackman said, a hawkish grin spread across his face.

Alex slid an arm around her waist and pulled her to his side. The wordless gesture was all Blackman needed to understand that Abby was accompanied.

"Thank you," she whispered.

Daniel pressed a finger to his earpiece and listened. "The guests are all seated," he said. "We need to get this process started. It will take a few moments."

Dr. Trent turned toward Henry Blackman. "I believe you can take it from here?"

"We can," he said.

Abby kept her distance from the display case, breathless, as she watched the pedestal turn on its axis. The diamond rotated ninety degrees and stopped, light glittering from its faceted surface. Sixty seconds later it turned another ninety degrees and paused again. This process repeated without interruption, 480 times every day.

Daniel stood to the side, feet spread and hands clasped behind his back. "Mr. Blackman, I have confirmed that your people are in the security terminus."

"Very well." He spoke into his headset "This is Henry Blackman. Let's begin the disarming sequence."

"Affirmative," came the reply.

Henry approached the case. "It will take a few seconds."

All eyes rested on the heavy marble and wood display. Deep within the base a slight metallic *click* sounded.

Abby's heart pounded as she waited through the countdown. After sixty seconds, the diamond remained still.

"Cut the alarm," Blackman ordered.

"Alarm disabled," crackled the voice from the security terminus.

"Open the case."

The room hushed as the hum of motors echoed through the room. One panel of the three-inch thick glass slid down into the display case. It took a full two minutes to descend, the security sensors deep within pacing the drop carefully.

"Everyone stay back," Blackman ordered. "There are still numerous security measures that must be disarmed."

Inside the case a series of clicks resounded in conjunction with the whining motor. "Please enter the security codes," Blackman ordered his assistant in the console.

There was a slight pause and then came the reply, "Codes entered."

Blackman took a deep breath, blinking as drops of sweat rolled into his eyes. "Disable the pressure sensor."

After a short pause came the reply, "Pressure sensor disabled."

Blackman motioned Abby forward, a triumphant look on his face. "Dr. Mitchell, I believe you get the honors."

Paralyzed, she gazed at the case just a few feet away.

"Are you all right, Abby?" Dr. Trent asked.

"Yes," she said. Her breath caught in her throat. "It isn't every day a girl takes the Hope Diamond out of its case."

Abby lifted the hem of her dress and moved toward the circular platform where the case rested. She looked over her shoulder, hesitant.

Dr. Trent nodded slightly, giving her permission, and Abby reached into the case. Her fingers stopped, a mere two inches from the diamond, and hovered. She took a deep breath and lifted it from the velvet podium with a trembling hand. The weight of the necklace was surprising—not just the Hope Diamond itself, but the setting and diamond-studded platinum chain as well. She stepped from the display, necklace in hand, waiting for something to happen. But the case simply sat open like a gaping mouth.

All eyes focused on the diamond in her hand. She lifted it slightly and asked, "Shall I put it on?"

A series of nods affirmed her.

Abby unfastened the clasp and placed the jewel against her neck, arms behind her head, attempting to fasten it. Her fingers fumbled with the clasp, and she frowned, trying to get it in place.

"Would you like me to help?" Alex asked.

Daniel Wallace clamped a large, heavy hand on Alex's shoulder. "Please don't. The only person with permission to touch the stone is Dr. Mitchell."

"Of course," Alex mumbled, stepping back. "I was just trying to help."

"I think I've got it, gentlemen." Abby released the clasp and let the diamond rest against her neck. She dropped her hands to her side and straightened her shoulders for full effect.

The necklace glinted in the light, complimented by her bare shoulders and DeDe's diamond earrings.

"Are we ready then?" Abby asked, regaining composure.

Daniel Wallace radioed to his security team downstairs. "Affirmative."

"After you," Abby said, waiting for Daniel to lead the way back downstairs.

<hr />

Most of the Smithsonian lay in shadow, all attention diverted to the main entrance. The marble steps hedged by massive stone pillars were awash with lights and activity. The remainder of the building, particularly the back wall that Isaac Weld ascended like a spider, lay still and dormant. He climbed the façade, squirming through the shadows, imperceptible to those below.

Isaac did not look at the ground as he slipped over the edge of the rooftop. The Rotunda loomed before him, light emanating from the transom windows. He peered through the glass panes, looking four stories down to the gathering below. The guests were seated, enjoying a meal of Beef Wellington and French wine.

The grin on his face spread to the crow's feet around his eyes. Isaac squatted and checked his watch. Right on time.

He spun away and made his way toward the maintenance entrance on the roof that serviced the HVAC components.

Isaac pulled a small magnetic device from the tool belt at his waist and stuck it next to the keypad beside the door. The screen shed blue light, and he pressed a series of buttons on the keypad. After a couple of moments a deep whine emanated from the box, and Isaac picked the lock. He slipped inside and closed the door tightly behind him.

The purpose of the small black box was not to open the door; he could have done that easily on his own. It was to make sure that security was unaware the door had been opened at all.

———◦◦◦◦———

With each step that Abby took, the burden around her neck grew heavier. The entourage of security personnel and museum staff was unnerving, and Abby held onto Alex's arm, seeking reassurance.

"You'll do just fine. Don't worry," Alex whispered.

Abby tried to take a deep breath, but the air caught in her throat.

Alex lifted her chin. "I'm here, okay? I'm not going anywhere."

She nodded, forcing herself to exhale.

Daniel held the elevator door for Abby and spoke into his headset. "We're at the elevators. Begin the introduction."

As Abby hung in the balance between the exhibition hall and the ground floor, she found her courage. All the details of her presentation came rushing back to her, long since memorized, setting themselves into a familiar place in her mind.

The audience had their backs turned as they watched a short film on the massive screen erected just for this event. Abby and her escorts slipped by on the edge of the room. They came to a stop before a set of risers leading to the stage and waited.

Peter Trent jogged up the steps and took his place behind the podium. "Ladies and gentlemen," he said as soon as the video wound to a close. "Thank you for coming tonight. It is a privilege to have you here for such an important event. This evening we welcome Dr. Abigail Mitchell as she presents the captivating story of our most renowned exhibit, the Hope Diamond. Dr. Mitchell received her masters in art history from Boston College and her doctorate from Cambridge University. She has traveled and written extensively on the Hope Diamond for the last ten years. Won't you please give a warm welcome to Dr. Abigail Mitchell."

An audible gasp traveled like a wave around the room as all eyes settled on her for the first time. Abby ascended the steps, grasping Alex's arm with one hand, and the hem of her dress with the other. Once on the stage, she graced Alex with a smile and nodded. He released her arm and took a seat at their table, right before the stage.

Whispers flitted throughout the room as she approached the podium, and guests wondered out loud if they were indeed seeing the Hope Diamond around her neck.

Abby straightened her shoulders to better display the diamond and leaned into the podium. "I know what you're thinking," she said, meeting as many glances as possible. "And this little trinket around my neck is not one of the eighty-dollar fakes you can buy in the gift shop down the hall." She smiled, relishing the moment. "Ladies and gentlemen, you are looking at the one and only Hope Diamond. As we begin this evening I think it's important that we take a moment to consider how a jewel that bears the name Hope can cause such despair. We all know about a French jewel merchant named Jean-Baptiste Tavernier and how he bought the diamond in sixteenth-century India. We know about King Louis XVI and how he lost his head to a guillotine during the French Revolution. Most people seated in this room are aware that Evalyn Walsh McLean graced the society pages in Washington, D.C., many times while wearing the Hope Diamond. You know those things so I won't bore you by repeating the story."

Abby scanned the crowd, looking for a familiar face. She found Alex seated a few feet away, his gaze transfixed on her. "What I will share with you tonight are the things you don't know, the hidden secrets of this jewel around my neck. We will see that the diamond does not treat kindly those who take it by force."

213

❦

The ventilation system that serviced the Smithsonian's Museum of Natural History was a tangled mass of ductwork, intricately woven throughout the building. Isaac Weld, consulting the schematic images on his iPhone, crawled through the maze of aluminum. At regular intervals he stopped, studied the plans, and either continued forward or veered off in a new direction.

On his right leg was strapped an emergency light stick that shed a pale green glow in the ductwork. Not only did it light his way forward, but the hole he punctured in the casing allowed the green phosphorous liquid to leak out; it would illuminate his way back. In a matter of hours, the gel would fade, leaving nothing but a greasy smear behind.

He rounded a particularly tight corner and heard the muted sounds of applause. Before him lay a thirty-foot stretch of ductwork and then a three-foot-square metal grate. Isaac inched forward and looked down on the festivities below. Abby leaned against the podium, the Hope Diamond hanging around her neck.

He lifted his watch and checked the time. The pacing in Abby's voice and her point in the narrative indicated that she was near the midpoint of her presentation.

Isaac pulled out a small black box, roughly the size of a computer battery, from his work belt and laid it before him. Beneath the lid was a single green button.

As with all venues in the Smithsonian, the Rotunda was armed with a series of security cameras, three per level on each of the three levels—nine cameras in all to disable. The familiar rush of adrenaline hit Isaac's bloodstream, and his heart pounded. The almost electric rush coursed through his veins. He pulled ten penlights from his belt and arranged all but one in a tripod. At the push of a button, each would send a beam of ultraviolet light directly into the path of the security cameras, reducing them to white screens.

Abby's speech was periodically interrupted with applause, and he waited until another such outburst occurred to unscrew the ventilation grate before him. The screwdriver he used was compact and noiseless, but he could not take the chance of being heard. Isaac loosened the screws and pulled the grate into the duct beside him. There was now little room to maneuver, but he had long since become accustomed to working in small spaces. He carefully aimed each of the penlights at an individual security camera.

Isaac clenched the last penlight between his teeth. In a few moments that one would be centered on the diamond around Abby's neck. Unique among blue diamonds, the Hope, when exposed to UV light phosphoresced a deep red, not unlike a swollen, angry eye. In a matter of seconds, the glowing jewel would be the only thing visible in the room.

───◦◊◦───

"What I find most interesting about the legacy of the Hope Diamond is not the drama that played out on a large scale in the lives of those associated with it, but by the private misery they endured behind closed doors." Abby lifted the diamond with a finger, "This thing has wrought more suffering than many human beings. Yet it is so much more than a blue rock dug from the bowels of India. It is a cultural icon, an object of spirituality, a symbol of greed at the deepest level. Those who long for power seek it, but rarely are they satisfied. It is a magnificent display of artistry, but ultimately, it is nothing more than a curse—"

No sooner had the word slipped from Abby's mouth than a loud pop was heard, and the room fell into utter darkness.

20

A STUNNED SILENCE SETTLED OVER THE ROOM, AS THOUGH THE GUESTS had yet to process the fact that they sat in the dark. Abby tried, unsuccessfully, to speak into the microphone and tell everyone to remain calm. Her voice fell flat, unmagnified.

Then pandemonium broke out. It was a woman who screamed first, her voice shrill and panicked. And like a series of dominoes tumbling over, the shrieks spread from table to table. Chairs scooted back, knocked over. Dishes and silverware fell to the floor. Abby remained at the podium, invisible, vulnerable, and terrified.

Everything in Isaac's line of sight was transformed into varying shades of green once he put on the night vision goggles. Chaos reigned below; people crawled like ants under a magnifying glass.

He set the timer on his wristwatch for ninety seconds, aimed the small crossbow at the medallion in the peak of the Rotunda, and pulled the trigger.

The anchor, attached to a fifty-foot line of thin climbing rope, whizzed toward the ceiling and entered the elaborately carved stone with a *chink*. Isaac pulled the rope taut, tested his harness, and swung headfirst into the open air above the crowd. He held the last penlight in his hand and aimed the ultraviolet beam toward the diamond around Abby's neck. An angry red began to burn within the depths of the jewel, growing brighter by the second. Isaac's harness whirred, as he descended five feet per second and then slowed to a stop. He dangled a mere two feet over Abby's head.

※

"Thirteen, fourteen, fifteen," Alex mouthed the words, opening his eyes on fifteen. He moved toward Abby, hands outstretched, as he navigated the room from memory. When his fingers met with soft black velvet he jumped onto the stage riser and pulled Abby into his arms. Her body stiffened in surprise, and she tried to pull away.

"Hey, it's okay. It's me."

Abby leaned into him, her breath ragged. "What just happened?"

"I don't know, probably a power outage."

"Please don't leave me. I don't like this."

Alex winced, but pulled her tighter. He wrapped his arms around her waist and laced his fingers through hers, knowing that Isaac dangled in the darkness above. The smile on his lips fluctuated between guilt and elation.

※

Isaac tapped Alex on the head with a gloved finger and waited for the signal. He watched his brother through the goggles, dismayed at the hesitance etched across his face.

Again he reached out and tapped Alex, counting down seconds they didn't have to spare. As if on instinct, their eyes met in the darkness, and yet Alex waited. Then, resigned to the inevitable, he shifted his weight and revealed the clasp that secured the Hope Diamond around Abby's neck.

Isaac descended the remaining two feet and with nimble fingers unclasped the necklace.

Abby heard the shriek before she realized it was hers. Yet it was different than the screams that echoed through the room from frightened aristocrats. Hers was primal and involuntary.

"What's wrong?" Alex leaned in to hear her above the noise.

Abby writhed frantically, trying to twist free from his grasp. "The necklace. It's gone!"

"What do you mean? I've been right here."

"I don't know," she panted. "Fingers. I felt fingers on my neck and then the weight of the necklace was gone."

The sob came from somewhere deep within, rushing from her chest with wavelike force. With it came fresh tears that sprang from her eyes, drawing from the well of intensity that descended on her like the tide.

By the time flashlight beams pierced the darkness below, Isaac had ascended thirty feet and was level with the ventilation grate, the diamond safely hidden in a velvet pouch beneath his shirt. As though he were a child on a swing, he rocked back and forth on the harness, spending precious seconds gaining momentum that would thrust him back to the opening. It only took a moment for Isaac to retreat into the safety of the ventilation shaft. He pressed the release mechanism on his crossbow and disconnected the anchor from the ceiling. A small hole, no wider than an inch, was the only evidence left on the medallion. The rope and anchor pulled back with a *whiz*, like a tape measure retracting. He reattached the vent cover, disassembled the tripod and pen lights, and replaced the equipment in the tool belt at his waist.

The mini-electro magnetic pulse only allowed ninety seconds of blackout, and his time was running out. Isaac followed the green residue from the phosphorescent light through the ductwork.

As he slithered on his belly through the maze of air-conditioning vents, Isaac Weld felt the weight of his greatest conquest resting beneath his shirt.

———⊗⊗⊗———

When the lights came on, it was not the muted lighting of the staged event, but the full, harsh, fluorescent glare produced by the emergency generators. The hundreds of panicked guests stood, relief evident on their faces. As they turned toward the stage, their expressions told Abby what she already knew. The diamond was gone.

The crowd's confused murmur grew into a cacophony of exclamations and gasps. Abby stood before the crowd, fully clothed, yet feeling totally naked. She shrank into Alex, seeking what protection she could find in his embrace.

———⊗⊗⊗———

Dow and DeDe remained seated the entire time, knowing full well what had happened the moment the lights went out. Their eyes remained fixed, unmoving during the ninety seconds of darkness as they held hands. When harsh light flooded the room, they saw the look of panic etched on Abby's face. Alex stood behind her, arms around her waist.

DeDe attempted to stand, but Dow laid a hand on her arm and pulled her back into the chair. A smile stretched the corners of his mouth. "Sit darling," he said.

"Shouldn't we—"

"No," he interrupted. "Let's see how this plays out."

∽∽∽

Blake Marshall's heart pounded as he counted down the seconds before the emergency lights kicked back on. He knew what had happened the moment the security cameras went white ten seconds before the power outage. He knew, and he was helpless to stop it.

As the generators clicked and chugged in the distance, building power, he shuffled in the dark toward the main security console, eyes focused blindly on the blank screens. When power returned to the small room, chaos played out on the monitors.

"Daniel is going to skin me alive," he gasped, throwing himself into the chair before the consoles.

"The cameras reverted to their default positions," Marshall yelled at the security crew. "Get her on the screen now! I don't care about anything else; I want to see Dr. Mitchell."

Technicians scrambled to adjust cameras throughout the Rotunda. A few seconds later Abby's panic-stricken face appeared on the screen. Her hands fluttered around her bare neck as she spoke with her date.

Marshall gaped at the screen. The diamond was gone. It took a moment before he regained control of his thoughts to insert his security card into the main processor. His fingers flew across the keyboard, typing in the distress code. Three seconds later, dozens of alarms went off, echoing down the halls of the Smithsonian Institute's Museum of Natural History, and every exterior door and window immediately locked. No one was going anywhere for a while.

⤫

Isaac Weld slipped through the door leading from the HVAC maintenance shaft onto the roof a mere two seconds before the alarm sounded. A steel rod jammed into the deadbolt, effectively locking him from the building. His original plan was to be clear of the door by twenty seconds. When Alex hesitated, it cut into Isaac's escape plan. Now the thief raced across the roof toward the back corner of the building.

⤫

Daniel Wallace plowed through the Rotunda like a bull at Pamplona, ready to charge anyone in his path. His bloodshot gaze locked on Abby. One hand pressed against his earpiece and the other held a small bullhorn.

"Cut the sirens," he ordered.

With nostrils flared, he took the stage steps two at a time and confronted Abby. She stepped back into Alex's protective embrace.

"Dr. Mitchell, do you want to tell me where that diamond is, or do we need to go about this the hard way?" Daniel challenged.

Abby gasped. "Daniel, you don't think—"

He leaned closer. "I'll tell you what I think—" His hot breath hissed against her ear. "—I think you are a very smart woman, Dr. Mitchell. And I think you have a great deal of explaining to do." Daniel locked glares with Alex, warning him not to interfere.

"Daniel, I . . . surely, you can't—" She shook her head in disbelief.

"I'm not a patient man. Talk to me now, or I can make this difficult. You don't want that to happen."

Tears welled up in her eyes, and she blinked them back.

"Okay, Dr. Mitchell, just remember that this was your choice," the security chief growled.

Daniel turned to the crowd and lifted the bullhorn to his mouth. His harsh voice echoed off the arched ceiling. "Ladies and gentlemen, we are in lockdown. We will remain so until we have recovered the Hope Diamond." He glowered at Abby's bare neck. "What that *means*," he continued, "is that every one of you is a suspect."

Stunned shouts of protest erupted from the guests.

"As suspects, you will be subjected to a body search and interrogation before leaving the Smithsonian tonight."

Daniel lowered the bullhorn and questioned Abby. "Am I correct in assuming that this is going to hurt the bottom line of your little fund-raiser?"

"You think I still care about that?"

"I think you planned this entire thing."

"You can't be serious!"

Daniel ignored her and spoke into the bullhorn again. "This is how it's going to work, ladies and gentlemen. Men will be escorted to the left into the Hall of Mammals. Ladies will be taken to the right into the Dinosaur Room. There you will undergo a physical search. Men will be searched by male security officers; women will be searched by female security officers."

Cell phones materialized among the guests; attorneys would earn their retainers tonight.

Horrified, Abby tugged at Daniel's arm and pulled the bullhorn down. "Are you insane? Do you know who these people are? You are looking at some of the most well-connected attorneys and politicians in the country. This will open the Smithsonian up to a class-action lawsuit that could destroy it forever."

"Then why don't you start talking, Dr. Mitchell?"

"Because I don't know anything!"

"I don't believe you."

"Daniel, think about what you're doing."

"The choice is yours, Abby. Where is the diamond?"

"I've already told you. I don't have it!" she yelled. Alex squeezed her arm in support.

"That's funny. You were the one wearing it five minutes ago."

Alex stepped forward. "What are you insinuating?"

"This is none of your business, Mr. Weld."

"I'm making it my business. You just accused Dr. Mitchell of a felony."

Daniel turned to Alex and eyed him closely. "Do you mind telling me what you were doing when that diamond magically disappeared from around her neck?"

"Standing right here with her."

"Is that so?"

"Yes, it is, as a matter of fact," Abby said. "He found me as soon as the lights went out."

"How convenient."

"What are you saying?" Alex gently moved Abby aside, shoving his face inches from Daniel.

"I'm saying that the Hope Diamond is gone. She was wearing it. And you were standing right next to her. You expect me to believe that neither of you know where it is now?"

"Alex had nothing to do with this!"

"And how do you know that, Dr. Mitchell?"

"His arms were around me the entire time. He came up here to keep me safe, not to steal the diamond."

"Safe from what, Dr. Mitchell? Are you afraid of the dark?"

"He's a gentleman, Daniel, unlike you."

"Apparently not. He stood there and let someone make off with a $250 million dollar necklace while it was hanging on your neck."

"Now wait just a minute! I had no idea—"

"You didn't know someone was taking it off her neck?"

"No."

"And what about you, Abby?"

"I felt someone unlatch the necklace, but it wasn't Alex. I'm telling you, he was right here. His arms were around me the whole time."

"Don't go anywhere," Daniel said. "I'll talk to you two later."

"We need to start the search, Dr. Trent," Daniel said. The head of the museum looked stunned. "The longer we wait the greater the possibility of losing that diamond."

"You can't be serious, Daniel. Do you know the lawsuits we would face by searching our patrons?"

"Someone in this room stole the diamond. If we don't search them, they could walk out of here, and you will never see it again. Are you prepared to let that happen?" Daniel ran a hand over his face. "It may already be gone."

Peter Trent paused and then leaned in, whispering, "Are we talking about *strip* searches?"

"No. Voluntary searches with full pat downs. The innocent have nothing to hide. Those who protest will be subjected to a vigorous interrogation. Now can we please do this?"

Peter closed his eyes and nodded.

⸺∞⸺

Isaac dropped to the ground and crouched in the shadows. The alarm fell silent, but he heard the roar of sirens approaching. He stowed the tool belt in the briefcase, along with the mask and gloves, and slipped into his sport coat.

With the Hope Diamond tucked safely beneath his shirt, Isaac headed down Constitution Avenue, away from the scene of the crime.

21

"**W**HAT DO YOU MEAN YOU CAN'T FIND IT?" PURPLE CAPILLARIES PRESSED to the surface of Daniel's nose, and his eyes bulged.

A security officer cowered before him, the harbinger of bad news. "We searched everyone, sir. Every single person. Some of them down to their underwear. No one has it."

"Do cavity searches then. I want that necklace found!"

"Er, yes . . . well . . . I doubt that would help."

"And why is that?"

"Sir, the diamond is too big to . . . fit . . . in a cavity."

"Is that so?"

"Yes sir."

Beads of sweat popped out on Daniel's forehead. This couldn't be happening—not on his watch.

Daniel observed Dr. Trent approaching him from the Hall of Mammals, jacket in hand and shirt partially unbuttoned.

"We have to let them go, Daniel."

"We haven't found the diamond, Dr. Trent."

"That is exactly why they have to be released. These people didn't do anything."

"I'm not letting anyone out of here until we find that thing."

"You are going to do exactly what I tell you, Daniel, because you work for me!"

"My butt is on the line here."

"No, Daniel, mine is. I made the decision to take the diamond out of the vault. The Board of Regents approved. You were just doing your job."

"And failed."

"Apparently, we all failed. But in the end I will be the one to answer for it. Now let these people go."

"I'm going to find it, sir. I promise you that."

Dr. Trent said nothing and just walked away in defeat.

———— ∞ ————

Abby listened as Daniel made the announcement on his bullhorn that everyone was being released. The irate crowd of guests collected their belongings and made their way to the front door. She stood a few feet from Dr. Trent, dreading the conversation they were about to have.

"You okay?" Alex slid an arm around her shoulders.

Abby lifted her eyes, meeting his briefly. It was answer enough.

Dr. Trent shifted from foot to foot. He finally cleared his throat. "We need to talk, Dr. Mitchell." He motioned with his head that he wanted her to come with him for a private conversation.

Abby nodded and followed him toward a corner of the room, holding her head as high as possible.

"I must say, Dr. Mitchell, there are no words. What I mean is, I just don't . . . how could you let this happen?" He spat out the angry question.

"Please, Dr. Trent. You have to believe me. I didn't have anything to do with this."

"You can understand why I have a difficult time believing that, Dr. Mitchell."

"I—"

"I cannot convey how disappointed I am. How angry I am."

"I know it looks bad. I do. But you have to believe me," she said, swallowing her tears, "I had no part in this."

Dr. Trent glared at her over the wire rims of his glasses. "Then who did?" His voice stayed calm . . . level . . . unnerving.

"I don't know!" Exasperated, Abby lifted her arms and then dropped them to her side.

Daniel Wallace pushed his way through the crowd, glowering at Abby as he approached. "Dr. Trent, have you made your decision?"

Abby looked back and forth between the two men. "What decision?"

"You must understand that this is very difficult for me, Abby."

"What are you talking about?"

"It all looks very bad, and the Board of Regents is already pressing me for action."

"I don't understand. What are you trying to say?"

Daniel broke in and spoke for Dr. Trent. "What he's trying to say is that someone needs to be held responsible for this, and that someone is you, Dr. Mitchell."

"Me?"

"You were wearing the diamond when it disappeared. All signs point to your involvement."

The edges of her face hardened, and she stood up straight, shoulders squared. "Is that so?"

Dr. Trent looked as though he was in pain, while Daniel appeared to be enjoying every moment.

"Yes, Dr. Mitchell, it is."

"Let's be honest, gentlemen," she said. "I made a ghastly mistake. But I'm not the only one who used poor judgment."

"Do enlighten me," Dr. Trent said.

Abby turned to Daniel, her fists clenched. "What about you, Daniel? This happened on your watch."

Daniel jerked. "Now wait a minute!"

"It was my understanding," she said, her voice rising above his, "that you spent the last twenty years in security management. Why couldn't you manage this?"

"I argued against letting you wear the diamond."

"This entire event rested on the assumption that you were fully capable of protecting that diamond, Daniel. I understand the situation that I'm in, but you screwed up too."

Daniel pulled a pair of handcuffs from his belt, shaking with anger. "This is a conversation we can finish later, Dr. Mitchell."

Her instinct was to pull away, but she remained where she stood and eyed the cuffs with disdain. "You're arresting me?"

Peter Trent pulled at his collar. "This is difficult, Abby, I know."

"And what are you arresting me *for*?" The question was simple, but both men shied away from the obvious answer.

"For stealing the Hope Diamond," Daniel said.

Abby laughed, her voice sounding harsh to her own ears. "For stealing the Hope Diamond! I assume you have some proof."

"You were wearing it when the lights went out, Abby," Dr. Trent mumbled.

"Yes, I was, on your orders. And I was searched just like everyone else." Abby met Daniel's gaze with fierce determination. "Did you or your security team find it on my person?"

"No."

"Did you find it in my belongings?"

"No."

"Tell me, Daniel, did you find that diamond at all?"

He flushed with anger.

Abby turned to her boss. "Dr. Trent, if you're accusing me of felony theft, I hope you have the proof to back up that accusation."

Trent hesitated, unable to meet her eyes, and spun his wedding band around his finger.

"Those are details we can attend to later," Daniel spat into the silence.

Abby shrugged. "Perhaps it will buy you some time. But it will also buy you the biggest headache you've ever experienced." She kept her eyes on Dr. Trent and weighed her next words carefully. "If I were you, I would remember the reason you hired me, Peter. I have certain connections you felt would be a great asset to this museum. I will not hesitate to use those in my favor."

A glance passed between them.

"Is that a threat, Dr. Mitchell?" Daniel asked.

"Yes, it is, but not in the way that you think, Daniel. As Dr. Trent would tell you if he could muster the courage to speak, I am fully prepared to defend myself."

"She's right," Dr. Trent whispered. His voice was barely audible above the clamor.

"Excuse me?"

"We don't have the grounds to arrest her."

"I beg to differ," Daniel insisted.

"You can beg what you like, but you will not be putting those cuffs on her, Daniel." Dr. Trent deflated like a circus balloon.

"You're making a huge mistake."

"Please don't tell me how to do my job. I'm not an idiot. Had you found that diamond in her purse I would be more than happy to let you take her to jail. But the fact is, Daniel, you have not found it at all."

Daniel's face contorted with rage.

Abby breathed a sigh of relief. "Thank you, Peter. Thank you. Now we can turn our attention to retrieving the stone."

"We?"

"Well, yes. I think I can be of assistance."

Dr. Trent placed a hand on her arm. "Abby, dear, I'm afraid you don't understand what's happening here. You won't be helping with anything."

"What do you mean?"

"Just because I don't have the evidence to have you arrested doesn't mean you are not the prime suspect."

"But that doesn't make sense!"

"The fact remains, my dear, that you were wearing that stone. You are the only person who had access to it. You are, unfortunately, at the top of the suspect list, and as such I will need your key card and all of your access codes."

"Please, Peter. You're making a big mistake. I can help."

"You are officially on administrative leave, without pay."

"This is the wrong move, Dr. Trent," she said, eyes narrowed.

"You haven't left me any choice."

"I don't have that diamond!"

"That remains to be seen."

"You can't be serious."

"Don't tell me what I am, Dr. Mitchell. I believe it is time for you to get your things and leave. You've done enough damage for one evening."

She grabbed her purse from the table and turned on her heel.

"Dr. Mitchell?"

"Yes?" she asked.

"Don't expect to get your job back."

Abby clenched her jaw. She dug through her purse and handed her badge to Daniel.

"Your security code, Dr. Mitchell."

"One nine seven eight."

Daniel spoke into his headset, "Security, this is Daniel Wallace. Eliminate code one nine seven eight from the system."

"I believe you were leaving," Dr. Trent said.

"Yes, Peter, I believe I was."

"Abby." Daniel addressed her for the last time. "If I were you, I wouldn't leave the country."

Her voice broke. "And why would I do a thing like that?"

"Just don't."

Abby brushed past Alex, tears pressing into the corners of her eyes. "Please, take me home."

22

Silence permeated the car as they drove back to Abby's apartment. Alex kept his gaze on the road while she looked out the window, eyes red and swollen.

After what seemed like an interminable amount of time, he came to a stop before her building and walked her in. Abby stood before her door, turning the keys over and over between her fingers. She wiped a stream of makeup away from her eyes.

"I'm sorry all this happened," he whispered. "It's not your fault."

"Even so, it isn't likely to matter. I will forever be known as the woman who lost the Hope Diamond."

Alex slid his arms around her waist and nuzzled her cheek. He pressed his lips to her temple and then pulled away. "Get some sleep."

She nodded.

He tipped her chin with his fingers. "I'm here if you need me."

She sniffled, wiping her face with the back of her hand, and offered him a weak smile.

"I'll call you in the morning."

"Okay," she whispered, then put her key in the lock and left him standing on the doorstep.

Alex left the building, guilt brewing beneath the surface. He knew quite well that he would never be calling her again.

———⊗⊗⊗———

Abby entered the silence of her apartment and took a deep breath as she walked to the window. She stared into the empty parking lot until Alex got into his car and left. He didn't look back. Raw emotion assaulted her when he pulled out of the parking lot, the wheels of his Mercedes spinning slowly at first, and then picking up speed

23

Versailles, France, June 23, 1789

"**W**HAT *RIGHT* DO THEY HAVE TO REVOLT?" MARIE ANTOINETTE SCREAMED, her voice shrill and hawkish like a bird swooping on its prey.

Her intended target was the rotund form of Jacques Necker, minister of finance. The statesman had been a member of the King's Privy Council for a number of years, but recently assumed the role of minister of finance amidst the turmoil caused by the Estates General. Although his mother was of French nobility, thus ensuring his power and title, his father was Swiss, giving him a distinct edge of indifference to traditional royal ineptitude.

"This is not some heathen republic like that of barbaric America. This is France for God's sake. The people have no right to dissent. And you," she said, pointing a bony finger at Necker, "have no right to suggest the king of France live on a budget like a common pig!"

Jacques leveled an unwavering gaze at the queen. "The people are starving, Your Majesty. Will you live in such opulence while they suffer?"

"Starve! How can that be?"

236

"There is no flour with which to make bread." His words were measured and careful, each syllable pronounced with marked impatience.

Marie Antoinette turned to him, her heavily painted lips parted slightly. She shrugged, *"Qu'ils mangent de la brioche."*

"Cake? Let them eat cake!" Necker gasped. "And just where do you presume they will find flour for cake when they cannot find it for bread? Much less the eggs and sugar to go along with it?"

Marie Antoinette crossed her arms across her chest and lifted her chin. "The dietary concerns of the common man are not my concern."

Jacques Necker would have responded most unwisely had the king not stepped forward, placing a white-knuckled hand on his wife's shoulder. She felt the icy grip and went silent immediately. Although turning to face her husband, she still held Necker with an aggressive stare, daring him to disagree with her.

Not one to be intimidated, even by the queen of France, he held her gaze until she averted her eyes and implored her husband, "It is obvious that Monsieur Necker is sympathetic to the Third Estate. He is the one that convinced you to give the *bourgeoisie* double representation during the Assembly. And with that privilege they have rebelled against us!" Without glancing at Necker she suggested, "Perhaps we need a new minister of finance. Our current one seems incapable of the job."

"May I remind you that Monsieur Necker is the third minister in two years? I hardly think it appropriate to replace him given the current circumstances."

"Circumstances that he brought upon us! He is sympathetic to common peasants! How can he possibly be of use to us?"

"It is the very fact that he is sympathetic to them, and the fact that they know it, which requires his presence here. They trust him, and we can use that to our advantage." Louis turned to Necker, a smile still toying with his mouth. "I hear that the National Assembly has drafted a constitution?"

Marie snorted, "National Assembly. What a preposterous name. Estate. They are the peasant estate, nothing more. And they claim to represent the people!"

Necker ignored the queen and replied, "Yes, Your Majesty."

Louis took a deep breath, exhaling slowly. "I am afraid that my only recourse to this little mess is becoming quite obvious, if not somewhat distasteful. Please summon Bertrand Laurent. I wish to make a declaration."

Necker nodded and gave the king a short bow as he left the chamber in search of the royal secretary. He found Bertrand Laurent cowering over a table of delicacies in the dining hall. The secretary followed Necker back to the king's chamber, somewhat reluctantly, as he crammed his mouth full of cold turkey and cake.

"I suggest you make yourself presentable," Necker said over his shoulder. "The king is in a foul mood . . . and the queen is with him."

Laurent hastily swallowed and wiped his mouth on his shirtsleeves. Before entering the room, he adjusted his wig, straightened his coattails, and took a deep breath.

"Ah, so glad you could join us Monsieur Laurent," Louis whined, motioning him to sit behind the large desk. "I wish to make a declaration to the National Assembly."

Bertrand Laurent hastily arranged parchment, inkwell, and pen. He seated himself and raised the feather pen as though holding a cup of tea, with his pinky erect.

Louis dove immediately into his declaration: "The King wishes that the ancient distinction of the three Orders of the State be preserved in its entirety, as essentially linked to the constitution of his Kingdom." He paused for a moment until he heard the scratching of Laurent's pen. "That the deputies, freely elected by each of the three Orders, forming three chambers, deliberating by Order can alone be considered as forming the body of the representatives of the Nation. As a result, the King has declared null the resolutions passed by the deputies of the Order of the Third Estate, the seventeenth of this month, as well as those which have followed them, as illegal and unconstitutional."

Necker gripped his hands behind his back and lowered his eyes while the king completed his declaration. He paced the outer reaches of the chamber, keeping near the wall as he listened to words that would no doubt herald the end of the monarchy as they knew it.

The queen, on the other hand, stood triumphantly beside her husband, head held high, a garish smile spread across her pale face.

Louis grasped the Golden Fleece in his right hand, thumb brushing across the inset blue diamond.

———⊗⊗⊗———

Three years later...
PARIS, FRANCE, JUNE 21, 1791

The heavy berlin coach came to a stop at the south end of the Tuileries Palace promptly at ten o'clock. History would note that it was the first of many mistakes that King Louis XVI made in his attempt to flee France. Although he had not sent for the royal carriage, he had nonetheless acquired one that hinted as to the importance of its occupant. Four white horses, each over sixteen hands high, snorted restlessly in front of the ornately decorated coach. The wooden doors and sidepieces were painted gold, while the steel frame was a deep burgundy. Thick velvet curtains covered the windows, while leather seats and padded silk walls embellished the interior.

The coach waited for just a moment when what appeared to be a Russian baroness and her butler made their way down the steps and nervously entered the carriage. Once inside, the butler pulled the heavy velvet curtains across the windows and ordered the coach to depart. It rolled away quietly, leaving the baroness within to remove her feathered cap with shaking hands.

"Do you think we were noticed, Your Majesty?" She whispered, fear evident in her voice.

"There is no need to whisper, Joséphine. Our detractors cannot hear us in this coach," responded the king as he settled into the seat.

"I still do not understand why we could not all leave at once."

"That is much too risky a proposition, Joséphine. Do you not think the king, his queen, his sister, his children, and their governess would be noticed leaving together? It is much safer this way. After circling the Tuileries once, we will return for my sister and son. On the last pass we will retrieve Marie and my daughters. And then we shall be off to Montmédy where we will be met by Austrian troops, courtesy of my wife's cousin. Only then will I be able to crush this cursed revolution and return power to the monarchy. So you see, this flight we take tonight is not just for our own deliverance, but for the good of the people. France will thank us in the end."

Joséphine nodded, but did not ask any more questions. A short while later, the carriage once again stopped at the south end of the palace, and the King's sister, Madam Élisabeth, dressed as a maid, and his only surviving son, Louis-Charles, slipped through the heavy double doors. They quickly descended the steps and did their best not to run for the carriage. The driver barely jumped down in time to open the door. Élisabeth and Louis-Charles scrambled into the coach as quickly as they could.

Once again the berlin pulled away and the governess began to look ill. No one spoke as they rolled through the grounds of Tuileries. It finally occurred to each of them just how close they were to escaping, and the anticipation of fleeing their captivity rendered them speechless.

At eleven-thirty, the carriage pulled to a stop one last time, and the occupants sat expectantly, curtain pulled aside as they peered out, waiting for the queen and her daughters to descend the steps. Several minutes passed with no sign of Marie Antoinette.

The summer evening grew still as the palace settled into sleep for the evening. Only a few windows glowed yellow with light, and even as they waited in the courtyard, those dimmed one by one.

"Something is wrong," Joséphine hissed. "We have been discovered."

"Do not come to such hasty conclusions," Louis dismissed, looking bored but unperturbed. "This is my wife we are speaking about. When have you ever known her to be punctual?"

"Given the circumstances you would think she would at least attempt to be on time," Élisabeth said.

Even as they debated the queen's chronic habit of keeping others waiting, she glided down the steps, looking every bit the queen of France, despite being dressed as a common maid. Each of her young daughters held a hand and struggled to keep up.

Marie Antoinette waited silently as the driver climbed down and opened the coach. He gently lifted each of her daughters into the cab, and then offered a hand to her as well. She climbed into the coach with exaggerated dignity, as a smile played at the corners of her mouth.

The coach, now crowded, rolled away a final time, and instead of circling the palace grounds, found its way into the streets of Paris. Once a safe distance away from Tuileries, a triumphant cry erupted from the passengers as they celebrated an apparent victory.

"Isn't this just glorious?" asked the queen, her face aglow with the flush of adventure.

Élisabeth looked sick to her stomach. "Will you just look at me? I'm dressed as . . . as . . . a courtier!"

"You didn't expect to walk out of the palace as the king's sister, did you?"

Élisabeth shot Marie a sour look and crossed her arms. "Some of us don't share your enthusiasm for dressing like peasants!"

"Considering this little costume will most likely save not only your place in the royal court, but also your life, I think you ought to show a little more appreciation for the lengths we have gone to get you out of Paris."

Élisabeth turned away from the queen, her eyes resting on the darkness outside the carriage as they rolled northeast toward the border with Belgium.

The tired children, at first terrified, lay their small heads in the nearest lap and were soon lulled to sleep by the rhythmic motions of the coach and the steady clip clop of hooves. They rested peacefully, unaware that their success was tentative at best, still reliant on the wisdom of parents who had never shown a great measure of the attribute.

One by one, the adults followed the children into slumber, far less comfortable in the crowded carriage. By the time they reached Meaux, all were fast asleep and the coach drove undetected through the French countryside. The brilliant escape plan of Marie Antoinette gave every indication of success. And yet, in all her months of scheming, the one thing she failed to take into account was her very nature and that of her husband.

Louis woke first, hunger drawing him from restless sleep, as the lowest edges of the horizon tinged with gray. Finding himself still alive on this new day, the king of France was infused with confidence. He straightened his wig of gray curls and opened the velvet curtain. Forests of pine, oak, cedar, and spruce stood sillhouetted against the quickly lightening sky. All was quiet. All was safe.

As the realization of freedom dawned on him, Louis's feelings of entitlement revived.

By God, am I not the king of France?

His brows furrowed at the indignity of fleeing his own country in a carriage hardly worthy to transport his tailor. The gnawing realization of discomfort and hunger did not help his mood. Why should they dine on stale bread, dried fruit, and cold cheese when they could sup at any number of small inns along the way? They had escaped after all. What was another hour added to their journey when their destination was just over the next hill, where awaited the king's army and the intervention of the Duke of Brunswick? Louis had gained the victory, and if he chose to celebrate a little earlier than anticipated, that was of no concern to anyone.

Yes, I would much prefer a hot meal to these beggar's provisions.

Louis reached overhead and pulled a braided cord that ran through the length of the cab; it rang a bell beside the driver. They slowed to a stop, and the driver jumped down to attend to the king.

"How much farther to Reims?" Louis asked.

"An hour and a bit," the coachman said, not quite daring to meet the king's eyes.

"I would like to stop for breakfast when we arrive."

A short time later the carriage rolled to a stop in the village of Ste.-Ménéhould, and the small party entered an inn in search of breakfast. As Louis pushed through the worn wooden doors, he was met by an old soldier. They exchanged a nod but nothing more.

As the king and his family dined on a breakfast of roast lamb, fresh bread, cheese, and fruit, the soldier, a man by the name of Jean-Baptiste Drouet, mounted his horse and raced to the next town. In Varennes, along with help from the outraged locals, he blocked the bridge across the Meuse River.

It was noon before the berlin coach, carrying the satiated royal family, approached a small river. When the coach slowed and stopped, Louis yanked on the bell, too lazy to stick his head out the window. He waited for the driver to dismount and open the door.

"Why have we stopped?" he demanded.

The coachman, pale with fright, lifted a hand and pointed to something Louis could not see. "We have been ordered to stop, Your Majesty," he gulped.

"Ordered! And just who would have the gall to order the king of France to stop anything?" he bellowed, tumbling from the carriage like a dizzy cat.

"I did," a voice sounded from the foot of the bridge.

Louis immediately understood his fatal error. "Jean-Baptiste Drouet," he murmured.

"You did not recognize me so readily this morning with the distraction of a hungry belly."

Louis was not ready to surrender so quickly, and he tucked a hand inside his jacket, searching for a bag of coins, now significantly lighter after their meal. "Come now, this is but a small matter, and I believe it can be settled for a reasonable fee."

Drouet smiled but it did nothing to warm Louis's heart. "You would buy me off, Your Majesty? I am not a man so weak as that." He stepped off the path to reveal a great number of peasants holding pitchforks and other makeshift weapons. "Besides, I doubt you will find them so easily bribed."

PARIS, FRANCE, AUGUST 13, 1792

It was the Knights Templar who first used stone, trowel, and mortar to construct the medieval fortress known as the Temple. At one time it was used for the more noble purposes of education, worship, and defense. But that was five hundred years before King Louis XVI found himself under arrest by armed guards. Now it served only as a prison.

The knights were less concerned with form than function and built a fortress of bare simplicity. A series of round turrets rose from the sharp square base, like spears pointing skyward with their butt ends rammed into the earth. Five-foot-thick stone walls rose seven stories high and were topped with a buttress notched at even intervals for archers. A long row of them stood now with needle-sharp points aimed squarely at the king of France, as his carriage rolled to a stop, its hinges creaking.

King Louis stepped from the carriage and set foot in the silent courtyard, with lips pursed and jaw clenched. He tilted his chin upward, taking in the height of the Temple. High above him flapped bright red triangular flags, cracking in the wind. Generations of harsh rain and biting wind had ground the stone walls smooth. Long thin windows were scattered irregularly across turret and walls, wide enough to see through, but incapable of allowing siege or escape.

The soldiers posted at the Temple allowed him the brief luxury of inspecting his prison. Many had never been so close to their sovereign before. Many felt this moment should have come years earlier.

The silence was broken by the slamming of a great door deep within the fortress, and it broke the stoicism of the soldiers. They whispered to one another and directed an occasional coarse gesture at their king. The rattle of footsteps echoed through the courtyard, followed by the grinding of wood upon stone as the massive wooden gates swung open, revealing twenty armed guards ready to escort Louis to his cell.

The king regarded them with chin held high, and his hands planted on his hips.

"Will citizen Louis Capet please step forward?" The call came from within the courtyard.

Louis's upper lip twitched, and he ground his teeth together at the familiar voice. He turned his head slightly to the left and beheld Jean-Baptiste Drouet. "I am Louis XVI, Sovereign King of France, and you will address me as such."

Drouet approached the king, with steady eyes and a commanding voice. "You are a criminal, a mere citizen of France. You are my prisoner. And you will step forward."

At Drouet's command, two foot soldiers approached the king from behind and gripped his elbows tightly. He shook loose of their grip before they could push him forward.

"Unhand me," he spat. He approached Drouet until they were practically nose to nose. "I see you have been rewarded for your betrayal. No longer a peasant grinding bread, hm? Captain of the guard. Are you pleased with yourself Jean-Baptiste Drouet?"

A smile of deep satisfaction spread across Drouet's face. "Immensely." The captain then took a step back and ordered, "Take him to the *Grosse Tour*."

The Great Tower to which Drouet referred was the largest turret at the Temple, stretching nearly twenty feet above the rest and home to The Keep, where many a prisoner met his end.

"Sir, the queen will arrive momentarily," said one of Drouet's captains. "Where is she to be taken?"

Drouet tilted his head to the right and looked upward at another tower, second only in size to the Great Tower. "Caesar's Tower will suffice for the queen. Now, why don't you see our most esteemed monarch to his cell?"

The foot soldiers again grabbed Louis by the arms, this time with a great deal more confidence, and shoved him forward through the heavy wooden gates. The armed guards parted as they passed, taking up ranks in the rear.

Louis was brought before a massive pair of solid wood doors that led to the Great Tower. These were parted with great difficulty by a set of four guards, two on each side. A cold gray staircase rose before them, disappearing into the blackness above. Two smoky oil torches were retrieved from brackets in the wall and handed to guards at each end of the procession.

Louis did not wait for the sharp nudge of the guard behind him, but stepped forward on his own, taking the steps lightly as though untroubled by the situation. Before long, the muscles along the fronts of his legs began to burn, and beads of sweat formed on his brow. Still they climbed, ever curving to the left as the steps took them up the circular tower. Halfway up the tower Louis's lungs, unaccustomed to physical exertion, burned and begged for oxygen. Yet Louis would not grant his captors the privilege of hearing him gasp for breath. He maintained his pace and sucked air between his teeth with all the control he could muster.

Before him the shaky torchlight bounced off the walls, a pale and sickly yellow, offering sparse light and no warmth. The pounding of his heart matched the rhythm of footsteps. The guards thundered up the staircase behind him. Just as his muscles buckled under his weight, they rounded a corner and, with it, took their last step.

Two soldiers reached out to steady the king, but he swatted away their hands. "Do not touch me," he panted, voice dry and cracking. "I do not need your help."

Before Louis stood a short wooden door, one foot thick, that opened into a bare stone room.

"Your chambers, Your Highness," said the lead guard with an exaggerated bow. "We pray you find our hospitality satisfactory."

The company of soldiers roared with laughter. Louis sniffed indignantly; his nostrils flared. He regarded the door with disgust, not because it led to his prison, but because to enter, he must bow and humble himself. He could not walk in with head held high.

"Perhaps we should help you in, Your Majesty," said the guard. He forced down the king's head, half pushing, half throwing the king of France into the small room. The door slammed shut behind Louis, and a large steel bolt fell onto brackets with a clang, locking him inside.

Louis clenched and unclenched his shaking hands. He faced the door and realized for the first time the reality of his situation. The door through which he entered his cell had no handle, latch, or grip on the inside. It was sanded smooth and flush with the stone walls.

Still panting from the climb, he approached the small window hewn into the rock. Through it he could see a patch of bitter gray sky and a sliver of courtyard below. No more than six inches wide, it was far too narrow to fit his head through. The king had even been robbed of the option of throwing himself from the window and choosing his own manner of death.

His lips quivered despite desperate attempts to bring them under control. Louis sniffed and shook his head.

"I will not cry," he hissed. "They will not break me. I am the rightful king of this godforsaken country, and I will not cry."

24

ABBY STOOD BEFORE HER LIVING ROOM WINDOW LONG AFTER ALEX WAS gone, the details of her plan falling into place. After some time, she took her hair down, and let it rest against her shoulders. She set her jaw in determination, and her moist eyes burned with a deep fire.

Abby peeled the evening gown off as though she were a snake shedding its skin and left it lying on the living room floor. In her bedroom she slipped into a pair of jeans, tennis shoes, and an old sweatshirt. She scrubbed her face and pulled her hair into a ponytail.

A quick glance at the clock on her nightstand proved she was running out of time. Abby grabbed the phone and stuffed clothing into a duffel bag. Her fingers were steady as she dialed the number from memory.

She was greeted by a familiar voice on the first ring. "Abby, are you okay?"

"I've been better, Dow."

"That was quite a . . . I mean I've never seen anything like—"

She smiled grimly. "They put on quite a show, don't they?"

"Oh, Abby, I didn't mean—"

"It's okay," she soothed. "You don't have to tiptoe around me. I'll be fine."

"I heard about Dr. Trent. That was a bad decision on his part."

"Yeah, I didn't see that coming. But there's nothing I can do about it now."

Dow paused on the other end. She knew he was trying to subdue his eagerness. "So do you think—"

"Yes, Dow, it was the Collectors." She tugged at the end of her ponytail, thinking over the events of the last few hours. "Don't forget I've been unlucky enough to be in the room twice now when they've struck. I must admit they do it with flair."

"Well, I honestly never thought I'd see the day that I'd witness one of their thefts."

"And here I thought that you always secretly wanted to."

"Perhaps from a distance, just to see how they work. But I didn't see a thing except the back of my eyelids." His voice took on a slight note of appreciation. "As much as I hate to admit it, their little display was quite impressive."

"Dow. These are the bad guys remember?"

"I have little chance of forgetting that."

"How's DeDe?"

Dow grunted. "She could have done without it. Never did have the stomach for that kind of thing."

"Tell her I'm sorry."

"It wasn't your fault, dear."

"I certainly feel like it was."

"I guess I need to ask how you're doing, I mean really doing?"

"Good question. Difficult answer. I don't honestly know."

"Let me know if there's anything I can do, okay? I'm here. DeDe is, too, and you know we love you like a *daughter*."

Abby swallowed the lump that rose in her throat caused by his genuine concern and the word *daughter*. Her voice wavered. "That's actually why I called. There is something you can do."

"Name it."

She took a deep breath, fully resigned to the course of action she planned. "I need you to get me on the next flight to Paris."

An uncomfortable silence lingered between them for a few moments.

"Paris?"

"My father. I have to find him, Dow."

"Abby, that is not a good idea."

"Dow, I have to try."

"Listen," his voice soothed, "I know you're really upset, and I know your dad disappointed you yesterday, but I don't think anything will come of you chasing him halfway across the globe. Why don't you let Interpol handle this?"

His words stung, and she physically recoiled. "Yes, he hurt me, but it wasn't the first time. My need to see him has less to do with our relationship than it does with the diamond."

Dow's words were measured. "Your father is a very powerful man, Abby."

"That's my point exactly."

"This is not a good idea. You were ordered not to leave the country."

"Dr. Trent is no longer my boss."

"No, but you are still a person of interest in the case."

"The last I checked, I haven't been charged with anything other than stupidity."

"Abby, listen—"

"Dow," she interrupted, "I'm getting on a plane tonight with or without your approval. It would be much easier if you just helped me."

"I have a bad feeling about this."

"And I don't have any other options. If I don't find my father in the next few hours, that diamond will be lost forever."

Dow clicked his tongue as he thought about the ramifications. "All right," he conceded after a lengthy silence. "When do you need to leave?"

Abby grabbed her duffel bag and walked toward the door. "As soon as possible."

⟐

Isaac greeted Alex on the tarmac at Warfield airstrip outside Columbia, near D.C., ready to celebrate the success of their biggest heist ever. Alex only glanced at his brother. He pushed past him and climbed the steps into the luxurious eight-passenger private jet. Isaac followed him.

"Tell me, Alex," Isaac growled, settling into an empty seat opposite him. "When did it happen?"

"What?"

"This sudden growth of a conscience."

Alex didn't look at his brother, nor did he answer the question.

"Because you know," Isaac continued, draining half his glass. "I remember a time when you were a ruthless crook and could get in the pants of twenty broads while keeping your head screwed on straight. Now one brown-eyed woman smiles at you, and you lose your edge. Great man. Just great."

Alex gripped the armrest until his knuckles turned white. "You know, it must be nice," he said, each syllable loaded with animosity.

"What?"

"Keeping your distance. Dealing with the logistics. Never getting your hands dirty."

"Are you saying I don't do my part?"

"Oh, you do it," Alex said, turning to Isaac for the first time. "You do it well."

"Then what is your problem?"

"You're so far removed from what's happening on the ground that you don't realize how complicated it gets down there."

"Complicated?"

"Yeah."

"The only complication I see is that you fell in love and almost ruined months of planning."

Alex winced at the truth; he had fallen in love with Abby, and now he was leaving. Looking out the window, Alex tamped down his emotions and watched the ground slip away. Soon the jet lifted into the sky, and as they approached cruising altitude, his thoughts turned to the brunette who remained on the ground far below.

Abby boarded the Boeing 747 at Dulles International Airport two hours later. The flight was less than half full. She moved through first class, holding nothing but her iPhone and a small carry-on.

"Ma'am," the flight attendant called after her.

Abby turned, her eyes bloodshot. "Yes?"

"You passed your seat. You're in B4."

"But that's first class."

"So is your ticket," the attendant said with a wink. "May I take your bag and get you something to drink?"

"No, thank you." Abby rubbed her tired, swollen eyes and settled into the seat. Wisps of hair escaped her pony-tail, and she still wore DeDe's diamond earrings. "I just need sleep."

"A Tylenol PM perhaps?"

"That would be great."

"I'll be right back."

Abby punched seven buttons on her cell phone and waited for Dow's voice. "Thank you," she said when he answered.

"It was the least I could do."

"It means a lot."

"You mean a lot to us," he said. "You deserve first class."

Dr. Abigail Mitchell could no longer compose herself. She muttered an unintelligible good-bye, buried her face in the headrest, and wept.

When the flight attendant returned, she laid the Tylenol on the seat beside Abby, along with a flight pillow and blanket. Abby slept before the plane left U.S. airspace.

———∽∾∾∾∽———

Although not a well-known tourist destination, *Hotel Le Bristol* was one of the most luxurious hotels in Paris. It sat in the middle of Paris's art and shopping district, across from the River Seine. Alex Weld and his brother met with the Broker in the Panoramic Suite several times a year and exchanged stolen goods for garish amounts of money.

Alex stood at the hotel window and observed the whitewashed building and manicured lawns below.

Isaac's mood lightened up during the flight. By the time they landed in Paris, he was so drunk that he staggered to the cab and then passed out. When they arrived at the hotel, Alex managed to wake up his brother and guide him to the suite. Isaac flopped on the bed and immediately began to snore. Yet try as he might, sleep eluded Alex.

It was not the jet lag that kept him awake all night, but a single thought of Abby, curled up on her couch, hair in a ponytail, wearing those hideous blue-and-orange toe socks. Try as he might, he could not erase her memory.

Once the sun rose above the skyline, Isaac emerged from the bedroom, showered, dressed, and ready for their meeting later. Room service delivered fruit, pastries, yogurt, and espresso, a traditional Parisian breakfast, and the brothers ate in silence.

Isaac drained his coffee cup and leveled a frigid stare at his brother. "I've been thinking."

"About what?"

"We've had this little arrangement going for what, nine years now?"

"Ten." Alex felt the tension between the two of them.

Isaac pointed a half-eaten piece of pastry at Alex. "I think it's time to dissolve our partnership. You're holding me back."

"I'm holding you back?"

"Yes. I'd prefer to work alone."

Alex's harsh laugh filled the room, but there was no mirth on his face. "Well, I'd prefer not to work at all."

"That can be arranged," Isaac said. Suddenly, he pulled a handgun from the holster behind his back. A silencer was screwed onto the end.

Alex jumped to his feet and backed away. "Whoa! What is this?"

"This," Isaac said, leveling the gun at Alex's head, "is a corporate takeover."

Alex opened his mouth to respond, but Isaac pulled the trigger before he could speak. The gun popped quietly, and a wisp of black smoke curled from the barrel. Alex fell to the carpet, blood pooling beneath his head.

25

PARIS, FRANCE, JANUARY 21, 1793,

THE DAWN DELIVERED A BLEAK AND DREARY DAY, SODDEN WITH RAIN and temperamental winds. More than 1,200 horsemen and hundreds of French citizens crowded the Place de Louis XV to carry out King Louis's execution. In the center of the plaza stood a scaffold holding the guillotine, and only there could a clearing be found. The people had come to see their king beheaded, but they did not want to be sprayed with his blood.

From a distance the heavy beat of a drum signaled the approach of the king's carriage. It was escorted by a contingent of horsemen, and a group of drummers announced his doom. They pulled into the plaza with all the drama and anticipation due such an event.

The doors to his carriage swung open, and out stepped the king of France, dressed in robes and possessed of the haughty expression for which he was so famous. Three guards immediately surrounded him and would have undressed him for the ritual beheading, but he gave them such a scowl that they backed away. King Louis XVI removed his own robes, undid his necktie, and opened his shirt, maintaining the dignity of nobility.

No longer taken off guard, the soldiers attempted to seize his hands but were rebuked sternly. "What are you attempting?" he asked.

"To bind you," replied a guard, feeling more and more uneasy.

"To bind me!" he shrieked, his voice breaking with anger. "No! I shall never consent to that. Do what you have been ordered, but you shall *never* bind me."

Louis took the arm of a priest as he made his way toward the scaffold. For the briefest moment, he appeared to lose his nerve, but once he reached the steps, he climbed them boldly to stand before the blade.

Such a fierce glare crossed the king's face that the drums fell silent. A hush settled over the crowd.

His words were laced with defiant anger as he announced, "I die innocent of all the crimes laid to my charge. I pardon those who have occasioned my death. And I pray to God that the blood you are going to shed may never be visited on France."

He would have continued with his speech were it not for a national guardsman on horseback who ordered the continuance of the drums. They roared to life again, pounding the death knell. With them roared to life the voices of those in the crowd who encouraged the executioners.

"Off with his head!"

"Death to the king!"

"Justice for the people!"

It was but a fleeting moment, and the king knelt before the guillotine. Only a blink of an eye later the axe fell upon him. A young guard, not more than eighteen years of age, seized the severed head by the hair and lifted it for the crowd to see. A macabre silence fell upon the witnesses, as though they realized for the first time that their king was dead.

Then a lone voice in the crowd bellowed, *"Vive la République!"*

One after another, the people took up the chant.

"Vive la République!"

"Vive la République!"

Within moments, it became the battle cry of a people deposing their monarch. The plaza reverberated with the sound of their protest, and then spontaneously, everyone tossed their hats into the air, darkening the sky and the ground on which laid the newly beheaded king of France.

26

WITH A BLANK EXPRESSION ON HIS FACE, ISAAC WELD STOOD OVER HIS brother's body, tilting his head to the side. He picked the discarded bullet shell from the floor and unscrewed the silencer. His eyes lingered on Alex's face for a moment as he tried to beckon memories from childhood. Nothing surfaced in Isaac's mind, and he turned away with a shrug.

Isaac picked up the Hope Diamond from his nightstand, hung the black velvet bag around his neck, and slipped it beneath his shirt. He felt emboldened by its weight. Checking his wristwatch, he pulled his cell phone from his pocket. Isaac waited patiently until a voice answered on the other end.

"Munson Financial, Sebastian speaking."

"This is Isaac Weld."

"I expected your call an hour ago, Mr. Weld."

"Yes, well, I was dealing with an unfortunate obstacle."

"Has this obstacle been removed?"

He glanced at the pool of blood that spread out in a circle on the floor. "It has. I'm ready to make the transfer that we spoke about previously."

"I can do that now if you like."

"Please do."

"The fee that we discussed will apply."

"That's fine."

"And you want to transfer the entire balance?"

"Yes."

"Very well. Eight hundred and twenty million dollars is being transferred from your Swiss bank account to an offshore account in the British Virgin Islands as agreed. It should only take a few moments."

"And this will be untraceable?"

"Yes, as I stated earlier."

"What about the other issue we discussed?"

"I have taken care of the details, and it is no longer a joint account."

"I don't foresee that being a problem, but I must cover all my bases."

"Of course, sir. All of my clients are careful men such as yourself. As a last precaution I need you to reconfirm your current account number."

Isaac rattled off a twenty-one digit bank account number beginning with CHkk, Switzerland's international banking code.

"Number confirmed. It will take about thirty seconds to transfer the full balance to your new account number—"

"I would prefer," Isaac interrupted, "that you not say it aloud."

"Of course. Please wait. I will let you know when the transfer is complete."

Isaac stood before the picture window in the *Hotel Le Bristol*. The previously arranged rendezvous with the Broker was no longer of interest to him. Now that Alex was out of the way, things were going to be different.

"Transfer complete, Mr. Weld."

"And the account will be active immediately?"

"Yes. You received the package I sent to you?"

"Yes."

"And you have your cards?"

"Yes."

"Then you and I have no further need of each other. Unless you need my services in the future we will not be speaking again, Mr. Weld."

"I prefer it that way."

"It's been a pleasure doing business with you."

Isaac flipped his phone shut, stuffed a small duffel bag with a few personal belongings, and left the room. Their suite was booked for three days, and he would be in another country by the time Alex's body was discovered. Isaac left his brother behind without a backward glance. Had he bothered to take the time, he would have been in for a great surprise.

Abby slept better on the flight to Paris than she had for a month at home. Perhaps it was the luxuries of first class, or the Tylenol PM she requested.

It was late morning by the time she found herself wandering the streets of Paris's shopping district, slightly bewildered and feeling the effects of jet lag. Despite six hours of solid sleep, her body insisted it was the middle of the night.

Abby stopped before Notre Dame Cathedral, known as the heart of Paris. Distances to anywhere in the city were measured from the cathedral, it being "point zero" for all French roads. It was a massive, ornate building, French Gothic in style, but not as gaudy as many scattered throughout Europe.

What held her attention were the ornate stained-glass windows, so reminiscent of the chapel across the street from her apartment.

Abby sat on a stone bench in the courtyard and dialed an international number on her iPhone. She counted the number of rings on the other end. Just as the message clicked on, it occurred to her that she had not really sorted through just what she wanted to say.

"Leave a message. I might get back to you." The familiar, yet brisk sound of her father's voice was just as startling to her on the answering machine as it was in real life.

"Dad, it's me," she said, realizing she'd been silent for several seconds after the beep. "I need your help. Please call my cell as soon as you can. This is important."

Her hope of actually connecting with him on the phone was slim, but she had to try. Things would be more difficult now. Abby took a deep breath and tried to gather her thoughts. Once again her eyes drifted toward the old church.

For a moment she was tempted to enter and offer a prayer for help. The task before her seemed impossible. Yet even as she looked with longing at the ancient place of worship, she could not urge her feet to move in that direction.

Abby tugged at her ear and studied her iPhone for a moment. Then she hailed a cab.

"I just want to get one thing straight," the Broker said, struggling to maintain a level tone on his cell. He sat in an open-air café, enjoying a light breakfast while Wülf stood a short distance away. His cheeks were flushed, and he gripped the phone tightly in his left hand. "You're changing the plan?"

"Yes," replied the voice of Isaac Weld on the other line.

"That won't happen."

"If you want your diamond it will."

"Are you threatening me, Mr. Weld?"

"Yes, I am."

"That is a dangerous proposition."

"If you want your diamond you will meet me at the rendezvous point in ten minutes."

Isaac hung up. The Broker shifted in his chair and looked at Wülf. "When this is over, I want him dead. Do you understand?"

"Perfectly."

Abby craned her neck and took in a charming hotel snuggled on the *Rue Du Faubourg Saint-Honore*. Each of the many windows was fitted with a wrought-iron flower box, now devoid of foliage. The glass front doors were trimmed in brass and welcomed guests into the elegant lobby.

Abby fingered her iPhone and pushed her way through the double doors, feeling at once underdressed. Reproductions of classic French paintings hung on the walls, and busts of French kings sat in niches, bathed in display lighting. Along the walls display cases featured Henry Winston and Pierre Cartier jewelry.

Abby would never have seen her father had he not stopped in the middle of the lobby to check a missed call on his cell phone. She flinched. Could it really be her father? Unmistakably. He was tall, his black hair tinged with gray at the temples. He wore a trim three-piece suit and a scowl. Abby could not remember the last time she had seen her father smile.

The Broker was not at all pleased to hear the message on his voice mail. Just as he hung up the phone, he lifted his eyes and saw her. Abby stood just inside the entrance of *Hotel Le Bristol*, watching him nervously.

"Dad!" she called out, her face at once hopeful and hesitant.

Douglas Mitchell, the man known to many as the Broker, could not control the look of fear that spread across his face.

27

Alex rolled onto his stomach, feeling as though a pitchfork had impaled the side of his head. While Isaac had made his call, Alex had played dead, struggling to stay conscious, so that he could control his breathing. If Isaac had known Alex lived, his brother would have unloaded another round into him, albeit as badly aimed as the first.

"He always was a lousy shot," Alex groaned, rising onto his hands and knees.

A swath of fire burned above his left ear, but he dared not touch it for fear of what he would find. Once on his hands and knees, Alex rocked back and forth gently, like a child learning to crawl. The bathroom was only fifteen feet away, but it may as well have been in Montana.

Alex crawled forward slowly, blood running down his cheek and dripping from his nose. Even on all fours he was dizzy, and spots swam before his eyes. Only when his hand met the cool marble of the bathroom floor did he lift his head. He sat back on his heels, grabbed the edge of the sink, and pulled himself into a standing position.

The bullet had ripped open a gash three inches long and nearly an inch wide above his left ear. Thankfully, it missed his temple by a hair's breadth. Alex ran his fingers over the wound, pressing gently as he looked for further damage. He took a trembling breath and teetered against the sink.

That was close.

What came next would not be fun, but it was necessary. Wincing, he pinched the skin together to close the gap. Blood oozed through his fingers and ran down the back of his hand. He stumbled to the minibar and grabbed a travel-size bottle of vodka. Back in the bathroom, Alex grabbed the sewing kit set out with the shampoo and hand lotion. It would be a quick fix that wouldn't last for long, but he didn't have time to find a doctor.

The black thread in the sewing kit could hardly be compared to medical sutures, but he had no choice. It took several attempts to thread the needle with shaky fingers, but he finally slipped the flimsy thread through the eye. Alex took a deep breath and dumped the bottle of vodka over his wound. He tucked his chin against his chest and held onto the sink until his knuckles turned white; the pain seared his skin like a branding iron. Tears dripped from his eyes and splattered into the bloody sink.

Alex took a deep breath, raised the needle, and stitched up the wound. He did it more by touch than sight, knowing full well that he was making a mess of things, but his main concern at the moment was to stop the bleeding. It took him ten minutes. His handiwork wasn't pretty, but it was effective.

He dared a quick glance at the clock, noting that Isaac had been gone for thirty minutes. He had to hurry. Peeling off his bloody clothes, he tossed them on the floor. He climbed into the shower and rinsed the blood from his head as carefully as possible so as not to damage his makeshift sutures.

Dizzy, he dried off and pulled on a pair of jeans and a tee shirt. He willed himself to remain conscious. To combat the nausea Alex forced himself to eat the rest of his breakfast. Then he chased down a few Tylenol with a glass of orange juice.

A linen table napkin folded into a rectangle made a fine bandage; he pressed it against the wound and covered his head with a baseball cap in case it started bleeding again.

If he had heard Isaac's money transfer orders correctly, he was operating on borrowed time and an empty bank account. Maybe, just maybe, he could intercept his brother before it was too late.

Abby could not remember the last time she had seen her father face-to-face. She also could not remember him ever looking less pleased to see her.

"Dad?" It was more of a question than a title.

"What are you doing here?" He finished the distance between them and took hold of her elbow, ushering her into a small seating area off the lobby.

"You said in your email that you would be in Paris." He grimaced, but she continued. "I need your help. Something's happened."

Alex Weld kept a firm grip on the handrail in the elevator as he descended to the first floor of *Hotel Le Bristol*. A deep, searing pain burned his skull, and his arms and legs argued against what he asked them to do. Cold beads of sweat formed an oil slick on his forehead, soaking through the baseball cap.

The narrow hallway joined the hotel lobby through an elaborate art gallery. It was the perfect place to watch for Isaac and the Broker.

His body, weak from blood loss, lagged several steps behind his mind, sharply alert from pain. He saw Abby and the Broker long before he could get his legs to stop moving toward them. He was not sure whether it was luck or accident that prevented either of them from seeing him, but he used the opportunity to step behind a large, square column, less than ten feet away. They spoke in strained whispers, emotion filling the air.

Although they bantered back and forth for several moments, Alex heard only a single word: *Dad*. It took a few seconds for it to register.

Seeing Abby in this place startled him. Alex leaned his head against the cool stone, putting the pieces together. The Broker had used them both.

———— ❦ ————

Douglas Mitchell hurried Abby to an open table tucked in the corner and pulled her into one of the plush chairs. He tossed an occasional glance over his shoulder.

His voice was neither kind nor gentle. "Why are you here?"

Abby recoiled from his tone. "Someone stole the Hope Diamond."

"How?"

"I don't know how. I was wearing it while I gave my speech, and then the lights went out and someone snatched it from around my neck."

Anger washed over his face, but he said nothing.

Abby dropped her eyes. "I'm losing my job over this."

"You think?"

"I thought you might be able to help." She stood up, suddenly desperate to escape his presence. "Apparently, I was wrong."

Douglas Mitchell grabbed her arm and pulled her back to the table. "I just don't know what you want me to do about it, Abby."

"I want you to help me."

"How would you suggest I do that?"

"You know people."

He did not respond, but watched Abby through narrowed eyes, waiting for her to continue.

"Nothing happens in the art world that you don't know about."

"I wouldn't exactly classify the Hope Diamond as art," he said.

"It's close enough, and you know it. You can find out what happened."

"I don't know that I want to get tangled up in this mess."

"Would you just get out of your self-preservation mode for one second and look at me. I'm your daughter, for God's sake, and I have never asked you for anything. *Never*. I need you on this one, Dad."

After a long silence, he conceded. "Okay. I'll do what I can."

"Thank you," she said, relief overwhelming her.

"But I can't do anything about it right now. You caught me right in the middle of something."

Her voice wavered. "What can be more important than . . . this?" Abby had almost said *me*.

"I wasn't expecting you."

"Obviously, *Dad*. We're not exactly close."

He ground his teeth and looked at his watch. "Look, I need to make a call. Wait here."

"How long?"

"Just wait."

She didn't want to oblige him but had no other option. "All right."

He waved toward a waiter. "Can I get a bottle of Pinot Noir for the lady?"

Without another word, Douglas Mitchell walked away, just as the waiter returned with the bottle of wine and two glasses.

⟨⟨⟩⟩

His mind spinning, the Broker punched in a number on his cell phone. In less than five minutes a carefully woven plan had disintegrated.

"Wülf!" he barked, as soon as his driver answered. "There has been a change of plans. I need you to pick me up. We're leaving immediately."

"*Ja,*" Wülf replied.

⟨⟨⟩⟩

The waiter poured Abby a glass of wine, and she reached for it with a trembling hand. After murmuring her thanks, he left to attend another table. She sat in the chair, lips pressed into a thin line, her finger tracing the rim of her glass. When someone dropped into the chair beside her, Abby jumped. It was a moment before she recognized the ashen face of Alex Weld. The hurtful emotions stirred up by seeing her father again soon melted into shock. The wine glass slipped from her fingers and tumbled through the air, splashing deep red wine over both their feet before it hit the tile floor and shattered.

"Daddy wasn't much help in getting the diamond back, was he?" Alex said, his words rash and laced with anger.

Her mouth dropped open. "What are you doing here?"

"Let's just say I'm on a business trip."

The Alex Weld she knew was gone, replaced by a cold, sharp man who stared at her with unnerving blue eyes.

The truth settled in layers. "You took it?"

"Guilty as charged. Now, where is your father?"

Abby recoiled, her heart trying to catch up with her head. "What does my father have to do with this?"

"You tell me." Alex reached for her arm, but she jerked it away. He closed his eyes and pursed his lips. "Listen, Abby, I'm not going to hurt you," he said, his voice taking on an apologetic tone.

She shook her head and blinked back tears. "You already have."

"I need your help."

A strange, cold laugh filled the air. Abby barely recognized it as her own. "Haven't I helped you enough?"

"Your father hired me to steal the diamond. I have to find out where he's going."

Abby leaned back in her chair and crossed her arms over her chest. She regarded him with disdain.

"I'm telling the truth."

"Alex, I'm beginning to wonder if you have ever told me the truth."

He reached into his pocket and pulled out an antique gold ring of woven vines and set it gently on the table.

Abby's eyes grew large and she gasped.

"Pretty ring don't you think?"

"That's mine!"

"I know." A sad smile washed over his face as he spun the ring around his middle finger.

She looked back and forth from him to the ring. "You?"

He nodded. "Who gave you that ring, Abby?"

"My father."

"Your father, huh? Let me guess. Last October?"

"Yes, it was a birthday present, but how—"

"Where do you think he got it?"

"I don't know. Bought it?"

"Sort of. You could say he bought it from me, and I stole it from a little old lady in Ireland who wore it every year on St. Patrick's Day. Poor old bat probably doesn't even know it's missing."

"How could you?"

"I was just doing my job."

Abby stood and lunged at him across the table, pounding her fists on his chest. "You're a thief and a liar!"

The other patrons in the gallery turned to stare at the scene, whispering among themselves about unrestrained and rude Americans.

Alex pulled her gently into the chair next to him. "The inscription says, 'Alligator Food' doesn't it?"

"You could have read that after you stole it from me."

"And the box? It came inside a pewter box with red velvet lining. What about that? You didn't have it with you in Rio."

Tears slipped unhindered down her cheeks. "How could you know about that?"

"Because I'm telling the truth."

The black Mercedes, carrying Douglas Mitchell, pulled around to the entrance of *Hotel Le Bristol*.

He leaned forward, addressing Wülf. "Don't do anything until I give the command. I'll let you know when I want him taken out."

Wülf nodded and parked as a lone figure stepped from behind a manicured topiary.

"Get in," the Broker demanded, rolling down the window.

Isaac settled into the dark gray leather seat. He avoided the fierce glance Wülf gave him in the rearview mirror.

"What do you think you're doing?" Douglas Mitchell asked.

Isaac grinned. "Let's just say I've gone into business for myself."

"What do you mean? Where is Alex?"

"My brother is dead."

Mitchell narrowed his eyes. "What exactly are you up to, Mr. Weld?"

"I am eliminating all the obstacles in my path, including partners and middle men like yourself, Mr. Mitchell." The Broker's eyes widened. "Oh yes, I know exactly who you are. As a matter of fact, I know everything about you."

"I would be very careful if I were you."

Isaac pulled the gun from his coat pocket and set it on his leg. "I'm tired of doing your dirty work and watching you make ten times more than I do for these little trinkets. Your services are no longer needed."

Douglas Mitchell began to shake, not from fear, but rage. "Then what am I doing here?" he growled between clenched teeth.

"You will take me to the rendezvous point so I can auction off our little diamond to the Collectors."

"No chance."

Isaac pressed the gun into the Broker's temple and tilted his head to one side, watching him seethe. Wülf observed the interaction but did nothing to intervene.

"What do I get out of it?" Mitchell asked, eyes darting between Isaac's expressionless face and the lethal weapon in his hand.

"You get to live."

28

EVALYN WALSH MCLEAN STOOD ON THE BALCONY OUTSIDE HER SUITE at the *Hotel le Bristol*, overlooking the *rue du Faubourg Saint-Honoré*. The narrow street, home to virtually every major boutique in Paris, began as a road extending from the Louvre and snaked its way through the high-end fashion district. Although somewhat cramped, it was nonetheless considered one of the most exclusive streets in the world. Mrs. McLean would not have considered staying anywhere else while in Paris.

From her balcony looking over the hotel gardens, she had breathtaking views of both the Eiffel Tower and the Louvre. Her long, elegant fingers gently wrapped around the wrought-iron balcony rail. The air was mild, temperate this late in September, and a faint breeze wafted scents of jasmine and gardenia from the garden below.

A few tendrils of her dark hair, which was curled and pinned high on her head, hung stylishly to the nape of her neck and brushed the three strands of pearls. She wore a light-blue silk gown, sashed at her narrow waist, and white lace-up boots. Tall and confident, she overlooked the city, a smile playing at the corners of her deep red lips.

It was in moments like this that Evalyn allowed herself to remember that she had been born the daughter of a poor Irish miner, living in squalor in the foothills of the Rocky Mountains. Then, in the most improbable, but often dreamed of, stroke of luck, she landed in her present life of luxury. Miners don't often strike the mother lode, but when they do, it changes their lives and that of their children forever. Evalyn closed her eyes and took a deep breath, drinking in the scent of what wealth could buy.

"Darling, he's here," her husband, Ned, called. Stretched out on a *chaise longue*, a cigar dangled precariously from the corner of his mouth. "The butler is bringing him up."

She turned, resting lightly against the railing, but she was in no hurry to make her appearance. Evalyn studied their room with an appreciative eye. It was the best hotel suite money could buy: elaborate woodwork, red toile curtains that draped the windows and puddled on the floor; matching bed linens; lush white wall-to-wall carpet, and a private bath of white carrara marble. Just then the butler rapped on the door.

"*Entrez*," Ned called, rising from the chaise.

Édourd swung open the paneled doors leading to the McLean suite and stepped aside as he ushered in their guest. "*Monsieur Pierre Cartier*," he said with a slight bow.

Evalyn observed Cartier with muted interest. He was a demure sort of man, self-possessed, and uninterested in making a statement of wealth with his physical appearance. Although well-dressed and of pleasant demeanor, he could have passed as any French businessman, as opposed to the most notable jewel merchant in the world. On that day he wore a modest three-piece suit of light gray wool, covered by a charcoal overcoat and black bowler hat. His wide smile showed large teeth, giving him an unfortunate resemblance to a horse. It was the small box he carried, wrapped in brown paper and sealed with wax that was of particular interest to Evalyn. Cartier held the package out before him, giving its entrance to the suite more priority than his own.

Ned crossed the room, shaking Cartier's hand firmly, while Evalyn swept in from the balcony, her dress lightly trailing the floor. "Pierre," she cooed. "So wonderful to see you again!"

He took her hand and brushed his lips against her fingers. "Madame McLean. Always a pleasure."

Evalyn beamed, never shy about receiving attention from the opposite sex. "Please do come in."

Pierre Cartier followed Evalyn and Ned into the suite, and they settled themselves in the living area.

"I trust that you are enjoying your vacation in France?" Cartier said.

"Oh, yes," she gushed. "Just yesterday we drove the most marvelous yellow Fiat coupe from Vichy. We had the top down the entire way. It was just *glorious*!"

"Vichy was it? Gambling I take it?" Pierre asked, a mischievous light in his eyes.

"My wife's favorite pastime," Ned jibed, offering Cartier a fine Cuban cigar.

"And a profitable one at that, darling," she said. "I added seventy thousand dollars to the coffers."

"No doubt money that will be spent before Monsieur Cartier leaves us today."

Evalyn turned her gaze to the parcel in Cartier's lap. "Do tell me what you have brought me today, Pierre. You know I am a great fan of yours, given that marvelous gem you sold us on our honeymoon."

"Ah, yes," Cartier said. "The Star of the East. Ninety-four carats, pure white, and in the shape of a tear drop, if I remember correctly."

"You astound me, Pierre. Such a mind for gems!" Evalyn exclaimed. "But, please, don't keep me waiting any longer. I simply can't stand it."

Ned rolled his eyes as he clipped the end of his cigar.

Pierre looked at Evalyn, a mysterious smirk on his face. "Tell me, Mrs. McLean, do you know anything of the Turkish Revolution?"

"Something of it. We were in Constantinople for part of our honeymoon, and we stayed with Sultan Abdul Hamid. Why he had the most glorious emerald and diamond studded porcelain cups!"

"Indeed. It was during your honeymoon that we first met."

"A most fortunate event in my life," she grinned.

"You told me then that you had seen a jewel in the harem, a great blue stone that rested against the throat of the sultan's favorite."

She thought for a moment, trying to recall those days spent with the sultan. They were, by this point, lost in a haze of alcohol and frequent heroin use. After a moment or two, she said, "It seems to me that I did see that stone."

"The woman who had that jewel from the sultan's hand was stabbed to death," Pierre said, leaning forward, his gaze locked on Evalyn.

She sat up stiffly in her chair. "Is that so?"

Cartier proceeded to tell her of Jean-Baptiste Tavernier and his journey to India, and she took special interest when he recounted the grisly deaths of King Louis XVI

279

and Marie Antoinette. Evalyn hung on every word and was not aware that Pierre Cartier bent the facts slightly to suit his purpose. The main players and general time frame of his story were all correct.

"Do continue," she said. "This is most fascinating."

"The stone disappeared after the Revolution. Simply put, Mrs. McLean, it was stolen," he said, a finger running lightly over the yet unopened package in his lap.

Evalyn glanced eagerly back and forth from Cartier to the brown paper box.

"It is my understanding," Cartier said. "That Tavernier had stolen the gem from a Hindu, perhaps a Hindu god. A most unfortunate decision, indeed, since Tavernier was later torn to pieces and eaten by wild dogs during a trip to Russia."

"Why, Monsieur Cartier, you make it sound as though all the violence of the French Revolution was just a repercussion of that Hindu idol's wrath."

"I am simply relaying the story of what I am about to offer you."

"And yet you do it in a most entertaining way."

Ned remained silent. He had long since learned that when Evalyn put her mind to something, there was little use in arguing. Eventually, she would get her way.

"It was some time later that the diamond appeared in London in the possession of the Hope family," Cartier said. "Lord Francis Hope's fortune as well as his marriage dissolved. The diamond was sold to Selim Habib and the Turkish sultan."

"I must see the thing!" Evalyn implored, nearly bursting from her ottoman.

With great flourish, Cartier unwrapped his package, breaking the wax seals and artfully unfolding the brown paper wrapping. Inside lay a black jeweler's box. He turned it to face Evalyn and flipped open the lid, revealing the stunning blue diamond.

With shaking hands, Evalyn reached out to take the box as Cartier continued his bloody tale.

"Now I simply can't vouch for everything I am about to tell you, Mrs. McLean," he said, "but I do believe it is worth solemn consideration. This diamond is supposed to be ill-favored and is said to bring bad luck to anyone who wears or even touches it. Selim Habib is said to have drowned when his ship sank after selling the diamond to the sultan. And we all know about the knife blade that sliced through Marie Antoinette's throat. Lord Hope himself had plenty of troubles that a superstitious soul might trace back to a heathen idol's wrath. And there are others, Mrs. McLean. Many others."

Evalyn lifted the diamond from its box, absorbed in the way light bounced from the dark blue facets of the gem.

"Bad luck objects are lucky for me," she murmured.

"Ah yes," Cartier said. "Madame told me that before, and I remembered. Myself, I think superstitions of the kind we speak of are baseless. Yet, one must admit, they are amusing."

Evalyn held the jewel up to the light. As she did, a resolve spread across her face. "I must have it."

29

ALEX AND ABBY SAT AT THEIR TABLE IN THE LOBBY, BROODING. ALEX swayed in his chair, trying to control the dizziness that threatened to topple him at any moment. As he rocked from side to side, his forearm brushed against Abby's, sending chill bumps across his skin.

"Every time I come to this city I understand why people believe in ghosts," he said.

"Been here a lot have you?" The sharp edge in her voice left little room for any whimsy he might impart.

Alex chose to ignore the venom and continued. "Everything here is so old. Every stone has a history. Our entire country is not half as old as this one city."

"Your point?"

" Generations of men and women have lived in this very place. You can almost feel their living history all around you."

"The only thing I feel right now is anger, Alex."

He turned and watched her gleaming hair fall across her shoulders. He had never wanted to kiss her more than he did at that moment, but he also knew there had never been a time it would be less welcomed. Pain and betrayal etched her face; he almost could not remember the shape of her mouth when she smiled.

Alex dropped his head and stared at his hands. "I didn't know he was your father."

"Sure you didn't."

He thought about his visit to the DMV and what he had learned there. "At least not until two days ago."

"Would it have mattered?"

"Not at first." He cringed at the truth. "But later on when I . . . yes, it would have mattered then."

"Would it have stopped you?"

He was silent.

"I thought not."

Alex could feel Abby stiffen next to him, and he knew she was about to leave.

"Please, don't go." He heard the desperate, pleading tone in his voice and felt weak for it.

"I told my father I would wait here."

Alex caught her eyes and tried to communicate that she hoped for the impossible. Her façade of strength was crumbling, and her lips began to tremble. Alex turned away so she wouldn't be ashamed of her own sorrow.

"He isn't coming back, is he?" she finally asked, just a word or two away from tears.

Alex shook his head.

"What do I do now?"

He grabbed her shoulders and pulled her closer. "Trust me."

She snorted. "I did."

"Do you care about your father, Abby?"

She hesitated for a moment. "Yes," she whispered.

"Then you have to help me find him."

"I don't feel very inclined to help you do anything right now."

"Then your father is going to die."

"What do you mean?" She looked up, startled.

"For the last ten years your father has been a broker for a group of men known as the Collectors."

"I'm listening."

"The Collectors put in an order. Your father—the Broker—gives my brother and me the marching orders, and we steal the piece. For the last ten years we have met him right here at the hotel to make the swap. He pays us, then takes the item back to the Collectors and auctions it off among them."

"I still don't understand why you think I can help."

"Because my brother tried to plant a bullet in my head this morning to remove me from the equation. We meet at this spot at exactly noon." Alex glanced at his watch. "That was fifteen minutes ago. And as you can plainly see, your father and my brother are nowhere to be found. So the plan has been derailed, and a lot of people are going to die before this is all over."

"Die?"

"Yes, die. This has gone far beyond the theft of some little trinket now. We're talking about the unraveling of the largest theft ring in the world. Don't you think they'd go to great lengths to keep their secret?"

"So your brother wanted you out of the picture?"

"You could say that."

"What? No honor among thieves?"

"Apparently not."

"How do I know you're telling the truth?"

Alex grimaced and peeled off the baseball cap. The bandage on the side of his head was soaked with fresh blood. "He didn't just try to shoot me, Abby. I was about two millimeters away from having my brains splattered on the wall."

She recoiled at the sight of his blood.

"You think I got what I deserved?" he asked.

"It crossed my mind," she said, with a weak smile. She turned away from him.

He grabbed her shoulders firmly. "Look, I know you could kill me yourself right now. Fair enough. I deserve it. But you need to decide what you're going to do because we don't have time to feel sorry for ourselves. That diamond will be gone forever in a matter of hours. How badly do you want it?"

"What happens if we find them?"

Alex grimaced. "I've got some unfinished business with my brother, and you get the diamond back. I'll do everything within my power to help you return it to the Smithsonian."

30

Douglas Mitchell led the way onto his private jet, parked on the tarmac at Charles de Gaulle International Airport, followed closely by Isaac Weld. Wülf disappeared into the cockpit and shut the door.

"I'm going to trust you just this once," Isaac said, reclining into the soft tan leather chair, "that you're telling me the truth about our destination." He pulled the gun from the inside pocket of his coat.

Douglas Mitchell had witnessed more than enough of Isaac's arrogance, and his tolerance was wearing thin. "Do you have a choice?"

"Do you?

The Broker cocked his head to one side and surveyed Isaac. "Would you like to know the truth, Mr. Weld?"

"I rarely have use for the truth."

"The *truth* is," the Broker continued, "you need me."

Isaac stared over the tip of his gun barrel.

"You may think that you know who I am and who I work for, but you know very little. You can't find them without me. You can't sell your merchandise without me. They will not listen to you without me. So," he said with a curt smile, "if I were you, I would put that little toy away, and the two of us can get down to business. I will make my offer once. Before you answer, I would remind you again, I do not like to be threatened."

Alex shivered, his jaw clenched tight to stop his chattering teeth. Dizziness swirled in his head, and he wobbled in the chair.

"You don't look so good," Abby said.

"I feel worse."

"What do you suggest we do?"

His mind raced through every option; his eyes shifted back and forth as though reading an unseen list. Finally, he squeezed them shut and shook his head. "There's nothing we can do," he muttered. "It's over."

"What do you mean, it's over?"

His face clouded. "There's no way we can find that diamond now. I'm sorry," he whispered. For the first time since meeting her, Alex allowed himself to feel regret. It hurt a great deal more than the searing wound above his ear.

Abby returned his gaze, but with a great deal less intensity. She struggled to keep a smile from spilling onto her face. "Alex—"

He winced at the reprimanding tone.

"I never said I didn't know where the diamond was," she continued, the satisfied note in her voice quite evident.

"What?"

"How much of a fool do you take me for?"

He said nothing, only just beginning to realize how badly he had underestimated her.

"Do you really think I would take the diamond out of its case, much less wear the thing, without taking appropriate measures? Do you think I'm that stupid?"

"I don't understand."

Abby pulled the iPhone from her pocket and handed it to him. Displayed on the screen was a grid of green lines with two red lights, one blinking and the other stationary.

"A GPS? That's how you tracked us here?"

She nodded.

His eyes filled with new light. "How far does it reach?"

"Anywhere on the planet," she said. "I know its exact location."

Alex looked at her with newfound respect. Suddenly, Abby Mitchell was transformed into someone he didn't know. He replayed the scenes from the event of the night before in his mind. "You weren't really having trouble with the clasp, were you?"

"No."

"Impressive." Alex returned her smile with an appreciative nod. "Okay, so the blinking light is the diamond on its way to God knows where, and the other light?"

"Me," Abby answered.

He looked her over carefully. "Where's the transmitter?"

She pushed her hair away from her face and touched one of the diamond stud earrings. Abby took the iPhone from him and tapped the screen a few times. "We've only got about five minutes to figure this out. They're at the airport right now, and my guess is they won't be there by the time we arrive."

31

LOUISVILLE, KENTUCKY, MAY 18, 1919

EVALYN WALSH MCLEAN WOKE AS THE DOOR TO HER SUITE SQUEAKED open. She watched Ned stumble into the room, unshaven and disheveled. Sunrise glowed on the horizon, announcing the arrival of a new day. She had lain awake most of the night, wondering where her husband might be. By his drunken appearance, she now had a fairly good idea.

Ned attempted to sneak to the bathroom without being noticed. Evalyn sat up in bed, the covers falling away to reveal a white satin nightgown. Around her neck she wore the Hope Diamond.

"Where have you been?" she snapped.

He staggered to a stop and ran into the back of a chair. "What?"

"Where have you been?"

"Celebrating our victory," he slurred. "Sir Barton won the Derby, darling."

"Yes. Two weeks ago."

"But the money. How much did we win again?"

"Eighty-five thousand dollars."

"Yes. Yes. That's what I was celebrating."

"From your condition, I'd say you were out spending it."

The color in Ned's cheeks rose, exacerbated by the flush of alcohol. "Don't lecture me about spending money!" he roared. "You're the one who spent $180,000 on that stupid blue rock."

Evalyn slid out of bed and grabbed her dressing gown from the back of a nearby chair. Her hair, now cut in a fashionable bob, fell into her eyes. She flicked it away and crossed the floor barefoot. Standing before Ned, hands on her hips, she thrust out her chin.

"I want to go home," she demanded.

"I'm not done here."

"Then I will leave without you."

Spectacularly drunk though he was, Ned was still a great deal stronger than Evalyn. He grabbed her thin arm and pulled her close, fingers digging into the skin. "You won't be going anywhere," he hissed, sour breath flooding her face, "without me."

Evalyn grimaced and turned her nose, yet she did not back down. "The children need us. We've been gone for a month."

"I'm sure the children are perfectly fine. Spoiled, in fact."

"What about Vinson? He's sick."

"That little retard?"

Evalyn hurled the palm of her right hand against Ned's cheek; the sound cracked like lightning through the room.

"Epilepsy!" she screamed. "He has epilepsy!"

The shadow of regret passed over Ned's face. Yet he gripped her arm until she gasped in pain. "We're not going."

Unable to look at his rage-contorted face, she dropped her eyes. For a moment she thought the dark red smudge on his collar was dirt. It took her but a moment to realize it was lipstick, and certainly not hers. The last kiss Ned and Evalyn shared came nine months before their youngest child was born. She understood then why he did not want to leave.

She tugged at his collar with her free hand. "Who is she?"

"What are you talking about?"

"I may be a fool for having married you, Ned McLean, but I am not stupid. Who is she?"

He glared at her for a moment, then released his grip, and shoved her away. "Get dressed," he spat. "You always did look like a hag in the morning."

McLean Estate, Washington, D.C.

The McLean residence, benignly named *Friendship*, rested on seventy-six acres just outside Washington, D.C. Ned's father bought the estate years earlier for its historic mansion. George Washington was said to have visited the mansion on occasion, and John McLean had taken a fancy to the idea that he could live in a home where presidents once slumbered. Many wondered if he was secretly considering a bid for the White House.

After Ned and Evalyn moved in after their honeymoon, she threw herself into renovating the house and grounds with great fervor. Open countryside converted to manicured lawns. She supervised the planting of new cedars throughout the estate, framing driveways, parks, and recreation areas. Fountains sprouted almost magically across the rolling terrain. Yet she was not content to stop just with the flora. Evalyn McLean wanted fauna as well. As much for her own fancy as that of her children, she collected a menagerie of donkeys, goats, cows, ponies, and all kinds of fowl. Her own favorites, however, were a pet llama, monkey, and parrot. The endless noise and mess of the McLean zoo drove Ned crazy, and in recent years he had spent less and less time with the family at the estate.

For their children, particularly nine-year-old Vinson, the grounds of the McLean estate were a never-ending wonderland. Born with his mother's stubbornness and his father's bent toward adventure, Vinson disregarded the accepted rules of conduct at the estate and wandered about as he pleased.

Slight of frame, yet sharp of mind, it was an unending frustration to Vinson that he could control neither mind nor body during one of his frequent epileptic seizures. Even at such a young age, he understood the look of worry in his mother's eyes, as well as the disgust in his father's. Two years earlier he took to escaping from his nanny so he could explore the acreage around the mansion, free of interference. One of his favorite places to loiter was near the front of the estate. He would climb the tallest tree, look out over the road, and watch the traffic as it passed. He told himself stories about the vehicle's occupants and where they might be going.

That is exactly what Vinson was up to that warm afternoon in mid-May. He lay on his belly, stretched halfway out on a great limb that overhung the road. Their old gardener, Henry Graber, was pulled to the side of the road, changing a flat tire. Vinson did not know why his father fired the man, but he heard the argument all the way up to his second-floor bedroom. Henry did not look pleased to have broken down right in front of the McLean family estate.

Vinson's mischievous streak rose to the surface, so he shimmied down the tree and snuck up behind the car. While Henry fiddled with a tire iron, the small boy crept inside the rear door and grabbed two small ferns from the backseat. He would have gotten away with his crime had his foot not slipped in the gravel beside the road, alerting the old man to his presence.

Knowing he was caught, Vinson darted into the road and ran for the front gates, quite sure that Henry would not dare to cross onto the McLean estate again.

The old man reached for him despite the fact that he was at least fifteen feet away by then. "*No*, Vinson!" he yelled. The gardener was not concerned for his ferns, for he had been a kind man, sorely used by Ned McLean, but rather his fear was caused by the oncoming Ford Wagon with wooden panels.

Vinson heard the concern in Henry's voice and stopped in the middle of the road. Perhaps it was the shock of seeing a moving vehicle at such near proximity, or it may have been the curse of a broken body that caused him to stiffen as his eyes rolled back in his head, unable to move from danger in that split second before the accident.

The Ford hit Vinson going only eight miles an hour, but Henry would forever remember the *thud*, almost wooden, as it collided with the child, knocking him to the ground, his head hitting the concrete. The seizure took full force of his little body, and Vinson lay in the road, twitching. Pandemonium ensued as the gardener and three women inside the car rushed to help the unresponsive boy.

"He came out of nowhere," the driver howled, her face streaked with tears.

With worn, gentle hands, the old man lifted the boy into his arms, calloused fingers kneading his throat, looking for a pulse. "He's still breathing. We must get him into the house."

"Who is this child?" asked one of the women.

"His name is Vinson," Henry said, running for the gate. "Son of Ned and Evalyn McLean."

Horror struck the three women, their mouths agape. As he scrambled through the gate, Henry could only hear pieces of their hushed conversation as they traipsed after him.

"That woman owns the Hope Diamond . . ."

"They say the thing is cursed . . ."

". . . not the child's fault he has such a foolish mother."

Without knocking, the old man burst through the front door of the mansion. At the sight of him holding the limp child in his arms, the entire household burst into a frenzy of activity. It was not until some time later that Henry realized the women who hit the child made a hasty departure once they saw that a physician had been called. Amidst the crisis, no one bothered to ask their names.

It was the butler's idea to call Dr. Brewster, a retired Army surgeon who vacationed in the area during that time of year. He arrived in a matter of minutes, face set in a permanent frown, bedside manor intimidating. Yet his hands were gentle as he lifted little Vinson's head from the pillow, pushing and prodding lightly with his fingers. He did everything he could to rouse the boy, but to no avail. Dr. Brewster parted Vinson's eyes gently, taking note that his pupils were fixed and enlarged—not responding to light.

With a tenderness that belied his gruff demeanor, he gently set the boy's head back on the pillow and rose from the bed. "His brain is swelling. This child's condition is serious and will decline with great speed. Where are his parents?"

"At the Kentucky Derby," the butler gulped.

"Summon them immediately. He needs emergency surgery and will most likely not survive the day," Dr. Brewster said, stuffing his medical instruments back inside his leather bag. "I will take him to the hospital immediately."

Henry and the butler looked at one another, understanding what a call to Ned McLean would mean. A dread, only matched by the fate of little Vinson, settled over them both.

"Dr. Brewster," the old man said as he rested a hand on the doctor's shoulder. "I think it would be a good idea if you made the call to Mr. McLean. He will take this news better from you than he would from any of the staff on the estate."

The butler gave Henry a look of appreciation, forever earning his gratitude.

"If you think it best," Dr. Brewster said. "Can you direct me to the telephone?"

———

Ned spent the greater part of the morning asleep, stretched across the bed on his stomach, still wearing his disheveled clothes. Evalyn cried in the tub, covered to her neck in warm soapy water, the salty tears coursing down her face. They dripped from her chin to the bathwater like a leaky faucet. She let the tears fall as they may. Rubbing would only give her puffy eyes.

An hour later, wrinkled and shivering, she pulled herself from the tepid water. It took another hour just to choose her pale pink satin gown, shin length and well-tailored. She strung pearls around her neck in layers, the familiar weight of her precious diamond resting against her throat.

Evalyn sat at her dressing table, gazing at her pale face, when the phone rang in the other room. She rose hesitantly, and then sat down again; she was in no mood to speak with anyone.

After six rings Ned shouted from the bedroom, "Won't you get that blasted call?"

"No darling, I will not," she cooed, her voice steady, as she applied another coat of lipstick.

Ned rolled out of bed and stumbled across the room, knocking over furniture as he went. He picked up the receiver.

"Ned McLean," he growled. "Dr. Brewster, I didn't realize you were back in town."

Evalyn's hands went limp and dropped to her lap as she strained to hear the conversation in the other room. Her heart pounded so fast that she could hear the blood rushing through her ears. Nothing but silence from the other room.

"I see. Is he all right? The hospital!" Ned gasped.

The faces of her children rushed through her mind as she listened.

"Yes, yes, Dr. Brewster. We can come home immediately. Thank you."

She heard Ned hang up the phone, but he said nothing. Evalyn finally composed herself enough to rise and walk into the other room. His face was white, and his arms hung at his sides. He did not meet her eyes.

"What happened?" she asked, hearing her own voice quaver despite her attempts at maintaining control.

"Vinson," he murmured.

"Oh, God!" Evalyn cried, collapsing to the bed. "What happened?"

Only then did Ned dare to look at his wife. He paused for a moment and said, "He merely has a bad case of influenza. They are taking him to the hospital for observation."

"My baby!" she wailed, throwing herself backward onto the pillows.

"We'll take the next train, Evalyn."

She sat up, her eyes fierce, "The next train doesn't leave for six hours. I already checked."

He crossed the room, towering over her. "Then I will *charter* one especially for us."

Evalyn would not say in that moment that she loved her husband, but she did appreciate him deeply, or better yet, she appreciated that his money could buy most anything—anything except the assurance that her child would be fine.

Ned changed without bothering to bathe, and they left their suite, leaving instructions at the front desk that their belongings were to be packed and shipped back to Washington on the next train.

Less than an hour later, a brand-new passenger train, consisting of engine, one mail car, two baggage cars, three day coaches, two dining cars, five sleeping cars, and caboose, pulled out of the Louisville train depot. There were only two passengers on board.

―――∞∞∞―――

While Ned and Evalyn McLean traveled through the night on their chartered train, Dr. Brewster was joined by a specialist from Johns Hopkins University, a brain surgeon from Philadelphia, and a physician from Washington.

They unanimously decided that the child's only chance of survival lay in a risky operation to relieve the swelling in his skull. It was performed at once, with all four doctors attending the procedure. Despite a combined one hundred years of surgical experience, little Vinson McLean did not survive the surgery.

"Have you read this?" Ned screamed, pushing the *New York Times* into Evalyn's face.

She turned her face, avoiding the glaring headline that read MCLEAN HEIR KILLED BY AN AUTOMOBILE.

He rattled the paper and held it six inches from his nose. "Let me just read it for you then, my dear." He took a long gulp straight from the bottle of whiskey in his hand before starting. They had buried their first-born child just the day before.

Sobs wracked Evalyn's thin body. She covered her ears with her hands as Ned read the account of Vinson's accident. Surely, if she could not hear him speak, the words would hold no reality.

". . . when news of the death of the boy spread throughout Washington tonight, it was at once remarked that this was another tragedy to be added to the long string of misfortunes that had followed successive owners of the Hope Diamond." Ned finished the article, his voice rising in a crescendo of anger. "Did you hear that, Evalyn? This is all *your* fault!"

"*My* fault! You think this is *my* fault?" she howled. Evalyn grabbed the paper from Ned's hand and wadded it into a ball. "*I* wanted to come home weeks ago. But you insisted on staying so you could fraternize with your little whore! If you had let me come home, this would have never happened!"

Evalyn ducked just in time to avoid the whiskey bottle that spun through the air and shattered on the wall behind her. Ned took a shaky step toward his wife, his hand raised. They locked eyes for a moment, defiant, and then he turned, grabbed his coat, and left the house.

With a wail of agony, Evalyn threw herself face first onto their bed, still wearing the black dress she'd worn to Vinson's funeral the day before. She lay there for some time, sobs wracking her body, until a soft knock rapped on the door.

"Mrs. McLean? Mrs. Florence Harding is here to see you," the butler announced.

Evalyn mumbled a response, and Florence rushed to her side and curled up on the bed next to her. Florence tried to comfort her, but Evalyn was inconsolable. Finally, Florence rose from the bed and summoned the butler.

"How can I help you, Mrs. Harding?"

"Please bring me some laudanum. I know that Evalyn uses it for the pain in her leg." The reality was that Evalyn used it for a great deal more than that, but neither the butler nor Florence Harding would be discussing that fact.

"Yes, ma'am." He opened an ornate cabinet in the corner of the room and picked up a beaker of clear fluid. He poured a generous amount into a crystal goblet.

Florence Harding took the glass from his hand and asked, "Is this too much?"

He met her eyes with a purposeful glance. "It is enough to ensure that Mrs. McLean will sleep for a long time."

"Good," she said. "You may go."

"Gladly," he murmured as he slipped from the room.

"Evalyn, my dear," Florence said. "I want you to take your medicine. It will relieve all manner of pain that you are feeling right now."

For the first time, Evalyn lifted her head from her pillow and looked at her friend. Without a word she grabbed the goblet and drained it in a single gulp.

"That's good, dearest; now you just lay right here. I promise to stay with you." Florence sat on the bed next to Evalyn and rubbed her temples as the grieving mother slipped into painless sleep.

32

"I NEED TO MAKE A CALL." ABBY PUNCHED A SERIES OF NUMBERS INTO the keypad and held the phone to her ear. "Wait here."

Alex watched this new, fascinating woman leave the small café.

"Yes, this is Dr. Abigail Mitchell with the Smithsonian. I need to speak with Director Heaton please," she said, turning her back to Alex.

He strained to hear the rest of what she said, but her words drifted in and out of earshot.

"I'm in Paris. . . . Yes, I'm fine, but I need your help. . . . a plane, chartered, if possible. . . . I know it's a lot to ask, but this is huge. . . . Let me know if you can make it happen. . . . Oh, there's one more thing." She looked at Alex from the corner of her eye. "I'll need a doctor to meet me on the tarmac. Make sure he has sedatives."

In his dealings with her, Alex approached their relationship with the assumption that Abby was a helpless victim, an unfortunate casualty in their plot to steal the diamond. He realized that he had treated her as such, with slight disdain. But as he watched her in action now, Alex wondered how he could have gotten her so wrong.

Normally, he kept a firm grip on his emotions, but his pain and the day's events had sent them ricocheting in a dozen different directions. The only constant was an overpowering affection for Abby that even now he struggled to admit was love. For the first time in his life, Alex Weld desired something he could never have. He had destroyed any possibility of a relationship with her by his actions the day before.

"Alex, are you okay?" Abby asked.

"Don't think so. Lightheaded," he murmured. Sweat dripped from his brow and splattered onto the tile floor. It took him a moment to focus on Abby. He hadn't noticed her return to the table.

"Listen to me." She placed her hands on his cheeks and pulled him closer. "Do you have your passport with you?"

"Back pocket." Her face faded in and out.

Abby pulled the passport from his jeans. "Come with me."

"Where are we going?"

"Do you trust me?"

He hesitated. "Yes."

"Then don't argue." She pulled his ball cap lower on his head, led him through the hotel lobby, and hailed a cab.

"Dangerous," he mumbled. "Cabs . . . crazy drivers . . . putting your life in their hands."

Abby helped him into the backseat of the car and reached over to buckle his seatbelt.

"Can you think of a faster way to get to the airport?"

"Nope."

Alex Weld fainted.

———✕———

When the cab arrived at the airport, a stretcher waited for them beneath the private jet, along with two paramedics and a physician.

"Dr. Mitchell?" the doctor asked, sticking out his hand. "My name is Aaron Baxter. I was told you were in need of medical assistance."

Abby pointed to Alex, now slumped over in the seat. "Not me. Him. He's been shot. I think the bullet grazed his temple."

Alex was barely lucid by the time they got him secured aboard the *Citation II*, a private chartered plane that Director Heaton had secured for Abby. After laying Alex flat on the floor, they ran an IV, cleaned his head wound, and pulled out the makeshift stitches. Because of the doctor's skill in re-stitching the wound, Alex would barely notice the scar when it healed.

Thank God for Interpol. Abby was grateful for the ability to bypass airport security. She watched the procedure, also thankful that Alex remained unconscious. The surgeon tied off the final stitch in Alex's scalp.

"Dr. Mitchell, we only gave him enough sedatives to knock him out for the duration of the surgery. I won't be accompanying you on this trip, so I can't give him any more general anesthesia."

"I understand."

"He'll wake up in the next hour or so, and he won't be feeling very well. Are you comfortable administering oral medication and tending to the bandages?"

Abby nodded. "I'll be fine."

"Once you arrive at your destination, he'll need additional medical care."

The paramedics disposed of the bloodied bandages and tape, and Dr. Baxter handed Abby a bottle of painkillers.

"I was told these orders came straight from the top," Dr. Baxter said. "Director Heaton himself?"

"That's right."

"So what did this guy do? They must want him pretty badly if they're putting him on a flight in this condition."

Abby furrowed her brow. "Yes," she said, "Alex Weld has been wreaking havoc for quite some time."

"Do you want him restrained?"

She gave the doctor a fierce look. "I can handle him."

He chuckled and threw his hands up in mock surrender. "I believe you."

When the medical staff exited the plane, the small flight crew prepared for departure.

Abby settled into her seat, and the pilot came back to confer with her.

"Dr. Mitchell, air traffic control has requested our flight plan."

Abby tapped her fingers on the tan leather armrest. "That poses an interesting problem."

"How's that?"

"We don't exactly have one at the moment," she said.

The pilot frowned and cocked his head to the side. "We're about to become airborne with no destination?"

She offered a shrug. "We're awaiting orders from Interpol."

"I see. Could you wait a moment?" He turned on his heel and walked back to the cockpit.

After a few moments, the pilot returned. "I've informed air traffic control that we're a diplomatic flight awaiting instructions. They've cleared us, but they still ask that we give them a ballpark idea of our heading for security purposes."

"All right," Abby said. She pulled her iPhone from her pocket and zoomed in on the grid of lines and blinking dots. She analyzed the screen for a few moments. "Will it suffice to tell them we are headed toward the continent of Africa?"

33

Table Mountain squatted above Cape Town, South Africa, engulfing the entire northern horizon. At a mere 3,500 feet above sea level, it was not tall enough to be intimidating, but its flat top and sheer rock faces gave it a certain landmark character. It was perhaps the contrast of blue ocean, white beaches, and lush vegetation that made the gray shale and sandstone monolith so impressive, as though angry gods had chucked the mountain from the heavens and it just happened to land at the mouth of Camps Bay on the southern tip of Africa. It loomed over the busy maritime city.

Isaac and the Broker remained silent as they drove through the bustling streets of Cape Town, the car darting in and out between clumps of tourists that loitered in the road. They had ignored one another for the greater part of the trip, and a fierce tension had settled between them. Held silent by their pride and ambition, neither wanted create an involuntary truce by speaking first. So they plodded forward at a snail's pace in the Black Audi, Table Mountain inching ever closer.

"To the hotel," the Broker ordered, speaking directly to Wülf. "We will take a cab from there."

Wülf nodded and navigated the vehicle through the narrow streets toward the Cape Grace Hotel, a prime five-story, red brick resort that sat on the Bay.

Isaac faced the Broker and narrowed his eyes. "What are you doing?"

"Do you want witnesses?"

"No."

"Then we go alone."

Wülf rolled to a stop beneath the hotel portico and opened the back door. The two men slid out, surveying their surroundings.

"Call a cab for us. You know what to do." The Broker met Wülf's gaze.

"Yes sir," he said, and then disappeared into the lobby.

Ten minutes later a chauffeured sedan pulled to the curb, and they climbed in.

"Destination, sir?" the driver asked.

"Table Mountain," the Broker responded. "Take us to the tram."

"Very well." He pulled into traffic and crawled through the tourist-clogged streets. Within a few moments they slipped onto a two-lane country road and wound their way toward the monolith that hovered over the city.

The Cocktail Bar at the top of Table Mountain in Cape Town could only be accessed by an aerial cableway that traversed a vast gorge laden with groves of cluster pine. The rented sedan pulled into a parking space at the lower cable station on Tafelberg Road, five miles outside Cape Town. Isaac Weld and the Broker left the car and headed toward the tram.

— ∞∞∞ —

Camps Bay Tabernacle nestled snugly in the tourist district of Cape Town, almost hidden among the shops. But it caught Abby's eye as she and Alex drove the rented Jeep through the city, following the GPS signal. It was an old structure of crumbling brick covered with cracked plaster. The large wooden doors stood open, and within she caught a glimmer of candlelight.

"Did you see something?"

Abby forced her eyes back to the road. "No. Just looking."

She had visited Cape Town a few times, but on none of her trips had she ever driven. As in Europe, South Africans drove on the opposite side of the road, and the driver sat in the right-hand seat. Later, she and Alex could compare notes to see who was more shaken by the experience.

"Do you have any idea why we're here?" he asked, looking a great deal healthier and more well-rested than he had the day before.

"I do now." Her eyes ran up the sheer rock face of Table Mountain.

"Care to explain?"

"See those sandstone cliffs?"

"You mean we're going up there?"

"Apparently so."

"Great."

A mischievous smiled danced at the corners of her mouth. "You're not afraid of heights are you?"

"Heights, no. Dangling several thousand feet in the air by a wire, yeah, that's a bit unnerving."

She smiled. "Don't worry. It's not the fall that kills you. It's the sudden stop."

"Funny."

"Oh, come on, Alex. It can't possibly be worse than some of the things you've done in your career." The last word came out as an insult, and she immediately regretted it.

He turned toward her, trying to catch her eyes now planted firmly on the road. "I've done a lot in my career. Much of it I regret."

She didn't respond, and they remained silent until Abby stopped the Jeep in front of the entrance to the cable station.

"Let's go," she said. "We need to finish this."

<hr />

Isaac felt the diamond tug against his chest as they rode the cable car up the mountain. The Broker remained silent, face turned toward the window. Isaac on the other hand looked up toward the cocktail bar two thousand feet above. As he did, he noticed the large black helicopter that touched down for less than a minute and then rose in the air again.

The Collectors, he thought, a triumphant grin spreading across his face.

34

Isaac and the Broker pushed through the glass doors leading to the cocktail bar. Although the restaurant could hold one hundred thirty people, fewer than twenty were scattered about the room, seated sparsely at the tables, sipping on a variety of wine and mixed drinks. Panoramic views spread along three sides of the restaurant, engulfing visitors with light from floor-to-ceiling windows. Clear blue water glinted off the white sand of Camps Bay below, and a cloudless sky stretched from horizon to horizon.

The Broker drifted to a table in the far corner, wedged between two windows that overlooked the cliff. He pulled back a chair and sat down, arms crossed and jaw clenched.

Isaac joined him at the table, his eyes wandering over the handful of customers. "What now?"

"We wait."

"I need a little more information than that."

The Broker clenched his jaw. "Pity you won't get any."

"Don't mess with me."

"Don't pick a fight."

Isaac patted his sport coat gently, reminding the Broker of the pistol tucked beneath the surface. "We have an agreement."

The Broker's lips twisted into a sadistic grin. "Do we now?"

The cable car chinked up the gorge, rocking gently in the wind. Empty except for Alex and Abby, only silence filled the space that would have normally accommodated twenty passengers. They stood at opposite ends, in an effort to balance their weight and the awkwardness they felt.

The sun flooded the city with caramel-colored light as it slipped toward the horizon, its arc almost complete for the day. Yet Alex's eyes were not on the breathtaking view, but rather on the brown-eyed woman who would not meet his gaze.

"I'm sorry," he said. "It wasn't supposed to turn out like this."

"I know. You were supposed to get away with it. The perfect crime."

"That's not what I meant." He ran the back of his hand across the stubble on his cheek. "I wasn't supposed to fall in love with you."

The words shocked Abby into a quick glance, but she looked away again, unable to absorb the intensity in his eyes.

"Abby, I've never loved anyone. Ever." He took a step toward her.

"Alex, please don't."

He inched his way along the cable car. "You were totally unexpected."

"And here I thought I was part of your plan all along. Isn't that how it works? Romance the girl. Steal the goods."

"Usually."

"But this time, you just happened to *really* fall in love? Wow! That's convenient."

"It's not like that!"

Alex scooped her into his arms in one fluid movement. Their lips brushed for a moment, and then he pressed in, desperate to communicate his sincerity. For a brief second, she softened and returned the kiss. But then she stiffened and pushed him away.

"Nice try." Abby wiped the kiss away with her forearm. But the look on her face left Alex unconvinced of her doubt.

He stood, eyes half closed, with the taste of her kiss still on his lips. Emotion erupted in his voice. "I'm sorry."

A shadow passed over her face as she glanced between the top of the mountain and Alex. She opened her mouth to speak, but closed it again. They were almost at the end of their ride.

Hardness settled around the edges of Isaac's face, and his demeanor cooled. "Double-crossing me is a big risk, considering I decide whether you live or die."

"True. But from where I sit, the risk is acceptable."

"Do explain."

"You've yet to prove you actually have the merchandise, Mr. Weld."

Isaac pondered for a moment and drew the black velvet bag from under his shirt. He lifted the diamond from the pouch and let it rest in his palm. "Satisfied?"

The Broker's ravenous eyes grew large. "Very."

"Good. Now when can we expect the Collectors to arrive?"

The Broker tapped his fingers together and fought to control the self-satisfied look that threatened to spread over his face. "Ah, yes. Let just say they won't be coming."

The edge in Isaac's voice was razor sharp. "I'm sure you're mistaken. Our agreement clearly stated that you would bring me to them." He spat the words as he leaned across the table.

"Actually," the Broker corrected, "I believe our agreement was to bring you to the rendezvous spot. And I did. This is where I've met with the Collectors for nearly twenty years."

Isaac's nostrils flared. "That diamond is for the Collectors."

"Not so." The Broker ran his eyes over the stone as light reflected from the faceted surface. "This is for my personal collection."

Isaac's hand crept toward the inside of his jacket.

"I wouldn't do that if I were you, Mr. Weld."

"As an unarmed man, I hardly think you're in a position to threaten me."

"True. I don't carry a weapon. I never have."

"Well, then, it seems I have the advantage."

"Ah, not so. I have a great distaste for guns, vulgar things that they are, but my assistant Wülf has quite the flare for them. Since he is standing but three feet behind you, I would think twice before pulling your weapon out."

Isaac turned. Wülf stood at the window, one arm resting on the window sill, the other tucked inside the pocket of his sport coat. The look he gave Isaac was merciless.

"I sent him ahead," the Broker said. "I would prefer he not kill you in here. You know, witnesses and all, but rest assured I will give the order should it come to that."

Isaac leaned back in his chair; his nostrils flared. "It seems our little game has come to an impasse."

"No, I believe you call this checkmate."

"Ah, but you see, I still have this." Isaac lifted the diamond and let it swing on its chain before the Broker. "And the truth is I don't believe you."

"What exactly do you not believe?"

"I saw the helicopter land, and I know the Collectors are here. I will get what I want."

A brief look of confusion crossed the Broker's face. "What helicopter?"

Even as Isaac enjoyed his moment of power, bedlam ensued.

35

WASHINGTON POST, JUNE 1, 1933

EVALYN WALSH MCLEAN STOOD AT THE WINDOW, HER BACK STRAIGHT as an arrow, as she watched the auction below on the front steps of the building. She wore a calf-length, black satin dress, fitted to her thin frame. Black heels, black mink coat, and a wide-brimmed black hat with netting completed the ensemble. As always, the Hope Diamond hung around her neck. The fingers of her left hand traced the facets of the jewel from memory. In her right hand she held a cigarette, smoke curling from the edges.

Her father-in-law had bought the *Washington Post* long before she and Ned married, but it had nonetheless been the primary source of her extravagant lifestyle throughout the years. Yet, like most things that Ned laid his hands on, it was poorly managed, and began to hemorrhage cash. During the year leading up to the bankruptcy, it lost twenty thousand dollars a month.

Ned stood three stories below, just to the left of the auctioneer, lost in a drunken haze. Alcohol had always been his preferred method of diffusing pain. Today was no different.

"Do I hear two fifty?" the auctioneer asked, scanning the crowd.

A bright red paddle flew into the air.

"Two fifty. Do we have three?"

Another paddle.

"Three, do we have three fifty?"

Three hundred and fifty thousand dollars. Just four years earlier, Eugene Meyer, head of the Federal Reserve, offered the McLean's five million dollars for the newspaper. Two years after that, publishing magnate William Randolph Hearst offered three million. In both cases Evalyn turned them down, hoping the paper would pass on to her children. Now here she stood, watching eager bidders salivate over the *Washington Post* for a mere three hundred and fifty thousand dollars.

As the numbers climbed in fifty thousand dollar increments, tears stung the corners of her eyes, and she blinked them back with a fury.

"Four fifty, do I hear five?"

Paddles everywhere.

"Five, five fifty, six."

"Six hundred thousand dollars. Do I have six fifty?"

The bidding slowed. Those who came to lowball the purchase of the newspaper dropped out.

"Six fifty. Do I hear seven?"

"Seven. Do I have seven fifty?"

She leaned forward in the silence as the sea of paddles remained lowered.

"Seven, going once . . ."

Then in the back, a paddle shot up.

"Seven fifty from the gentleman in the back. Do I have eight?"

That gentleman in the back was none other than Eugene Meyer, the very same man who had offered five million dollars for the paper such a short time ago.

The auction narrowed down to two people, ironically the same two who had offered millions for the paper in better days: Eugene Meyer and William Randolph Hearst.

"Seven fifty going once, going twice . . ."

"Eight from Mr. Hearst. Do I have eight fifty?"

An agonizing pause.

"Eight going once, eight going twice . . ."

"Eight fifty from Mr. Meyer! Do I have nine?"

Silence. Interminable.

"Eight fifty going once. Eight fifty going twice. Sold to Eugene Meyer for eight hundred and fifty thousand dollars!"

The crowd below erupted in applause, and Eugene Meyer made his way up the steps, grinning as spectators slapped him on the back.

At some point during the last few moments, Ned had slipped away, too embarrassed to remain.

Evalyn was so absorbed in the scene below that she did not hear the door open behind her.

"It's over then, I guess," he said.

In disgust she examined her disgraced husband from head to toe, and then sucked on her cigarette holder. "It was over a long time ago."

Ned remained by the door. His forehead looked clammy, and as usual, his breath was sour. Although he cleaned up for the auction, he was but a shadow of his former self.

"That's what I've been saying for years," he said, "but you still contest the divorce."

"There is no divorce," she said, a vindictive smile playing at the corner of her mouth.

"Apparently, you didn't get the papers I sent you at Christmas, wrapped in red and green paper?"

"Oh, I got them," she said. "We both know that. And I contested them. And I will continue to do so every time you try to put me out by drawing up papers in some god-forsaken Third-World country because no judge in the States will grant your wishes. I am not that easy to get rid of Ned McLean."

Three decades of heavy drinking had caused many of the capillaries in Ned's cheeks and nose to burst, giving him a permanently ruddy complexion. His face grew redder and redder as they argued. "You just said it was over, Evalyn! You said it!"

"I was not speaking of our marriage, Ned. I tried to end that seventeen years ago, but you sent me those blasted telegrams, all sixty of them for God's sake, *professing your love*. And I believed you! What a fool I was!" Her hands were shaking, but her face remained still. "I was referring to this kingdom we have built. Nothing but a house of cards. Millions squandered. Six homes gone. *The Washington Post* gone. Our marriage nothing but a sham for the last twenty years. And Vinson!" Her voice broke. "My baby is gone. All because of *you*!"

She paced the floor in front of him; her expression was rabid and tense with anger. The edges of his scowl trimmed with fear, and he backed away.

"No, Ned," she continued. "After all that you have put me through, you will not be rid of me that easily!"

"I want a divorce!"

"Never!"

"What good can this possibly do, Evalyn? We haven't been together in years."

"That is not my fault. I've always been here. You're the one who's chosen scores of women over me. *Scores*! Don't you think I know about what you and Warren Harding did at your father's home on H Street? I know you two called it the *Love Nest*! I know about the women that came and went! Oh, and Florence knew too. And still, after Warren died, she tried to protect him—protect the both of you. What do you think she was doing for those eighteen days she spent at Friendship after he died?"

Ned stared at her, unsure how to answer.

"Burning papers, that's what! For *eighteen* days. You think you're in trouble now? You think you're humiliated now? Had she not destroyed the most incriminating evidence of your business dalliances with Warren, you'd be in prison. You owe me, Ned, and I will never forget. It would be best if you didn't, either."

Evalyn stopped her rant and glared at Ned again. No tenderness remained in her heart. She could muster only apathy for the shriveled man that stood but ten feet away. All the sadness, pity, and anger were gone. It had all been spent over the last miserable twenty years. The only thing that stirred in her heart as she looked at a once great and wealthy man was power. For the first time since she met Ned McLean, she felt as though she had the power. Even better, Evalyn Walsh McLean had a plan.

She took a long drag on her cigarette and exhaled the smoke from her nostrils, then lifted her purse from the desk and walked from the office, her head held high.

SHEPPARD AND ENOCH PRATT SANATORIUM
TOWSON, MARYLAND, OCTOBER, 1933

"It seems you have made the news again, Mrs. McLean." Enoch Pratt, director of the upscale mental institution said, handing Evalyn a copy of the *Washington Daily*

News. They sat in his office, overlooking the opulent grounds of the sanatorium.

She took it with a gloved hand and read the front page headline, MRS. MCLEAN WANTS HUSBAND ADJUDGED OF UNSOUND MIND. Her face was expressionless. "Not so, Mr. Pratt. We all know he is of unsound mind. I want him committed."

He offered her a polite smile. "Well, if that be the case, you have most certainly gotten your wish. It was three days ago, was it not, that your husband was declared insane?"

"Four days ago, Mr. Pratt, but who's counting?"

"Indeed," he said. "Now, if you will come with me, I will give you a tour of our facilities." Enoch Pratt stood and ushered Evalyn from his office.

Hardly what one would imagine when thinking of a mental institution, the Sanatorium was a sprawling campus of manicured lawns, lush gardens, and winding sidewalks. The numerous buildings were scattered throughout the grounds in an uncluttered sort of way. The only hint of it being a guarded facility was the ten-foot brick wall that surrounded the estate, but even it was covered in English ivy and climbing roses. To the casual observer the complex appeared more like an elite boarding school than a housing facility for the mentally unstable.

"As you can see," Dr. Pratt said, as he led Evalyn down a sidewalk toward the edge of the property, "your husband has been given his own private cottage."

"And where is he now?"

"Sedated, actually. Even though his mental evaluation showed that he is not a danger to himself or others, he still did not take kindly to being admitted. Would you like to see him?"

"Yes, Dr. Pratt, I believe I would."

"Very well then, please come with me."

A small white cottage with a wood shingle roof and green shutters sat on the edge of the property. Though benignly surrounded by gardenia bushes and climbing jasmine, Evalyn did not fail to notice the ornate wrought iron bars on the windows, or the fact that the door could only be locked from the outside.

"Charming," she said.

"We thought you would approve." Dr. Pratt approached the door. "Our medical team is inside, so depending on your husband's current condition, we may not be able to stay long."

He swung the door open, and Evalyn entered the cottage, consisting of bedroom, bathroom, and living area. Much to her satisfaction she noted that the entire house was smaller than the living area of their suite at The Hotel Bristol so many years earlier.

"Given your husband's notoriety, we felt it would be best to isolate him from the general population. These are the mentally ill we are dealing with after all."

"Of course, Dr. Pratt. I trust your judgment."

The bedroom door was closed, and Evalyn could hear rustling and hushed voices on the other side.

"If you will wait here a moment, I will just check on his progress." Dr. Pratt slipped behind the bedroom door for less than a minute, then stuck his head out and beckoned Evalyn to enter.

Ned McLean wore his favorite gray satin pajamas and thick-soled house shoes. He lay on his back, eyes closed, strapped to the bed by three thick yellow belts, one across his chest, another across his waist, and the third across his shins. Beads of sweat dripped from his forehead, and a five o'clock shadow covered his thick jaw and double chin.

Two doctors and three nurses populated the room, but they stepped back from the bed when Evalyn entered. They peered at her with curiosity, as though she were an oddity in a store window to be ogled. The gaze of all five settled on the large blue stone that rested against her collarbone. Even after all these years, the Hope Diamond still elicited strong reactions from those who saw it.

Dr. Pratt approached the bed and whispered in Ned's ear. "Your wife is here to see you, Mr. McLean." He motioned Evalyn to the side of the bed.

Ned's eyes cracked open and rolled back and forth as he tried to focus on her.

One of the physicians stepped forward and explained, "He may be a little groggy. For a man of his age he was putting up a considerable fight, and we had to give him a sedative to settle him down."

Evalyn took a step forward and leaned toward her husband. "Hello, Ned," she said.

He twitched, as though the very sound of her voice scalded him. Finally, his eyes locked onto hers, and he struggled against his restraints. Though he could not speak, low gurgling sounds escaped his mouth as he thrashed his head back and forth.

"Oh, my," Evalyn gasped, "he is just overcome at the very sight of me."

"He must miss you terribly, Mrs. McLean," the doctor said.

Evalyn threw a hand across her forehead and turned away. "I simply can't bear to see him like this."

"Of course. How insensitive of me. I can't imagine how disturbing this must be for you. Perhaps you should come back on a day when he is feeling better."

"I think that might be a good idea."

As Dr. Pratt escorted Evalyn from the room, she turned to her husband. He lifted his head and followed her with his eyes. She offered him a slight grin, without mercy and full of malice. It was a smile that Ned McLean knew well after all these years of marriage. He thrashed about so fiercely on his gurney that the wheels started to rise off the floor.

One of the physicians stepped forward, needle in one hand. "You probably don't want to see this, Mrs. McLean. I fear you will find it quite disturbing."

As tempted as she was to stay and witness the procedure, she left the cottage, forever turning her back on Ned McLean.

Dr. Pratt gently shut the door. "I apologize for you having seen that, Mrs. McLean, but I also fear it may have been necessary. Your husband is in a very poor condition."

"He has been quite ill for some time, Dr. Pratt. This is nothing new to me."

"I'm sorry for all that you have been through."

"So am I."

"I do feel, however, that your husband is in very good hands here."

"I concur, Dr. Pratt, and I trust your staff wholeheartedly."

He led the way through the hospital grounds, and they returned to his office. "Just so you are aware, Mrs. McLean, your husband is suffering from acute psychosis and alcohol saturation. You need to understand that this is not a temporary situation. Your husband will spend the remainder of his life in this sanatorium."

Evalyn nodded, averting her eyes as she struggled to suppress a smile. "I see," she murmured.

"It is difficult news, I know, but I must be honest in our prognosis."

"I understand, Dr. Pratt."

"Now, would you like to tour the rest of the grounds?"

"If you don't mind, I have seen quite enough, thank you. I think I would like to go home."

"Of course. I will walk you to your car."

"Actually," Evalyn said, placing a gloved hand on his arm, "I need a little time to myself. If it's all the same to you, I'd like to go alone."

"I see. Yes, that might be the best thing after all. I know you have had a difficult day."

Evalyn shook his hand. "Thank you for all that you and your staff are doing for my husband, Dr. Pratt. I am most grateful."

Enoch Pratt gave her a curt bow, and Evalyn walked away.

As she navigated her way through the grounds, passing various patients and staff, it was debatable whether she garnered more curious looks for the Hope Diamond strung casually around her neck, or for the broad grin spread across her face.

MCLEAN ESTATE, SATURDAY, APRIL 26, 1947

A single lamp illuminated the ornate bedroom on the second floor of the *Friendship* estate. A small crowd gathered around the bed where the withered form of Evalyn Walsh McLean lay swallowed beneath a down comforter. Her unblinking and watery eyes, always large, now consumed her thin face. The Hope Diamond sat lightly in the palm of one hand. She did not have the strength to lift it.

An hour earlier, Dr. Baxter administered a final dose of laudanum, and although it relaxed her to the point of immobility, it had yet to draw her into an unending sleep. The few people present grew restless.

Beside her bed sat two men, heads bowed in hushed conversation.

"Where's her family, that's what I want to know?" Frank Waldrup, managing editor of the *Washington-Times Herald*, whispered to Thurman Arnold, Evalyn's attorney.

"That's her son-in-law over in the corner."

"I hardly count him as family. He's here to keep watch over the money in her daughter's stead, Thurman. I suppose he wants to make sure you don't administer any legal matters without family present."

"As if I would do something like that at a time like this. For a U.S. Senator, the man doesn't know much about the law, does he?"

Evalyn drew a deep breath, and those keeping vigil leaned forward, anticipating it to be her last. She tightened her fist around the diamond and coughed, lungs desperately trying to eject the mucous that filled them. The pneumonia rendered her helpless, fighting for breath. Yet after several moments, the coughing stopped, and she drew another shallow breath. She licked her cracked lips with a dry and swollen tongue.

"She's trying to speak," said Thurman. He reached out from the chair at her bedside and laid a hand on her arm. "Evalyn, just lie still."

She swatted at him in irritation.

"Let her be, Thurman. You know she'll do as she pleases." Frank Waldrup had known Evalyn McLean for twenty years, and he knew better than to interfere if she wanted to speak.

A calm washed over her face, and she almost smiled. Her voice rang out startlingly clear. "There are those who would believe that somehow a curse is housed deep in the blue of this diamond." She wrapped her fingers around the stone, caressing it gently.

A panicked hush fell over the room. None present wanted to be part of a discussion on the rumored curses that haunted Evalyn's life, yet none were willing to miss what she had to say.

"I scoff at that in the privacy of my mind, for I do comprehend the source of what is evil in our lives," she continued. Her dilated eyes stared across the room. "The natural consequences of unearned wealth in undisciplined hands."

Arnold waited for her to continue, but she had fallen silent. After a moment he reached out and patted her wrist, deciding that a noncommittal, "There, there," would suffice as an answer.

Her bony hand, with its paper-thin skin, was cold to the touch. Not wanting to alert the others yet to his suspicion, Thurman rested his hand lightly on her wrist, searching for a pulse. Her eyes were still open, large and staring, but her chest no longer rose and fell with shallow breaths. Evalyn had spoken her last words.

Her son–in–law, Robert Reynolds, sat in the corner with his arms crossed over his chest, brow furrowed.

Also present, but only from a sense of duty, was the vice president of Georgetown University, and Frank Murphy, associate justice of the Supreme Court. The five of them awaited her demise, all for different reasons.

Thurman rose from his chair. "Frank, would you summon Dr. Baxter, please?"

"Of course." He jumped to his feet and slipped from the room.

Evalyn's son-in-law leaned forward with great eagerness, no longer looking tired. "You mean she's dead then?"

"I believe," said Thurman, his words measured and angry, "that your mother-in-law has passed on to the next life."

Robert's face twisted in disbelief. "Why are her eyes still open if she's dead?"

"Because," said the voice of Dr. Baxter. "When the body dies, it remains in the exact position it was in during its last breath." Carrying his black bag, he moved to Evalyn's bedside. It took only a moment to check her pulse, listen for breath, and declare her dead. He then ran his palm over her face and closed her eyelids.

"Well then," Robert Reynolds said, jumping to his feet. "I believe we have the matter of a will to attend to."

"Are you serious, man?" Thurman asked, aghast.

"You are the executor of her will, Mr. Arnold."

"Yes, but this is hardly the time."

"I don't intend for you to read it now. I simply want to know when it will take place and who will be in attendance."

Thurman clenched his fists, "You and your wife will just have to wait, Mr. Reynolds."

The carefully placed barb had its intended effect, and Robert said nothing else about the will.

Thurman turned to Frank with a knowing look. "Will you help me gather her effects?" His eyes darted to the diamond still clenched in Evalyn's hand.

"Certainly." Frank slipped into her closet.

"Effects, what effects?" her son-in-law asked.

"Her jewels, Mr. Reynolds. They must be secured."

"You can't possibly think that I am going to let you walk out of this house with her jewelry," Robert said, eyes fastened on the Hope Diamond.

"You don't have a choice, Mr. Reynolds."

"By heaven, I don't! I'm here to represent her family."

Thurman locked eyes with Richard. "And I am here to represent her. My instructions were to secure these jewels after her death. That is exactly what I am doing. Are you going to challenge my authority before a Supreme Court justice, Mr. Reynolds?"

Reynolds took a step back, not ready to give up. "And just what do you intend to do with them, Mr. Arnold?"

"Secure them in a safe deposit box as instructed, whichever bank is open, being that it is a Saturday night."

"You will be taking a witness with you, I presume?"

"And why would you presume such a thing?"

"To ensure that all things are done in a legal and upstanding manner, of course. We wouldn't want any of my mother-in-law's jewels to mysteriously disappear now, would we?"

Thurman bristled. Before he could answer, Frank Waldrup returned from the closet, shoe box in hand. "I will accompany, Mr. Arnold."

"I want a full inventory before you leave," Reynolds demanded.

Although Thurman Arnold did not consider the demand worthy of an answer, Associate Justice Frank Murphy made a detailed list of each gem that was taken from Evalyn's dressing room and placed in the box. Seventy-three gems lay in the box, including The Star of the East, her first purchase from Pierre Cartier.

Thurman Arnold and Frank Waldrup stood by her bed and tried to decide on the proper etiquette for removing the jewel from a dead woman's hands. Frank lifted her hand, and Thurman pried open her fingers, strong even in death.

The weight of the jewel felt heavy and unnatural in Thurman's hand. He braved only a single glance at the deep blue stone before adding it to the shoebox with a shudder. He then kissed the back of Evalyn's hand and laid it across her chest.

Frank put on his hat. "Shall we?"

"Let's get it over with."

They said their good-byes to Evalyn, nodded to the other men gathered, except for her son-in-law, and left the room.

"It's late," Frank said. "We won't find a bank or jewelry store open."

"I know. I've been thinking about where to take these jewels, and I have an idea," Thurman said, leading the way downstairs. He paused in the main hallway, next to the only telephone in the house. From deep inside his coat he drew a small black book and flipped through it in search of the name he had in mind.

Thurman Arnold dialed the number, thick fingers maneuvering the rotary dial. He cast a skeptical glance at the clock, which read close to midnight. The phone rang eight times. Just as he was about to hang up, a gruff voice answered.

"Hello, John; this is Thurman Arnold." He paused and waited for the man on the other end to wake and gather his senses. "No, there's no emergency. I need a favor. Yes, I know it's very late."

A curious Frank Waldrup furrowed his eyebrows and waited.

"I need to store something in your office for safekeeping . . . in your safe actually—"

Thurman chuckled for a moment and scratched his head. "Well, actually I'm holding a shoebox that contains the jewels of Evalyn Walsh McLean, and frankly I need to keep them away from her family long enough for the will to be read. . . . Yes, sir, she passed on this evening, less than an hour ago. . . . You will? Thank goodness. . . . No, sir, you don't have to meet us there, just as long as you call ahead and make sure we can get in. Thank you so much. . . . Good night to you, too, sir."

Thurman placed the receiver on its cradle and turned to Frank with a triumphant look.

"Do you mind telling me where we're going?" Frank asked. Thurman simply smiled in reply. "You take this safekeeping business seriously, I take it?"

Thurman tipped his hat lightly and said, "Just doing my job, Frank, just doing my job."

As they left the McLean estate, servants were already turning out the lights and covering all the mirrors in the house with black cloth. For the first time since Evalyn Walsh McLean set foot within the walls of *Friendship*, calm reigned at the mansion.

Thurman Arnold and Frank Waldrup slipped from the house and walked toward Thurman's black Plymouth coupe. Frank climbed into the passenger side and set the shoebox on his lap. The coupe started with a rumble, and they drove out of the grounds just as a light mist began to fall.

The drive took less than thirty minutes. Thurman Arnold parked illegally at the corner of Pennsylvania and Constitution.

Frank Waldrup gave him an uneasy glance as they climbed from the car. "This is the Department of Justice."

"I'm an attorney," Thurman shrugged, leading the way up the steps.

Upon entry they were met by a security guard. "Names please," he ordered.

"Thurman Arnold and Frank Waldrup."

The guard quickly checked a manifest at the security desk and waved them on.

"Good. He called it in," Thurman said with a relieved sigh.

"Who called what in?" Frank asked.

"John."

"Oh. John. Of course." Frank rolled his eyes in defeat.

Thurman led him to a bank of elevators and pushed the button for the fifth floor. It rose with a slight hum. The door opened with a ding, and they marched down the thickly carpeted hall, Frank trailing behind, looking somewhat mystified.

Thurman stopped before a heavy wooden door and double-checked the nameplate on the wall to make sure they were in the right place.

"My word!" Frank Waldrup exclaimed, stumbling backwards. "You can't be serious?"

"About what?"

"When you were on the phone, I didn't . . . you were talking to someone named John. I didn't realize it was *John Edgar Hoover!*"

"Well, who else would it have been, you fool? This is important." Thurman turned the knob and pushed the heavy door open.

"J. Edgar Hoover. As in Director of the F.B.I. The Federal Bureau of Investigation!" he hissed. "You can't just walk straight into his office."

Irritated, Thurman scowled at Frank. "Were you with me in Evalyn's house when I made that call, Frank?"

"Yes."

"And were you with me just now when the security guards checked the manifest and waved us through?"

"Yes."

"Well, both of those things are clear indicators that we have permission to be here. Now if you don't mind, I'm exhausted, and I want to go home and get some sleep."

Thurman Arnold placed the shoebox full of jewels into the safe of J. Edgar Hoover for safekeeping. "Such a pity, really," he said. "She was an absurd woman at times, but she didn't deserve many of the cards that life dealt her."

36

ABBY LED ALEX INTO THE COCKTAIL BAR ON TOP OF TABLE MOUNTAIN.
No sooner had they passed through the door than she
pushed him into a corner to avoid the stampede of people
that raced through the room.

Alex saw several things happen at once, and yet he could
not process any of them. Sitting at a table on the other side
of the bar with the Broker, was his brother, Isaac. The
Hope Diamond dangled from his hand, light refracting a
series of small rainbows off the blue facets. Even as his
brother and the Broker stared at the diamond, a swarm
of people ran toward them with guns drawn.

Isaac jumped to his feet, clenched the necklace in one
hand, and pulled a pistol from his coat pocket with the
other. He scanned the room in an effort to find an escape
route.

It was only when Alex saw Dow move purposefully from
behind the bar, Interpol badge hanging from his neck and
a Glock nine-millimeter held firmly in his hands, that he
understood what was happening. He turned to Abby, both
impressed and bewildered.

"You did this?"

She offered him a pained smile. "It sucks to be used, doesn't it?"

Though a small army of Interpol agents descended on Isaac, he saw only one face in the crowd, that of his brother—a man who ought to be dead.

"You traitor," Isaac hissed, his words shaky and full of rage.

"I had nothing to do with this," Alex said.

Isaac clicked his tongue. "You've gotten bad at lying, Alex. I just wasn't aware you were in the business of betrayal as well."

"Betrayal? You're one to talk!"

"I should have done it sooner."

"You always were a terrible shot."

"Something I can remedy." Isaac turned the barrel of his gun an inch to the right. A smile twitched at the corner of his mouth as he pulled the trigger.

In the split second before a barrage of gunfire riddled him with bullet holes, Abby screamed.

Isaac Weld fell backward over his chair and then dropped to the floor, already dead. The diamond slid from his hand and landed a mere six inches from where The Broker cowered beneath the table.

Douglas Mitchell watched his daughter stumble to the floor, but the sight of her blood-stained shirt only held his attention for a moment. He crawled beneath the table and grasped the Hope Diamond with a trembling hand. The weight of the jewel, its curves and facets, felt just as he'd dreamed it would all these years.

From the corner of his eye he saw Wülf pinned to the floor with arms behind his back. Pandemonium still raged at his periphery. Glass fell. People yelled. Gunsmoke hung acrid in the air. But he cared for nothing except the feeling of the diamond in his palm.

And then a voice shattered his reverie.

"I don't believe that belongs to you."

He lifted his eyes from the jewel and found Abby kneeling beside him on the floor. Behind her stood at least a dozen armed Interpol officers, guns leveled at him. His fingers wrapped tighter around the necklace, and he jerked back.

"Yes, it does."

"No, it doesn't." Abby held out her hand, palm up.

"No."

"Give it to me. Please." Her voice wavered, and her eyes filled with tears. They both understood in that moment that she was asking for more than the diamond, she was asking for something she had never received from him.

Douglas Mitchell searched the eyes of his daughter and pummeled her with words that had an impact like an atomic bomb in her heart. "There is nothing in this world that is more important to me than this diamond. Nothing. Do you hear?"

He had said those words, in one form or another, for the last thirty years of her life. Yet she had never heard them come from his mouth. Abby recoiled and rocked back on her heels.

He looked at the thin trail of blood that dripped from her shoulder. "He shot you?"

"Apparently, he's a bad shot."

"Pity."

Dow Heaton, Director of Interpol's Art Theft Division, rushed forward and hit Douglas Mitchell with the butt of his gun. The Broker slumped to the floor. Dow pried open his fingers, nearly cracking his bones with the force, and set the necklace in Abby's limp hand. He could not look her in the eyes. He knew the pain that resided there. Instead, Dow took out his aggression on her father. He jerked the Broker to his feet and cast him toward a group of waiting officers.

Tears dripped from Abby's chin as her father was dragged away. Douglas Mitchell looked at her over his shoulder, his face contorted in disgust.

Dow helped Abby to her feet and sat her down at a table. Abby clutched the diamond as though it were the last feeble connection to her father. Dow then turned to Alex, ready to unleash the remainder of his fury.

"Please," Alex said with a flinch. "I'm not him."

"Maybe not, but you had no problem doing his dirty work."

"And I'll regret it for the rest of my life." Alex bit his lip as he blinked back unfamiliar tears. "But I'm here, okay? I came back. I tried to make it right."

"You will never be able to right your wrongs, Mr. Weld."

"Let me try."

Dow turned and pointed at Abby. "Do you see that girl? She's the closest thing to a daughter I have, and I won't let you hurt her again."

"I see her," Alex said. "I see her more clearly every moment. You can hate me if you want, but you won't chase me away."

Abby lifted her tearstained face. "Dow."

"Don't worry, I'll get rid of him," he said.

"No. Let him stay."

"Abby—"

"Please. We have a lot of unfinished business."

Dow shook his head. "You're hurt."

"I'll be fine. It's just a nick."

"I don't think this is the time—"

Abby held up her hand. "Now is the only time."

Dow wavered for a moment and then relented. "Are you sure?"

She nodded and held the necklace out for him. "Would you take this? The sight of it makes me sick."

⁂

Abby motioned toward the empty seat across the table. "Sit down, Alex."

"Your shoulder—"

"Is not nearly as bad as your head—"

"You really should have it looked at."

"I'll be fine. I owe you an explanation."

"No," Alex said. "You don't owe me anything."

"I did this." She looked at the aftermath of the cocktail bar. "I've known for years that my father wanted to get his hands on the Hope Diamond. I've known about his connection to the Collectors, and I've known that he would eventually try and use me to get the stone. It was inevitable. You were just a pawn."

Alex gnawed on his bottom lip. "When the game is over, the pawn and the king go back in the same box." He couldn't look at her. He tried to lift his eyes, but they were paralyzed, locked on his hands that lay across the top of the table. "I'm sorry," he finally whispered.

Her voice was gentle. She beckoned him to look at her. "You weren't the first person to use me, Alex. My father has been doing it for years."

He braved a quick glance and found not condemnation as he expected, just sadness. "It was wrong. For both of us."

"I was trying to give him the opportunity to be the dad I've always needed him to be, trying to give him the chance to choose me. It's hard to admit that he never will."

"I helped him do this."

"No, Alex. He made his choice long before he met you."

"I'm sorry," he said again, unable to find words that mattered.

"Abby," Dow said as he stood behind her, hand on her shoulder. "I have to take Mr. Weld into custody now."

Abby nodded and gave Alex her own apologetic look. "I'm sorry. There was nothing I could do. They told me your sentence may be lightened for your cooperation at the end, but I can't get you out of this."

"It's not your job to rescue me." Alex stood and looked Dow squarely in the eye. He held his wrists together and lifted them up so Dow could easily place him under arrest.

───※───

For Abby's sake Dow hid his gleeful smile. He clasped the handcuffs on Alex's wrists with such force that they dug into the younger man's skin, causing it to pucker and turn pink.

Alex fought his own smile. "I don't suppose I have any chance of a plea bargain?"

"There's nothing you could offer me that would come close to satisfying the debt you owe, Mr. Weld."

"I wouldn't be so certain of that." Alex let the words hang in the air, enjoying the sudden looks of interest from both Abby and Dow.

"Speak quickly, Mr. Weld. Time is running out."

"Would my freedom be worth names, addresses, and phone numbers of all five Collectors, as well as detailed lists of every piece of art my brother and I have stolen for them in the last ten years, including locations of those art pieces today?"

Dow shook his head. "I don't believe you."

"Do you really think I would put myself in such a precarious situation that I don't know who I'm working for? Let's just say that I'm a great deal smarter than my brother ever gave me credit for, and I've been keeping detailed records for quite some time."

"You're a good liar, Mr. Weld."

"I have proof."

"I want to see it."

"I want your promise that the information I give you will buy my freedom."

"I can't let you loose in the art world again."

Alex looked at Abby for some time and then said, "I've lost my taste for theft."

Dow considered for a moment, deep in thought. He popped the knuckles on his left hand. "*If* you have the information you claim, I may be able to get clearance."

"You're the Director of Interpol's Art Theft Division, Mr. Heaton. I doubt you need clearance from anyone."

Dow shrugged. "Fair enough."

"Then put it in writing. Right now. That if the information I give you is what I claim, you'll plea bargain me out of this."

Getting the Hope Diamond back was a major victory in their fight against the Collectors, but the offer of their identity and the whereabouts of every major work of art stolen in the last ten years, was a temptation that even Dow Heaton could not resist. He grabbed a sheet of paper from the bar and scratched out his plea deal. "You have these men and women as your witnesses, Mr. Weld, that if your information is what you claim, you can have your freedom. You will have immunity from prosecution from all your past crimes."

"In my wallet is a flash drive. On it you will find everything you're looking for."

"Get it," Dow ordered an assistant.

The small drive was quickly inserted into an Interpol laptop. Names and numbers flashed onto the screen, and it took all of Dow's self-control not to stumble backward.

"I told you the information would be worth my freedom," Alex said. "You'll notice the second file contains pictures. I believe they will come in particularly handy during prosecution."

37

AFTER BEING PATCHED UP, ABBY SLIPPED FROM THE COCKTAIL BAR AND jogged toward the cable car. It was a relief to escape the noise and activity inside and breathe the fresh air. She never once looked back as she began the long descent to the bottom of Table Mountain.

The tram rocked almost imperceptibly in the breeze. It physically hurt to look out on the breathtaking view of mountains and blue water and contrast it with the darkness in her heart. The pain of her father's rejection stabbed her again, and Abby slid down the wall of the cable car. No tears came. There were none left. Instead, an unfamiliar calm embraced her.

She sat alone, the voice of her father echoing through her mind. Her greatest fear had been confirmed. The man who gave her life could care less if she lived or died. It was a devastating blow, but not in the way she expected. Abby always assumed it was how he felt, but she thought the confirmation would destroy her. Yes, it hurt, but she would go on with her life.

She closed her eyes and pulled her knees to her chest. Two images battled in her mind: the ruthless, cold, uncaring look on her father's face, and the solid, welcoming form of the stone chapel that sat outside her apartment. It beckoned her heart even now.

Alex turned to the window just as Abby stepped into the cable car. He wanted to call after her, to beg her to stop, but knew his words would be wasted. She couldn't hear him.

"Let her go." Dow rested a hand on Alex's shoulder as he moved toward the door.

"Could you?"

Dow paused, his expression conflicted. "I suppose not."

"Then please let me make it right."

"Don't you think she's been through enough?" Dow wavered, unsure, as he read the ardor on Alex's face.

"More than enough. But I have to do this."

Dow shifted and pulled an iPhone from his back pocket. He handed it to Alex. "You'll need this."

Alex gave Dow a curious look.

"How did you think we were tracking the diamond? It was a tight race, but we managed to get here before the Broker."

Alex took the phone and shook his head. "I really underestimated that woman."

"Don't make the same mistake again."

Alex rested a final glance on his brother, now covered with a white sheet, before hurrying toward a cable car. He would deal with those emotions later.

Candles flickered in Camps Bay Tabernacle; the church was empty. Abby stood in the doorway, her heart engaged in a tug of war. Tears slipped down her cheeks, and she wanted to run away, as she always did, and not surrender to the pull from within the church.

I'm tired of running.

Finally, Abby stepped across the threshold. A quiet love permeated the room and released the chains around her heart. Her father's cruel words, Alex's plea for forgiveness, Dow's gentle encouragement, all fell by the wayside as she approached the rough wooden altar and sank to her knees. Only one other time had she found herself in such a position, and now, as then, her knees pressed into the wood floor.

Her voice sounded weak and timid to her ears as she whispered in the empty sanctuary. "I'm tired of hating him." And then she sobbed. It was an act of cleansing that prepared her heart for a conversation she had feared for years.

She rocked back and forth, her words louder and stronger as she cried out her heart before the altar.

"I've been running for so long . . . and all the while you were trying to show me . . . that you were here waiting to give me what he couldn't—"

Of all the places that Abby could have gone, this was the one that Alex least expected. He felt like an intruder as he stood just outside the church. He did not want to eavesdrop, yet he was compelled by the intensity in her words. Alex Weld had no history with God, had given Him little thought in his thirty-five years. Yet as he listened to Abby weep, his heart was troubled.

"This is too much," he whispered, pressing his forehead against the doorframe. Alex closed his eyes, unable to escape the vision of his brother, covered by the white sheet. Isaac was dead, and for what? Money? Everything he knew, everything he had strived for, suddenly felt so wrong.

"Alex?" He jerked and saw Abby standing in the doorway. "What are you doing here?"

He tried to answer but choked on his own tears.

She stepped closer, only inches away now, her eyes boring into him.

"I followed you," he said, holding up Dow's iPhone. "I just . . . I just wanted to make it right. But the truth is I don't know how."

Abby listened to him, and then wiped a tear off his cheek. "I used you, too, Alex. To get what I wanted. We're no different."

"Don't." He pulled her to his chest and buried his face in her neck. "You're nothing like me. I'm a liar and a thief!"

They held on to one another in the doorway of the small church in Cape Town, South Africa, two lost and lonely souls trying to make sense of the chaos in their lives. And they wept together.

"Please don't be angry with me," Alex cried. "I wasn't trying to intrude. I just—" His voice trailed off. "I just want to be with you, Abby. I don't want to lose you. Whatever we're doing with our lives, I want to do it together."

She pulled away and held him at arm's length. "There's something I need to do first."

"What?"

Abby pulled the ring off her finger and held it up for Alex to see. "For the longest time I imagined this to be a symbol of my father's love, because it was all I had. But now I see it for what it is, a bribe, and a stolen one at that."

Alex winced as she continued.

"I need to return it to its rightful owner."

"Then let me come with you. No one knows better than I where to return it."

"I can't do that, Alex. This is something that I need to do."

"Listen." He gripped her shoulders. "I'm involved in this, whether you like it or not. I have amends to make as well."

38

Daniel Wallace burst through the door of Peter Trent's office just as his secretary gave him the day's mail. On top of the stack was a package marked Priority Overnight Delivery, postmarked Cape Town, South Africa.

"We've got her, sir! My connection at the State Department tracked her leaving D.C. She arrived in Paris two days ago."

Peter furrowed his brow and pulled a letter opener from his desk drawer. He tore into the package as Daniel continued.

"We can have Paris police pick her up." Daniel finally realized that Dr. Trent was not paying attention.

"Sir? Did you hear me? We found Dr. Mitchell."

"What?" Peter looked up, eyes large, blood draining from his face.

"I *said*, we found Abby Mitchell. In Paris." And then Daniel saw just what had captured Dr. Trent's attention. His jaw fell open. "I don't believe it!"

"I don't think Dr. Mitchell's whereabouts is a concern any longer." Peter Trent dug into the box and pulled out the Hope Diamond.

Epilogue

Dr. Abigail Mitchell wrapped the trench coat around her waist and slid into the black government sedan outside the U.S. Embassy in Dublin, Ireland. For the first time in many years, she did not feel the oppressive weight of the Hope Diamond over her shoulders. She bathed Dow, DeDe, and Alex in a radiant smile.

"You ready?" Dow asked.

"Yes."

"It was a brilliant touch, Abby," DeDe said. "Returning the diamond to the Smithsonian the way it originally arrived, in a plain brown box sent by regular mail. Peter Trent could never have expected that."

"I'm sad to say the poor man never expected any of it."

"Will you be returning to the Smithsonian, my dear?" Dow asked.

"No," she said with a grin. "My work there is done."

Dow nodded, an eager light in his eyes. "You know, I'd love to put you to work."

"I'm sure you would."

"Is that a yes then?"

"Was that a job offer?"

"Of course."

Abby gave Dow a peck on the cheek. "Let me think about it."

"Take all the time you want."

Abby locked her seatbelt. "Shall we go then?"

"Just give the driver the address." Dow pulled Abby into a hug. "Call us when you get back to the States." He and DeDe slipped from the car and left her alone with Alex.

Abby looked at him with a smile, and he leaned over the seat, handing the chauffeur a slip of paper. "Take us here, please."

Fifteen minutes later, the sedan rolled to a stop on the south side of the River Liffey before a set of upper-class row houses. The building, clad in warm brownstone, rose four stories above them. Small, manicured yards were filled with the remnants of summer flowers.

"That one, right there." Alex pointed to an apartment on the ground floor adorned with lace curtains and a series of window boxes. He got out of the car and opened her door. "Shall we?"

Holding the pewter box in one hand, Abby rang the doorbell. It took several moments, but they soon heard a shuffling within and the door swung open to reveal a tiny wisp of a woman. Wrapped in a pink housecoat, the elderly woman blinked into the sunlight, observing her visitors with a startling pair of blue eyes.

"Good morning." Abby took a step forward, the box in her outstretched hand. "I think this belongs to you?"

"Oooh, yeh found me ring!" the old woman exclaimed, taking the box with a frail hand. "I was wondering where eh 'twas."

"Yes," Abby said after a long pause. "We found it."

347

The old woman turned her crisp blue eyes on them. "Thank yeh." Her smile turned her face into a maze of wrinkles.

Suddenly unsure of what else to say, Abby nodded and turned to go. Alex followed, unable to meet the gaze of the sweet old woman.

"Wait," Abby said, turning around. "What does the inscription mean? On the inside. Why Alligator Food?"

Laughter filled the street, like the sound of silver bells ringing in the wind. "Me husband was such a prankster," she said between peals of laughter. "He always thought it looked like yer lips were saying, 'I love yeh,' when yeh said the words Alligator Food. He inscribed the words on me ring so I would never forget." She leaned forward, her eyes ablaze. "And I never did. We spoke those words to each other every day for fifty years, and I've said them every day since I buried the man."

"Thank you," Abby said. "I needed to know." She and Alex turned to go.

"Wait," the old woman called. A mischievous grin spread across her face. She tossed the box to Abby with surprising strength. "I don't need this anymore. Why don't yeh keep it? It might do yer love some good." Then she closed the door and left them speechless on the doorstep.

Alex took the box from her and slipped the ring on her finger. "So, Alligator Food, huh?"

She looked at him, pensive. "Give me some time and maybe so."

He took her hand and rubbed it softly with his thumb. "There's something I need to tell you." His voice was hesitant, filled with trepidation.

"What?"

"My name isn't really Alex Weld."

Discussion Questions

1. *Eye of the god* is told in third-person through a variety of characters, both contemporary and historical. Which historical character did you resonate with most? Why? Which contemporary character did you resonate with most? Why?

2. Dr. Abigail Mitchell, director of the Smithsonian, plays a leading role in the contemporary narrative. Why is Abby so driven in her career? What are the inherent dangers of that kind of determination and focus?

3. The thieves, Alex and Isaac Weld, have an interesting relationship. They are brothers, business partners, and at times foes. What talents do each of them bring to the table, and how does it create tension between them?

4. At the outset of the story, we are introduced to the "curse" of the Hope Diamond. As the story proceeds, we see that each character grows to love or need the diamond for different reasons. How might their lives be different if they did not allow the jewel to play such a prominent role? In what ways do they bring the curse upon themselves?

5. Each of the three historical narratives is accurate in detail and context. Which one did you find most interesting? Why? How do Jean-Baptiste Tavernier, Louis XVI, and Evalyn Walsh McLean each succumb to the curse of the Hope Diamond?

6. The Hope Diamond plays a key role in this story, almost becoming a character itself. How would you describe the jewel to someone about to visit it at the Smithsonian? What is so special about it? Why has it captured imaginations for hundreds of years?

7. The relationship between Abby and her father is troubled and at times hurtful. What are the issues in that relationship? How do they affect Abby? Can you relate to the longing she has for her father, as well as the fear of him?

8. Alex Weld finds it easy, and in fact quite enjoyable, to manipulate women. Yet when he meets Abby, he begins to struggle with using her. What effect does Abby have on him? Why does it cause him to feel guilty? How do his developing feelings affect the relationship with his brother?

9. In many ways, Dow and DeDe are surrogate parents for Abby. How do they affect Abby in her job and in her relationship with Alex? Why is Dow's role in Abby's life of particular importance?

10. Throughout much of the book, the Broker is a shadowy figure, manipulating the lives of each character. How does he complicate the lives of both Alex and Abby? What is his stake in the story?

11. Just like each of the other characters, Abby is obsessed with the Hope Diamond. Yet how does her obsession differ from the others? Is it a good or a negative influence on her life? How does it affect her choices and her relationships?

12. How would you describe Abby's spiritual journey? What role does her father play in it? Why is she so afraid to enter each of the various churches? Can you relate to her hesitance in the pursuit of spirituality?

13. How will Abby be different as she moves forward with her life? How has Alex affected her? What has she learned about herself through her contact with the Hope Diamond? How do you think she will grow spiritually from this point forward?

Want to learn more about author
Ariel Allison and check out other great
fiction from Abingdon Press?

Sign up for our fiction newsletter at
www.AbingdonPress.com
to read interviews with your favorite authors, find tips
for starting a reading group, and stay posted on what
new titles are on the horizon. It's the place to connect
with other fiction readers or to post a
comment about this book.

Be sure to visit Ariel online!

www.arielallison.com
www.inspire-writer.blogspot.com
www.steppingstonesforwriters.blogspot.com